prologue

CW01500803

Marmalade's Preliminary Observations

IF ONLY HUMANS paid attention to the important things.

Like the way a visitor's fingers linger too long on doorframes. Or how certain men smell of ambition and deceit rather than merely bergamot and wool. Or perhaps—and this seems rather obvious to those of us with superior senses—how the particular texture of a footfall can reveal everything about a person's intentions.

But Clara doesn't notice these things. She's too occupied with her herbs and tinctures, her endless fretting over bank statements, and her habit of speaking to empty corners of the shop as if her grandmother might answer. (She might, actually. I've suspected for some time that I'm not the only observer in this establishment, though I maintain a dignified silence on the matter.)

If Clara had simply watched the man's eyes when he asked

for henbane—how they darted to the ceiling beams, the walls, the counter's edge—she might have realized he wanted more than herbs. The unsteady hands and slight hitch in his breathing told their own story, though Clara remained oblivious to these signs of distress. If she'd noticed how he measured the shop with his gaze, counting paces when he thought no one was looking, perhaps she would have been prepared. If she'd checked the jar—*that* jar—before the Inspector arrived, perhaps none of this would've happened.

But no one ever listens to me.

I'm just a cat.

A very *observant* one.

And now I'm obliged to watch a mystery unfold because humans insist on being oblivious to the obvious. It's exhausting, truly, being the only one who sees everything clearly in a world of fog-minded bipeds.

I suppose I'll have to guide them through it. Again.

At least it keeps my afternoons interesting.

murder at her door

A Cozy Victorian Mystery of Herbs, Hauntings, and a
Most Unladylike Suspect

tarot and tea leaves mysteries - book 1

Zia Bellamy

one

A curl of lemon balm steam spiraled up from the brass kettle as Clara Wetherly pinched dried lavender buds into a muslin sachet. Her fingers moved with practiced precision, though her thoughts wandered. It was nearly eight in the evening, and Hawthorne & Wetherly still smelled of rosemary, rose hips, and rain—her favorite combination.

Marmalade was curled in the open tarot drawer again, paw batting at a cluster of calendula petals he'd knocked loose in his sleep. The great orange beast gave her a look when she passed, as if daring her to move him. She didn't.

"I ought to start charging you rent," Clara murmured, shaking the petals from the hem of her apron.

She glanced up at the faded sign above the apothecary counter: Hawthorne & Wetherly, Est. 1827. Grandmother had insisted on keeping the original name even after Grandfather died. "A woman's reputation in business is hard enough to establish without changing the letterhead every time a man departs," she'd said with that familiar spark in her eye. Now Clara found herself uttering the same words to Mr. Pinkett from the bank whenever he came round suggesting she might be "better suited selling the property to a proper business." As if three generations of Wetherly women hadn't built something proper.

Clara glanced at the evening newspaper, still folded beside the register. Another article about railway expansion plans and the former Crimean soldiers seeking work. London was changing rapidly in this spring of 1856, and Bloomsbury seemed to be at the center of it all.

The shop was quiet this early, the sort of quiet that breathed—not silent, exactly, but alive with the creak of old floorboards, the scent of London rain on brick, and the faint whisper of something unseen moving between the shelves. The sort of quiet where one might imagine their grandmother's voice was just a little louder than memory.

Clara caught herself humming a tune her grandmother used to sing while steeping tinctures. She paused mid-measure, frowning at the foolishness of it. But she didn't stop. Grandmother always said the plants responded better to music.

The bell above the door jingled.

"Miss Wetherly," Mrs. Penfield announced, her steel-gray curls trembling while her opinions remained rigid as ever. "You've mixed that nervine blend I requested?"

Clara motioned toward the polished counter where a parchment-tied bundle waited. "Hops, passionflower, a hint of valerian. I swapped the licorice for lemon balm this time."

"Mercy, I'll sleep for a week."

"If you let yourself," Clara replied, arching an eyebrow.

Mrs. Penfield sniffed, offered Marmalade a disdainful glance, and tucked the bundle into her handbag. "Your grandmother would have kittens if she knew that beast was napping atop her tarot cards."

"Grandmother adored cats. She always claimed they could see what we couldn't."

"Yes, well," Mrs. Penfield pursed her lips. "Speaking of seeing things, did you hear about Lady Ashmore's séance last week? Three women fainted when the table lifted clean off the floor."

"How extraordinary," Clara replied, not bothering to hide her skepticism. "Though I suspect Lord Pennington's special brandy might have lifted more than furniture."

As Mrs. Penfield left, muttering something about proper respect for the beyond, Clara noticed her neighbor Mr. Jenkins locking his tobacco shop door across the street. The 'SOLD' sign had appeared in his window just yesterday—the third business on the block this month. She was beginning to feel surrounded.

Clara wiped her hands on her apron and surveyed the shop. Shelves lined with labeled jars. Dried herbs hung in orderly braids above the worktable. The Gilded Leaf sat open on its wooden stand, a pressed violet marking the page where she'd last left off. The book had been her grandmother's most prized possession—a leather-bound collection of remedies and observations passed down through generations of Wetherly women. Clara's inheritance, along with the business loan statements from Mr. Pinkett's bank that she pretended not to notice when they arrived each month.

She moved to close the book when the door opened again. A man stood in the threshold—proper coat, polished shoes, but something in his expression that didn't match the attire. His fingers trembled against the doorframe, and his gaze swept briefly along the ceiling beams and stone walls, assessing them with an architect's precision before settling on her.

"Miss Wetherly, I presume?"

Clara nodded, suddenly aware of a peculiar stillness in the shop. Even the kettle seemed to hush its whisper.

"I require something specific."

She waited, hands folded at her waist.

The man stepped closer, his voice dropping. "Henbane."

A beat of silence passed. Marmalade uncurled in the drawer, leapt down, and slinked toward the counter. He stopped a few feet from the man, tail high, then hissed.

Clara didn't flinch. "Henbane isn't sold here. Not to strangers. And certainly not to men who cannot meet my eyes when speaking."

The man inhaled slowly. "I'm not a fool, Miss Wetherly. But I am quite desperate." He held out his trembling hand. "These tremors worsen daily. Nothing helps. I can hardly hold a pen."

"Then see a physician."

"I have. He prescribes treatments that only seem to make it worse." He stepped forward, but only slightly. "I was told your shop offered more... discretion. And results."

"By whom?"

He hesitated. "My doctor mentioned it—though quite unofficially. He admits his treatments aren't progressing as quickly as he'd hoped."

Clara folded her arms. "We offer alternatives. I can prepare something to calm the mind. Lemon balm. Valerian. Skullcap. Even mugwort, if you're insistent."

He considered her for a long moment, then nodded. "I'll take whatever you recommend. Stronger than what's at the chemist's."

Clara turned to her shelves, measuring the blend with steady hands. Behind her, she could feel the man's gaze like steam.

When she returned, he placed two silver coins on the counter—more than the mixture required. "For your trouble."

Clara said nothing as she passed the parchment-wrapped blend across.

He left without another word. She waited until the door shut fully before glancing down. Marmalade was perched on

The Gilded Leaf, one paw splayed over the page. Henbane. The flame of the candle beside the counter guttered sideways, though no draft disturbed the air.

Clara frowned. And quietly reached for the bolt on the door.

She locked the door, turned the sign to CLOSED, and turned back into the warm hush of the shop. The kettle hissed from the corner hearth—nearly empty, but still coaxing breath from the lemon balm.

Clara filled a cup and took it to her small writing desk, setting it beside The Gilded Leaf. The book remained open where Marmalade had marked it earlier. The cat had abandoned his post for his usual perch on the windowsill, his orange bulk hunched like a silent guardian.

She ran her fingers along the spine before flipping it open to the page he'd marked. Henbane. The ink had faded in places, but her grandmother's handwriting was unmistakable: "When the hands tremble and the mind betrays... only truth binds the spirit to the body." Below it, a warning in her grandmother's sharpest script: "Beware those who seek the plant but fear the truth it brings."

Clara read it twice. The teaspoon in her empty cup gave a soft, inexplicable tap. A breeze with no source brushed her cheek, carrying with it the faintest scent of lavender water— her grandmother's signature perfume.

Marmalade growled low, eyes fixed on a space just beyond her shoulder. She didn't turn. Instead, she sipped the tea and stared down at the page—at that one word: Henbane.

The man today—his pallor, the tremor in his fingers, the barely veiled panic—he reminded her of something. No. Someone. Her father, at the end. Before the fits, before the shame, before the doctors with blank eyes and leeches and no answers. The same desperation. The same trembling hands growing worse with each treatment. The same fear in the eyes.

She'd been too young to understand it then. But Grandmother had known something more, she was certain. Why else keep her father's name from The Gilded Leaf when every other Wetherly was chronicled within?

She closed the book gently and placed her hand atop it. "What aren't you telling me?" she whispered.

Marmalade meowed softly, like punctuation. And in the silence that followed, Clara no longer believed it was just the rain she heard outside.

She rose from her chair to douse the lamps, pausing by the window. A soft sound—sharp, like a crate tipping or glass tapping against brick—echoed faintly from the alley.

She pulled aside the curtain and peered into the fog. Nothing moved. Just the glow of the gas lamp and a thick drift of mist curling along the cobblestones.

Marmalade leapt up beside her, landing with a grunt and flattening his ears. He pressed his nose to the glass, tail twitching with precision.

Clara squinted harder. Was that a figure leaning against the wall? No, just a shadow—she thought.

"Nothing but wind," she muttered.

But Marmalade didn't blink. And neither did the shadow when the gas lamp flickered.

Clara stepped back, one hand instinctively reaching for the drawer where her grandmother had kept a small pistol. The drawer that Clara, against all propriety, had never emptied.

A soft creaking came from across the room—the precise pattern of Genevieve's footsteps, though no one stood there.

Clara pulled the drawer open, her fingers finding the cold metal of her grandmother's pistol. But by the time she returned to the window, the shadow—if there had truly been one—was gone. The alley appeared empty, nothing but mist and darkness.

After a long moment, she returned the pistol to its drawer,

latched the window, and retired upstairs, unaware of what transpired in the alley below long after she had fallen asleep.

MARMALADE'S OBSERVATIONS – Entry No. 1

The man didn't belong here.

I recognized him immediately—the same man who had asked Clara for henbane earlier today. The one who made my fur stand on end. The one who couldn't meet her eyes when speaking.

He'd returned, but this time not for herbs.

Humans rarely look properly at buildings. They see doors and windows, not the bones beneath. This visitor was different. He examined the very stones as if he might purchase them. As if I would allow such a transaction to proceed without my approval.

Clara hadn't noticed his return. She was upstairs, fretting over receipts as usual, speaking softly to empty air (she does this often, imagining her grandmother can hear—perhaps she can; I make no judgments about human oddities. I'm far too sophisticated for that).

The trembling-handed man moved with quieter steps now. A different purpose. He knelt beside the herb crates in the alley, examining something in the dirt. Humans and their fascination with dirt. I bury things there for good reason—he was obviously an amateur.

Then came another man. Something glinted on his hand in the lamplight—gold catching the glow. Words exchanged like sharpened knives. Something passed between hands. A twist, a gasp, a fall.

I watched from the kitchen window, tail swishing against the glass with perfect timing. The air suddenly chilled around me, my fur rising along my spine. I wasn't the only one watching. And I'm never wrong about these things.

One man left. One remained, growing colder in the mist.

Typical human inefficiency.

Clara would find him come morning. The evidence would speak wrongly. The shop would be threatened.

I would, of course, need to intervene. It's exhausting being the only competent one in this establishment.

I stretched, yawned, and considered waking her. But humans rarely understand the things cats try to tell them. Their limitations are truly boundless.

Instead, I'd watch. I'd wait. I'd notice what they missed.

After all, that's what I do best. Someone in this household must maintain standards.

two

Clara's morning ritual never varied. Water for tea. Sachet of dried mint. Windows opened to dispel the night's shadows. She moved through her grandmother's apartment—no, her apartment now, though after nearly three years, she still couldn't think of it as truly hers.

Genevieve's presence lingered in every corner, from the faded cushion of the reading chair to the collection of pressed herbs framed on the wall. Clara had changed nothing after her grandmother's passing, finding comfort in the familiar arrangement, as if maintaining the rooms exactly as they had been might somehow preserve a piece of the woman who had raised her. Soft morning light traced patterns through the lace curtains Genevieve had crocheted decades ago, casting patterned shadows across the floorboards.

Clara finished her tea, washed the cup, and descended the narrow staircase behind the curtained archway that connected her private world to the shop below. The steps creaked in precisely the same places they always had, a familiar music that had accompanied her every morning since she was tall enough to navigate them alone. Then came the final part of her ritual

—the quick trip to the alley to check her potted herbs before opening the shop for the day.

Spring in London meant new growth, and the seedlings required daily attention. But this morning, as she unbolted the back door and stepped into the narrow passage, a different kind of stillness awaited. The herb crates had been disturbed, and behind them—a sprawled form in a familiar coat, face down on the cobblestones.

The pot of chamomile slipped from her fingers, shattering on the threshold between her ordered world and the chaos that had arrived overnight. Clara's breath caught in her throat as she took one cautious step forward, then another. The morning fog still hung low in the alley, wrapping the scene in a gauzy shroud.

Part of her wanted to retreat, to bolt the door and pretend she'd seen nothing. But the rational part—the part Grandmother had cultivated since childhood—compelled her forward. The face, turned sideways on the cobblestones, belonged to yesterday's visitor—the man who had asked for henbane.

His eyes were open, fixed in a vacant stare, and his lips bore a distinctive bluish tinge. Not the purple-black of nightshade or the foam-flecked red of hemlock, but something else entirely. Clara's mind catalogued the symptoms automatically, her botanical training impossible to suppress even in shock.

"Good heavens," she whispered, the sound barely disturbing the morning stillness. Death had a scent all its own —one Clara recognized from preparing grandmother's body three years prior. It mingled strangely with the spring herbs and the damp stone, creating a discordant note in the usual morning perfume of her alley.

Clara knelt beside him, heedless of the damp seeping through her skirts. Professional instinct took over as she pressed two fingers to his neck, finding the skin cold and unyielding. No pulse throbbed beneath her touch. He had been dead for hours, likely since sometime in the night. His hands were partially curled, revealing ink stains on the fingertips and paper cuts along the index finger—the marks of a man who worked with documents. Not the rough calluses of a laborer or the pristine hands of a gentleman. Something in between, much like his attire yesterday. The peculiar discoloration around his mouth drew her attention.

Clara leaned closer, noting the subtle patterns that spoke of specific compounds. Not monkshood or foxglove—she knew those signs intimately. This was something more unusual, perhaps a combination. The faint smell of bitter almonds lingered, but mixed with something else she couldn't immediately place. Her gaze traveled down to his partially open coat, where a corner of paper protruded from an inner pocket. Some sort of notebook, perhaps containing the identification she should be seeking rather than analyzing symptoms.

But before she could reach for it, something else caught her eye. A small glass jar had rolled partially beneath his shoulder, nearly hidden by the fold of his coat. The morning light caught its surface, revealing the remnants of a familiar label—one she recognized immediately as her own. Clara's heart quickened.

The jar bore the distinctive amber tint she used for her more potent mixtures, though the label appeared to have been partially scraped away. She reached toward it, fingertips just brushing the glass. If she could examine the contents, perhaps she might determine what had happened to this man. What had been in that jar? Had he stolen it from her shop somehow? Or had someone else— The crunch of boots on gravel froze her in place.

"Step away from the body, Miss." The voice cut through the morning air with the precision of a surgeon's blade.

Clara withdrew her hand from the jar and slowly rose to her feet, turning to face the source of the command.

A tall man stood at the alley entrance, his silhouette sharp against the misty light. Dark coat with silver buttons that caught the wan sunlight. Broad shoulders held with military rigidity. He stepped forward, revealing a face that might have graced a portrait in some aristocratic home—were it not for the hardened look in his eyes and the faint scar along his jawline. Clara did not move.

"I was checking for signs of life."

"From your position, it appeared you were searching his pockets." Each word was measured, clipped at the edges like precisely trimmed herbs. He closed the distance between them with unhurried steps that nonetheless conveyed authority. "The man is clearly deceased."

"Yes. He is." Clara stood her ground, though she took a half-step away from the body. "His skin is cold. He's been dead for hours."

The man's gaze sharpened at her clinical assessment. He stopped a few feet from her, close enough that she could see the silver threads at his temples despite his relatively young face. When she didn't continue, he prompted, "Your name, Miss?"

"Clara Wetherly. This is my shop." She gestured toward the open back door, broken pot shards still scattered across the threshold. "I found him when I came to check my herbs."

"Inspector Graham Redgrave, Detective Branch, Metropolitan Police." He studied her face with the same methodical attention he'd given the scene. "A neighbor reported a disturbance in this alley last night, and a body discovered this morning."

Clara's brow furrowed. A neighbor had seen something in the night? Had someone witnessed what happened and waited until morning to report it?

Before she could formulate a question, the inspector continued. "When I arrived, I did not expect to find the shop owner examining the deceased rather than alerting the authorities."

His tone made the statement an accusation. Clara felt heat rising in her cheeks. "I only just discovered him. I've had no chance to—"

"And yet you had time to kneel beside him and conduct what appeared to be a rather thorough examination." He didn't raise his voice, which somehow made it worse. "Including reaching for that jar."

The jar. Clara's eyes flicked briefly to it, still partially hidden beneath the dead man's shoulder. The inspector followed her gaze, his expression unchanging save for a slight narrowing of his eyes. "You recognize it, then."

"It appears to be one of mine," Clara admitted, seeing no benefit in denial. "Though I can't be certain without examining it."

Inspector Redgrave circled the body with measured steps, his gaze never leaving Clara even as he assessed the scene. He stopped beside the corpse and, with a gloved hand, carefully extracted the jar without disturbing the body. He held it up to the light, studying the remnants of the label before turning his attention back to Clara. "You found a dead man in your alley, Miss Wetherly, and your first action was to examine his pockets?" The question hung in the air between them.

"My first action was to confirm he was beyond help, Inspector. My second was to look for identification." Clara kept her voice steady despite the thundering of her heart.

"Most ladies would have swooned or screamed."

"Most ladies haven't prepared bodies for burial since they were sixteen. I find swooning rarely improves a situation." She regretted the words as soon as they left her mouth—revealing too much, too defensive.

A flicker of something—surprise, perhaps—crossed his face before the impassive mask returned. He placed the jar carefully into an evidence pouch, then knelt to examine the body himself. "You know this man?" It wasn't really a question.

"He came to my shop yesterday. Asked for henbane."

The inspector's hand stilled momentarily over the victim's coat. "Henbane. A poison."

"A medicinal herb when properly prepared," Clara countered, fingers briefly straightening her cuff. "Though certainly toxic in untrained hands."

"And did you provide him with this... medicinal herb?" His tone made clear what he thought of such a distinction.

"I did not. I refused him." Clara watched as the inspector examined the victim's hands, noting the same ink stains and paper cuts she had observed. "I offered safer alternatives to whatever he claimed to need it for."

"Which was?"

"He didn't specify. Just said he was desperate." Redgrave looked up at her, his hazel eyes assessing.

For a moment, neither spoke. Then he reached into the victim's inner pocket and withdrew a small notebook bound in worn leather, its pages dog-eared from frequent use. "Did you examine this as well, Miss Wetherly?"

"No. I noticed it but hadn't yet—" She stopped, realizing how her words would sound.

"Hadn't yet searched through it?" Redgrave finished for her, a grim satisfaction in his tone. The distant sound of approaching footsteps announced the arrival of constables. Redgrave rose, tucking the notebook into his own coat.

Two uniformed men appeared at the alley entrance, followed by a third in plainclothes carrying a medical bag.

"Secure the scene," Redgrave ordered without looking

away from Clara. "And escort Miss Wetherly back into her shop. We'll continue our discussion there."

One of the constables approached Clara. "This way, Miss."

She hesitated, looking back at the jar now secure in the inspector's evidence pouch. If she had examined it first—if she had confirmed its contents before Redgrave arrived—perhaps she might have understood what truly happened here. Now it was evidence against her, its secrets sealed away.

three

The shop felt smaller with Inspector Redgrave inside it. He moved with surprising care among the shelves of herbs and tinctures, examining labels with a scholar's attention while the constable stood by the door like a sentinel. Clara remained behind the counter, her domain becoming an interrogation chamber.

Through the front window, she could see curious faces gathering—Mrs. Penfield's pinched expression, Mr. Jenkins's concerned frown. News traveled quickly in this part of Bloomsbury. Redgrave completed his circuit of the shop and came to stand before the counter. He placed the evidence pouch containing the jar carefully between them. "Tell me about your inventory system, Miss Wetherly."

His gaze swept over the labeled drawers and bottles lining the walls.

"Each jar and drawer is labeled with the herb's common and Latin name." Clara kept her hands folded before her, refusing to fidget under his scrutiny. "Medicinal preparations are stored in those amber jars, organized by purpose rather than ingredient."

"And poisons?" The question came sharp and quick.

"I don't stock poisons as such, Inspector. I stock herbs, many of which can be harmful if improperly used." She met his gaze directly. "Just as many medicines from a physician can kill if misadministered. The difference lies in intention, not inventory."

"A convenient distinction." Redgrave tapped the evidence pouch. "This jar bears your label—partially removed, but recognizable. Do you deny it came from your shop?"

Clara studied the jar through the pouch. "The glass is similar to what I use, and the remaining label appears to be in my hand. But I cannot confirm its contents without examining it directly."

"You keep quite an extensive collection of potential poisons, Miss Wetherly." His gaze shifted to a shelf of amber bottles behind her.

"I keep an extensive collection of medicines, Inspector. Whether they heal or harm depends entirely on knowledge and intention." Clara felt her grandmother's words flowing through her, a lifetime of defending their craft distilled into this moment. "Rather like questions and accusations, wouldn't you agree?"

"And which are you offering me?" Redgrave indicated the kettle still steaming on the small shop stove.

"That remains to be determined." The words slipped out before she could catch them, earning a raised eyebrow from the inspector.

He opened the notebook he'd retrieved from the victim, turning pages with methodical precision. Clara caught glimpses of small, neat handwriting, numbers arranged in columns, and what appeared to be property assessments. "Do you recognize this man's name?" Redgrave asked suddenly. "Silas Barrett."

"No. He didn't introduce himself when he visited."

"And yet you knew immediately who I meant when I arrived." His tone suggested this was somehow damning.

"I recognized his face, Inspector. Not his name." Clara tightened her grip on her folded hands.

"What interest did Mr. Barrett have in my shop beyond requesting henbane?"

Something shifted in Redgrave's expression—surprise, perhaps, that she would ask questions of her own. He considered her for a moment before turning the notebook around and placing it on the counter between them, open to a page that made Clara's breath catch. A careful sketch of her building, annotated with measurements and calculations.

In the margin, in the same neat hand: "FINAL HOLD-OUT" underlined twice.

"It appears, Miss Wetherly," Redgrave said quietly, "that Mr. Barrett had significantly more interest in your property than in your herbs."

Clara stared at the notebook, her mind racing. Property assessments. Measurements. Her building labeled as the "FINAL HOLDOUT." Barrett hadn't come for henbane at all. "He was evaluating my shop," she said softly, more to herself than to Redgrave. "The way he looked at the walls, the ceiling beams..."

"You noticed his interest in the structure?" Redgrave's tone sharpened.

"I thought it odd at the time." Clara looked up from the notebook. "But I didn't connect it to the recent property sales until now."

"Recent property sales?" Redgrave prompted, watching her closely.

"Three businesses on this block have sold in the past month. Mr. Jenkins across the street just yesterday." Clara nodded toward the window where curious onlookers still gathered. "I didn't realize they were connected."

Redgrave turned another page in the notebook, revealing a list of addresses with prices and dates noted beside each. Every building on the block was listed—with check marks beside most. Only Hawthorne & Wetherly remained unmarked. "According to these notes, Mr. Barrett was acquiring properties for a company called Blackstone Development." Redgrave studied her reaction. "Does that name mean anything to you?"

Clara shook her head. "No. But I've received several offers to sell in recent months. I declined them all."

The constable at the door was joined by the plainclothes man Clara had seen earlier, now entering with his medical bag. He nodded briefly to Redgrave before addressing him. "Preliminary examination suggests poison, Inspector. The discoloration and residue are consistent with plant-based toxins." His eyes slid to Clara as he spoke. "Without laboratory analysis, I cannot be more specific, but the symptoms align with several botanical compounds."

"Thank you, Dr. Morris." Redgrave gestured toward the evidence pouch on the counter. "We've found what may be the source. From Miss Wetherly's shop."

The doctor looked at Clara with undisguised suspicion. "Indeed? How convenient to have the poisoner and her supplies so readily at hand."

"I am not a poisoner," Clara said firmly, meeting his gaze. "I'm a botanical practitioner, like my grandmother before me."

"A distinction without a difference, in my experience." Dr. Morris sniffed. "Your experience is lacking then, Doctor."

Clara kept her voice level despite her rising anger. "A skilled preparer of remedies knows precisely how to heal. A poisoner knows only how to harm."

"Fascinating semantic debate," Redgrave interrupted. "Dr. Morris, please continue your examination of the body. I'd like a complete report as soon as possible, with particular attention to any evidence of the specific compounds used."

As Morris gathered his bag to leave, Clara noticed something unexpected - the way his fingers lingered briefly over her shelf of dried aconite, his eyes assessing the quality with what appeared to be professional appreciation before his expression reverted to disdain. His hand moved with the practiced grace of someone accustomed to handling botanical specimens, though he seemed determined to project nothing but contempt for her profession.

As the doctor left, Redgrave turned his attention back to Clara. "I must ask you not to leave town, Miss Wetherly. This investigation is just beginning, and you are, at present, our primary person of interest."

"You believe I poisoned a man and then left his body in my own alley to be discovered?" Clara couldn't keep the incredulity from her voice.

"I believe very little at this stage, Miss Wetherly." Redgrave's expression remained largely unreadable, though something in his eyes suggested a mind less certain than his words conveyed. "But I find it curious that a man seeking to purchase your property ends up dead behind your shop, apparently poisoned, with one of your jars nearby." He closed the notebook with a snap. "Particularly when you specialize in precisely the knowledge required to administer such a poison."

The bell above the shop door jingled, drawing their attention. Mrs. Penfield stood in the doorway, her face a mask of concern and barely disguised curiosity. "I've come for my tonic, dear," she announced, as if there were no police presence at all. "Though I see you're otherwise engaged."

"The shop is closed for the investigation, Ma'am," the constable informed Mrs. Penfield, moving to block her entry.

"Nonsense. I've been purchasing my sleep tonic from the Wetherlys for twenty years." Mrs. Penfield drew herself up with the authority of a longtime customer. "I witnessed the commotion and thought Clara might need a friendly face."

Her gaze traveled to the evidence pouch on the counter, then to Redgrave's stern expression. "Though I see she has enough attention already." Redgrave studied the older woman.

"You're acquainted with Miss Wetherly?"

"With three generations of Wetherly women, Inspector." Mrs. Penfield sniffed, her tone making clear she found his question nearly offensive. "Genevieve – God rest her soul – would be appalled to see her granddaughter treated like a common criminal."

Clara felt a rush of gratitude despite the awkwardness of the situation. "Mrs. Penfield, I'll prepare your tonic as soon as I'm able. Perhaps tomorrow, if—"

"There's been a death, Mrs...?" Redgrave interrupted.

"Penfield. Agatha Penfield." She peered at him with narrowed eyes. "And yes, I'm quite aware. Half the neighborhood is watching your men carry that poor man out of the alley." She lowered her voice to a stage whisper that somehow carried perfectly. "Poisoned, they're saying. Though I can't imagine Clara having anything to do with that. The girl refuses to kill even garden pests."

"Did you happen to see this man visit the shop yesterday?" Redgrave asked, his tone shifting subtly to draw out information.

"I did." Mrs. Penfield seemed pleased to be consulted. "Arrived just as I was leaving. Nervous sort. Kept looking at the shop like he was appraising it rather than shopping in it." Clara caught the slight stiffening in Redgrave's posture. Mrs. Penfield had unwittingly confirmed a connection between Barrett and property assessment.

The bell jingled again as Mr. Jenkins entered, removing his cap. "Pardon the intrusion. I saw Mrs. Penfield come in and thought I might..." He trailed off, looking uncertainly at the constable and Redgrave.

"This is not a social gathering, sir," Redgrave stated firmly.

"Albert Jenkins, Inspector. Tobacco shop across the way." He nodded toward the window. "Or it was, until yesterday. Sold to those development fellows."

"Blackstone Development?" Redgrave asked sharply.

"That's the one." Jenkins twisted his cap in his hands. "Same company that's bought up half the block. Their man was everywhere these past weeks, measuring and assessing. Offered fair prices, I'll give them that."

"Their man?" Redgrave prompted. "Would you recognize him?"

"Oh, certainly. Thin fellow, precise like a clockmaker. Always making notes." Jenkins looked toward the alley.

"Is that who...?" His expression confirmed his suspicion before Redgrave could answer. Mrs. Penfield gasped softly. "That was the gentleman I saw yesterday! Quite nervous, he seemed."

"Did he mention what he was seeking in Miss Wetherly's shop?" Redgrave asked, tone deliberately casual.

"Henbane," Clara supplied before Mrs. Penfield could respond, aware of Redgrave's intense focus. "Which I refused to provide."

"Henbane!" Jenkins echoed, his face paling.

"My word. Isn't that—"

"A poison," Jenkins finished, his face paling. "My father warned me about it when I was a boy. Said witches used it to —" He stopped abruptly, glancing at Clara. "Begging your pardon, Miss Wetherly."

"I refused his request," Clara stated firmly, for Redgrave's benefit as much as the others'. "I offered safer alternatives."

"Of course you did, dear," Mrs. Penfield patted her hand. "Just as your grandmother would have. Though perhaps..." she lowered her voice again, "this isn't the time to mention the family's expertise in such matters." The whisper carried easily to Redgrave, whose expression darkened slightly. "

Thank you both for your... contributions. The constable will take your statements outside." He nodded to the officer, who began ushering the neighbors toward the door.

"Oh, but I haven't gotten my tonic," Mrs. Penfield protested.

"I'm afraid Miss Wetherly's business is suspended until further notice," Redgrave replied, his tone brooking no argument.

Clara's grip tightened on the edge of the counter. "Inspector, my customers depend on these remedies. Some for conditions that cannot wait days or weeks. Surely you don't intend to—"

"The scene of a potential murder takes precedence over sleep tonics, Miss Wetherly," Redgrave informed her, adjusting his cuffs with fastidious precision. "The sooner we resolve this matter, the sooner you can resume your... practice."

"Every day closed is income lost," Clara pressed, thinking of the loan payment due to Mr. Pinkett at month's end. "Perhaps I could dispense existing preparations under supervision?"

"Not possible," Redgrave stated with finality, nodding for the constable to continue.

As they were guided outside, Clara caught fragments of whispered conversation from the growing crowd. "Poison... witch's shop... the last one who wouldn't sell..." The weight of suspicion settled over her like a shroud. Redgrave waited until the door closed behind Mrs. Penfield and Mr. Jenkins before turning back to Clara. His expression had shifted subtly—still suspicious, but with a thoughtfulness that hadn't been there before. "You're something of an anomaly, Miss Wetherly. The last holdout on a block being systematically purchased. A woman running a business alone. A dispenser of botanical remedies with knowledge of compounds that most doctors would struggle to identify." He paced slowly before the counter. "And now a potential murder suspect."

"I did not poison anyone." Clara kept her voice steady. "He came seeking henbane. I refused him. That is the extent of our interaction."

"And yet one of your jars was found beside his body." Redgrave tapped the evidence pouch. "A jar containing what appears to be a toxic compound, according to Dr. Morris's preliminary assessment."

"I'd need to examine it to—"

"Yes, you've made that clear." Redgrave cut her off. "Unfortunately, allowing a suspect to handle evidence is not standard procedure."

Clara felt her patience fraying. "If I had poisoned him, Inspector, would I have left incriminating evidence beside the body? Would I have placed it in a jar bearing my own label? I may be many things, but I assure you, 'foolish' is not among them."

A flicker of doubt crossed Redgrave's face, lingering longer than before. "Criminals often make such mistakes. Particularly those unused to murder." His tone lacked its earlier conviction, as if he were reciting words he didn't entirely believe.

The shop door opened again, this time admitting a second constable. "Inspector, we've completed the initial inventory of the scene. Dr. Morris requests your presence."

"In a moment." Redgrave turned back to Clara. "I'll need a complete inventory of your herbs and preparations. Especially those with toxic properties."

"That's nearly every shelf in this shop, Inspector." Clara gestured to the walls of labeled drawers and bottles. "Most herbs can be harmful in incorrect dosages or preparations."

"Precisely my concern," Redgrave replied. "Constable Fletcher will remain to observe while you compile the list." He moved toward the door, then paused. "I'd be particularly interested in which preparations you store in amber jars identical to the one found with Mr. Barrett."

As he stepped outside, Clara heard Dr. Morris's voice drifting in from the alley. "...unusual presentation, Inspector. The discoloration suggests botanical toxins rather than mineral compounds. I'll need to conduct further tests, but this appears to be the work of someone with considerable knowledge of plant properties."

The door closed, cutting off the rest of the conversation, but Clara had heard enough. Morris's description triggered her professional interest despite the circumstances. Botanical toxins... that wasn't something commonly found in nature or in standard medical preparations. She moved to begin the requested inventory under the watchful eye of Constable Fletcher, her mind racing. The amber jars on her shelves contained her most potent mixtures—tinctures for serious ailments, compounds for pain relief, sleep aids for those with severe insomnia. None contained poisons in the concentration Dr. Morris was describing.

As she worked, Clara became increasingly certain of one thing: whatever was in that jar by Barrett's body, it wasn't one of her preparations. Someone had gone to considerable trouble to make it appear so, scraping away most of the label but leaving just enough to identify its source. The sound of approaching footsteps announced Redgrave's return. This time, he was accompanied by Dr. Morris, whose clinical gaze swept the shop with undisguised suspicion.

"Miss Wetherly," Redgrave began without preamble, "Dr. Morris has made an interesting observation about the poison used on Mr. Barrett."

"I haven't yet determined the exact compound," Morris interjected, "but the symptoms suggest a sophisticated botanical knowledge. The kind only found in..." he paused meaningfully, looking around the shop, "certain circles."

"Medical circles, perhaps?" Clara suggested, unable to keep a hint of challenge from her voice.

"Hardly." Morris sniffed. "No reputable physician would maintain such an extensive collection of potentially harmful substances."

"Your knowledge of poisons is unnervingly comprehensive, Miss Wetherly," Redgrave observed, watching her reaction carefully.

"As is your knowledge of criminal investigation for someone with such refined manners," Clara retorted before she could stop herself. The tension of the morning had worn her patience dangerously thin.

Redgrave stiffened visibly. "We all have pasts we carry with us."

"Indeed," Clara met his gaze evenly. "Some more useful than others."

Dr. Morris cleared his throat. "I'll continue my examination at the laboratory. I expect to have preliminary findings by tomorrow morning." His gaze swept over Clara's shelves once more. "Though I believe the source is rather... evident."

"Evidence requires proof, not assumption, Doctor," Clara replied. "Something both botanists and investigators understand."

Redgrave's eyes narrowed slightly at her retort. "Constable Fletcher will remain here while you complete that inventory, Miss Wetherly. I expect it to be thorough."

"Of course, Inspector. I have nothing to hide." Clara reached for her ledger book beneath the counter. "Though you might find it more efficient to simply tell me which specific herbs or preparations interest you. My complete inventory contains over two hundred items."

"All of them, Miss Wetherly." Redgrave paused at the threshold. "I expect that inventory to be complete when I return. You are not to leave these premises without my express permission. Is that understood?"

"Perfectly, Inspector." Clara met his gaze steadily. "Though you should know that jar you found—the one with my partial label—couldn't possibly contain what Dr. Morris described."

Redgrave hesitated. "And why is that?"

"Because I don't prepare poisons," Clara said simply. "And because a compound of that complexity would require specialized equipment I don't possess. Whoever created it wanted you to believe it came from my shop."

"A convenient theory." Redgrave's expression remained unreadable.

"Not convenient, Inspector. Accurate." Clara began writing in her ledger. "I would suggest you investigate who benefits from Barrett's death—and from my implication in it."

Redgrave studied her for a long moment. "Good day, Miss Wetherly."

As the door closed behind him, Clara continued her inventory with determined precision. With her shop closed and suspicion mounting, she needed to clear her name quickly. Barrett's interest in her building as the "FINAL HOLDOUT" suggested something larger at work than a simple request for henbane.

Marmalade, seemingly satisfied with Redgrave's departure, stretched languidly before leaping to the shelf above the counter. He paced the length of it once, twice, then settled beside the row of ledgers and journals, his tail occasionally brushing against their spines. The shop felt unnaturally quiet without customers, the only sound the scratching of her pen and the constable's occasional shifting. Then, from the small shelf above the counter, a book slid forward and fell open to the floor with a sudden thump.

Marmalade hadn't moved—indeed, he appeared to be watching the fallen book with expectant interest rather than feline surprise, his whiskers twitching forward as if sensing something the humans could not.

Constable Fletcher startled. "What was that?"

"Just a draft," Clara murmured, bending to retrieve the fallen book—her grandmother's old business ledger. "These old buildings settle."

As she lifted it, she noticed it had fallen open to a page dated fifteen years earlier. An entry in her grandmother's flowing script caught her eye: "Refused offer from Blackstone. Property not for sale at any price." Clara's breath caught. She glanced at the constable, who had resumed his position by the door, then carefully placed the ledger on the counter. Perhaps this wasn't merely about her refusal to sell. Perhaps history was repeating itself. A faint humming of a tune her grandmother had favored drifted through the quiet space, though no one sang.

For an instant, Clara could have sworn she caught the faint scent of her grandmother's lavender water. "I understand," she whispered under her breath, too softly for the constable to hear. "I won't sell either."

four

The scratching of Clara's pen against paper filled the silent shop as Constable Fletcher shifted his weight from one foot to the other. She'd been cataloging her inventory for hours, her fingers cramping around the pen but her resolve unwavering. Each jar, each drawer, each pouch precisely documented under the watchful gaze that followed her every movement.

"Nearly finished?" Fletcher asked, stifling a yawn. He had maintained his post by the door for hours, shifting occasionally from one foot to the other.

"Three more shelves," Clara replied, refusing to rush despite her cramping fingers. Precision mattered now more than ever. One mistaken notation, one overlooked item could be misconstrued as deliberate omission—further evidence against her.

Marmalade had claimed the windowsill, his orange bulk spread luxuriously across the fading sunbeam. Every so often, his eyes would open to narrow slits, assessing the constable before drifting closed again in feigned disinterest.

The silence between them stretched, broken only by the

scratch of Clara's pen and the ticking of the shop clock. The constable cleared his throat.

"Unusual profession for a woman," he ventured, clearly uncomfortable with the prolonged quiet.

"Not in my family," Clara responded without looking up. "We've been dispensers of botanical remedies for generations."

"And the... other things?" His voice lowered slightly. "The readings and such."

Clara's pen paused momentarily. "We provide medicinal preparations, Officer Fletcher. The rest is merely conversation."

A conversation her grandmother had often conducted over delicate china cups, with subtle readings of leaves and whispered consultations that had more than once uncovered fevers before they flared or infections before they festered. Genevieve had always known which customers needed more than mere tinctures.

As Clara reached for the valerian root drawer, a slight movement caught her eye. The Gilded Leaf, still open on its stand from earlier, had a page turning gently, though no draft stirred the air. Marmalade's head lifted slightly, his attention fixed on the space beside the book rather than the book itself.

Clara said nothing, but moved closer to the counter, using her body to shield the sight from the constable. The page had settled on a detailed drawing of monkshood with her grandmother's precise handwriting below: "Never to be confused with common blue delphinium—one soothes, one silences."

Below the drawing, in the margin, a small annotation Clara had never noticed before: "B. tried to purchase this knowledge once. Some things aren't for sale."

B. Blackstone? The same company that had sent Barrett to acquire her property?

The shop door opened with such force that the bell jangled sharply. Inspector Redgrave entered, his footsteps sharp against the floorboards, each step conveying authority. Behind him followed Dr. Morris, clutching a leather folio to his chest, his expression one of barely restrained triumph.

"Miss Wetherly," Redgrave acknowledged, his gaze moving to the ledger before her. "I trust the inventory is proceeding satisfactorily?"

"It's nearly complete, Inspector," Clara replied, closing The Gilded Leaf with deliberate casualness. "Though I doubt you'll find anything unexpected within it."

Redgrave's eyes narrowed slightly at her tone. "Dr. Morris has completed his preliminary analysis of the substance in the jar found at the scene."

Clara met his gaze steadily, refusing to display the anxiety coiling beneath her calm exterior.

"I've identified the primary compounds," Morris announced, laying his folio on the counter with theatrical precision. "The victim displays symptoms consistent with aconite poisoning - the distinctive blue-tinged lips and sudden heart failure. The peculiar odor noted at the scene suggests other possible agents were combined with it." His eyes fixed on Clara. "The pattern suggests deliberate poisoning, not accidental ingestion."

"Such combinations aren't used in traditional botanical practice," Clara responded, keeping her voice even despite the accusation in his tone. "And you'll note that aconite produces very different symptoms from henbane, which is what Barrett requested from me."

Morris raised an eyebrow. "So you admit knowledge of various poisons and their effects?"

"I possess knowledge of medicinal plants and their properties, Doctor. The same knowledge your medical texts contain, though perhaps with more practical application."

Morris's lips thinned. "Practical application indeed. The difference being, Miss Wetherly, that physicians are bound by oath and rigorous training. We don't dispense dangerous compounds to anyone who walks through our door."

"Neither do I," Clara replied. "Which is precisely why I refused Mr. Barrett's request."

"Yet somehow," Morris said, examining his fingernails, "a jar bearing your label was found beside his body. A most curious coincidence."

"Equipment like those?" Morris gestured to the small collection of brass stills on her shelf.

"Those are for essential oils and tinctures. They couldn't possibly—"

"The victim shows clear signs of aconite poisoning," Morris interrupted. "The distinctive blue tinge to the lips, the cardio-respiratory failure. Death would have come within minutes of ingestion." He turned to Redgrave. "The jar contained traces of all three compounds, Inspector. A deliberate mixture."

"And that particular combination," Redgrave addressed Clara directly, "is it documented in your shop's records?"

"Absolutely not." Clara's response was immediate and firm. "Such a mixture would serve no medicinal purpose. It would only cause harm."

"Then perhaps you might explain this," Redgrave withdrew a folded paper from his coat. "The label from one of your amber jars, recovered from our evidence. It bears your handwriting and indicates contents consistent with aconite preparation."

Clara stared at the list, the blood draining from her face. "That's impossible. I don't stock—"

"The label was partially removed," Redgrave continued, "but what remained matched your handwriting precisely. Dr. Morris has confirmed the contents match the residue found in the victim's mouth."

Marmalade leapt suddenly from the windowsill, landing

with a solid thump on the counter between Clara and the inspector. He fixed Redgrave with an unblinking stare before turning to brush against Clara's trembling hand.

"I did not prepare that mixture," Clara stated, drawing strength from the warm weight of the cat against her fingers. "I've never combined those herbs. They're antithetical to every principle of botanical healing."

"The evidence suggests otherwise, Miss Wetherly." Redgrave's expression remained impassive. "I'm placing you under house arrest while we complete our investigation. Constable Fletcher will remain posted outside your door. You are not to leave these premises or conduct business until further notice."

Clara felt the room tilt slightly. "For how long?"

"Until we've completed our inquiry. Days. Perhaps weeks."

"I can't survive weeks without business, Inspector." The words escaped before she could consider them, revealing more vulnerability than she intended. "My customers—"

"Should seek proper medical attention," Morris interjected. "Rather than folk remedies of questionable efficacy and safety."

Clara's gaze snapped to the doctor. "My botanical preparations have helped this community for three generations. When your leeches and purgatives failed, Inspector, where do you think people turned? Who tended the cholera victims you abandoned as hopeless during the last outbreak?"

A flash of something—respect? surprise?—crossed Redgrave's face before he masked it. "Your financial concerns are not our primary consideration, Miss Wetherly. A man is dead."

"A man who sought to purchase my property," Clara countered. "Have you investigated Blackstone Development with equal scrutiny? Or those who might benefit from Barrett's failure to acquire my shop?"

Redgrave's silence was answer enough.

"I'll expect that inventory completed by morning," he said finally. "Dr. Morris will review it alongside our own examination of your supplies."

As they moved toward the door, the bell above it jangled again. A portly gentleman in an expensive but slightly outdated suit entered, his gold watch chain catching the last rays of sunlight. His small eyes widened at the police presence.

"Inspector," he nodded, then turned to Clara with a smile that didn't reach his eyes. "Miss Wetherly. I'd hoped to catch you before closing." He glanced pointedly at the constable. "Though I see there's been some trouble."

"Mr. Pinkett," Clara acknowledged, her stomach tightening at the banker's appearance. "As you can see, I'm otherwise engaged."

Marmalade's fur bristled along his spine, his low growl vibrating through the counter beneath Clara's palm. The cat's amber eyes fixed on Pinkett with such focused hostility that the banker took an involuntary step backward.

"George Pinkett, Metropolitan Merchant Bank," he introduced himself to Redgrave with an obsequious nod. "I handle Miss Wetherly's business accounts."

Redgrave studied the banker with newfound interest. "Your timing is fortuitous, Mr. Pinkett. We're concerned about certain financial pressures that might be relevant to our investigation."

Pinkett straightened, clearly pleased at being consulted by the police. "Indeed? Well, I've come about precisely such matters. In light of recent... developments, the bank must reconsider certain arrangements."

"What developments?" Clara asked sharply.

"The sale of every property on this block except yours, for one." Pinkett's tone suggested she was being deliberately obtuse. "And now a murder at your doorstep. The bank must protect its investments."

"You mean you're calling in my loan," Clara translated flatly.

"Not immediately," Pinkett demurred. "But we must insist on accelerated payment or consider foreclosure options. Unless, of course, you were to accept one of the many generous offers Blackstone Development has extended."

Clara caught Redgrave's sudden attention at the mention of Blackstone.

"Mr. Pinkett," Redgrave interrupted, "are you suggesting Miss Wetherly sell her property to the same company that employed the murder victim?"

"Employed?" Pinkett blinked. "Barrett wasn't an employee, Inspector. He was a freelance property assessor. He worked for multiple development companies, including Blackstone and their competitor, Halston Properties."

Clara and Redgrave exchanged a glance. This was new information.

"In fact," Pinkett continued, warming to his subject, "there are multiple developers quite interested in this block. Blackstone Development has made the most visible offers, but I understand Halston Properties has been making inquiries as well."

"Both seem determined to acquire these properties," Pinkett added. "Quite competitive about it, from what I hear. Barrett worked with both companies at different times - not uncommon for property assessors to have multiple clients."

"My financial circumstances are not public knowledge, Mr. Pinkett." Clara's voice had chilled considerably.

"No indeed," Pinkett agreed, though his expression suggested otherwise. "However, I happened to notice Constable Fletcher posted outside earlier today. I can only assume this means disruption to your business." He lowered his voice with false concern. "In such circumstances, I imagine your financial situation will become considerably more strained."

"How fortunate for the developers," Clara observed, watching Pinkett's reaction carefully. "A murder that implicates me, closes my shop, and creates financial pressure to sell. One might almost think it... convenient."

Pinkett's face flushed. "I hardly think anyone would resort to murder over property, Miss Wetherly."

"Someone did," Redgrave interjected, his gaze moving between Clara and the banker with new interest. "And it appears Mr. Barrett worked for multiple interested parties. Perhaps he discovered something that made him dangerous to someone."

Dr. Morris, who had remained silent during this exchange, cleared his throat. "We're getting rather ahead of ourselves, Inspector. Let's not forget the evidence points quite clearly to botanical poisoning." His eyes flickered briefly to Clara. "And to a very specific source."

Marmalade's growl deepened, his tail lashing sharply against the counter.

"That animal seems unwell," Pinkett observed, taking a step back. "Perhaps it should be contained during business discussions."

"Marmalade stays," Clara stated. "And this is not a business discussion, Mr. Pinkett. Not while I am under house arrest."

Redgrave's eyebrow raised slightly. "Indeed. Your financial negotiations will have to wait, Mr. Pinkett. However, I would appreciate your statement regarding Halston Properties and their interest in this location."

"Certainly, Inspector. Always happy to assist the authorities." Pinkett offered another ingratiating smile. "I could share the details of Miss Wetherly's loans as well, if that would be helpful."

"That won't be necessary," Redgrave replied before Clara could object. "Focus your statement on the property acquisitions."

After Pinkett and the police departed, with Constable Fletcher taking up his post outside the front door, Clara finally allowed herself to sink into the chair behind the counter. Marmalade immediately leapt into her lap, uncharacteristically affectionate as he pressed his warm weight against her trembling hands.

"What a mess," she whispered, stroking his fur. "Someone has gone to considerable trouble to frame me, Marmalade. But why?"

The cat's eyes fixed on hers with an unnerving intelligence. He blinked once, deliberately, then leapt to the floor with sudden purpose, padding toward the curtained doorway leading to her private quarters. At the threshold, he turned, tail lashing the air impatiently, and released a commanding meow that echoed through the empty shop.

Clara followed, grateful for the simple distraction of the cat's demands. Her rooms above the shop felt like sanctuary after the tense confrontations below. She lit the lamps against the gathering darkness, then set about preparing a simple meal, more from habit than hunger.

Marmalade watched from his perch atop a bookshelf, tail twitching occasionally, his gaze following something Clara couldn't see. A familiar prickle ran down her spine—the same sensation she'd experienced countless times since her grandmother's death. The sense of being observed by benevolent eyes.

"I know," she said softly to the empty room. "I'm not selling. Not now, not ever."

A chill swept through the room, sharp enough to raise

gooseflesh along Clara's arms. The candle on her small writing desk flickered with unusual brightness. The scent of lavender water—her grandmother's signature perfume—filled the air, as distinct as if a bottle had been freshly opened.

Clara approached the desk, drawn by a sense she couldn't articulate.

The desk had been her grandmother's, its many small drawers containing decades of correspondence, receipts for simples, and personal papers. Clara rarely opened them, finding comfort in keeping things as Genevieve had left them. But tonight, her fingers were drawn to a particular drawer— one she couldn't recall having explored before.

Inside lay a bundle of letters tied with faded ribbon, the topmost bearing a wax seal she didn't recognize. Clara untied the ribbon and carefully opened the first envelope, revealing elegant handwriting on expensive stationery.

MARCH 12, *1841*

Mrs. Hawthorne,

I must express my disappointment at your continued refusal of my most generous offer. The property you cling to so stubbornly will inevitably be required for the advancement of this neighborhood. Your sentimental attachment to a small shop is impeding progress that could benefit many.

Your insistence on maintaining this establishment rather than accepting fair compensation is shortsighted. The property alone is worth more than you could earn in a decade of selling tinctures and reading leaves for superstitious housewives.

Consider carefully the future of your granddaughter. A woman alone faces many hardships in this world, particularly one without proper connections or security. My final offer stands until month's end. After that, I cannot guarantee the continued favorable terms or protection from those who might view your practices with less understanding than I have shown.

Regards,
Lord William Blackstone

CLARA'S HANDS trembled as she set the letter down. Blackstone had made repeated offers?

She quickly scanned the remaining letters. Each showed increasing frustration from Lord Blackstone, culminating in a final letter dated 1842 that merely stated: "You have made your choice, Mrs. Hawthorne. Time will reveal its wisdom."

Clara leaned back, her mind racing. The current Blackstone Development must be connected to the Lord Blackstone who had pressured her grandmother. And now, fifteen years later, they were still pursuing the property—by any means necessary.

She returned to the drawer, searching for her grandmother's responses, but found none. Instead, her fingers brushed against a small leather notebook wedged at the back. Pulling it out, she found a list of names, dates, and notations in Genevieve's precise handwriting.

One entry caught her eye immediately: "Refused Blackstone's offer again. No price worth the home where Clara was raised. Our legacy is not for sale."

The next entry chilled her blood: "B. suggested financial difficulties might force my hand eventually. Said development was 'inevitable progress.' Will not surrender what three generations of Wetherly women have built."

Clara closed the notebook, a new clarity settling over her. This wasn't merely about purchasing her shop. The systematic acquisition of every property on the block suggested something larger—a comprehensive development plan. And someone had murdered Barrett, using herbs to implicate her, ensuring the shop would be closed and financial pressure would mount.

They expected her to sell out of desperation.

Instead, she would fight.

Clara strode to The Gilded Leaf with renewed determination, her fingers running along the worn leather binding before she opened it to the page she'd seen earlier—the monkshood illustration. The detailed drawing seemed to capture the plant's deadly beauty, the intricate purple-blue flowers almost vibrating with subtle menace under her touch.

If Barrett had been poisoned with aconite, commonly known as monkshood, that was significant. But why had he asked for henbane? Clara recalled his visit—how his eyes had wandered to the ceiling beams, the wall dimensions, the counter placement.

"Barrett had no interest in henbane," Clara murmured, the realization dawning. "He merely needed a pretext to enter the shop, to examine its structure and value firsthand. Something specialized enough that I'd be distracted explaining its properties while he studied the beams and foundation."

Or had there been another reason? His trembling hands, his desperation... those weren't the mannerisms of a calculating property assessor. He had seemed genuinely unwell, almost afraid. And aconite poisoning, with its distinctive symptoms, would have begun well before his death if administered gradually. Had Barrett been seeking henbane on someone else's instruction? As treatment for his symptoms, perhaps?

Clara frowned, recalling Dr. Morris's swift certainty about the poison. Most physicians she'd encountered dismissed botanical knowledge entirely, yet Morris had identified the compounds with unusual precision. Almost as if he'd known exactly what to look for.

Someone versed in toxic botanicals had created that

poison mixture deliberately—someone who knew enough to use Clara's jar and label to implicate her.

Clara turned to her herbs, taking a deep breath of the familiar scents that usually brought comfort. Tonight, they reminded her of darker possibilities—how easily healing knowledge could be twisted toward harm.

She wouldn't wait passively for Redgrave to discover the truth. She needed to learn more about Blackstone Development, about Halston Properties, and about Barrett's work for both. Even under house arrest, there were ways to gather information.

Tomorrow, Mrs. Penfield would undoubtedly return, propriety and police orders be damned. The widow's endless gossip, which Clara had often found tedious, might now provide exactly the neighborhood intelligence she needed.

And perhaps Inspector Redgrave, despite his suspicions, might be made to see that looking beyond the obvious suspect served his investigation as well as her freedom.

Marmalade leapt onto the counter and pawed at The Gilded Leaf, drawing Clara's attention to a previously overlooked notation in the margin of the monkshood page:

"Trust fox rather than wolf when walking in the forest—at least the fox admits its nature."

A riddle? Or a warning? Clara pondered her grandmother's cryptic note. Wolf and fox—predators both, but with different approaches. One open about its danger, one deceptive. In this tangle of developers, bankers, and physicians, who wore their true nature openly, and who disguised their intentions behind respectable facades?

Lord Blackstone made no secret of his desire for the property. His family had pursued it openly for years. Dr. Morris, however, had appeared from nowhere, his interest in the poison surprisingly specific, his condescension toward her botanical knowledge immediate and pointed.

Clara studied the monkshood illustration, tracing the delicate petals with her fingertip. Physicians had access to botanical compounds. They understood chemistry, dosage, effects. And Morris had identified the poison with remarkable confidence for someone examining a day-old corpse.

A warning about deceptive partners, perhaps? Clara couldn't be certain. But one thing was clear—her grandmother had refused to sell this property for fifteen years, and Clara would honor that determination. This shop wasn't merely her livelihood and home—it was her last connection to the grandmother who had raised her, the physical embodiment of three generations of Wetherly women.

She closed The Gilded Leaf with a decisive snap, her mind already forming plans. Mrs. Penfield would come tomorrow, police orders or no—the widow had never missed a Tuesday tonic in twenty years. Clara needed to learn more about both development companies, about Barrett's connections to each, and about Dr. Morris's unusually specific knowledge of botanical poisons. Someone in the neighborhood must have seen or heard something valuable.

"They think they've trapped me," she whispered to Marmalade, who watched her with approving eyes. "But they've only given me reason to investigate."

five

"**A**bsolutely not! The shop is closed by order of Inspector Redgrave!" Constable Fletcher's voice carried up the narrow staircase to Clara's sitting room, interrupting her inventory of remaining tea stocks.

"Nonsense!" The familiar, imperious tone of Mrs. Penfield cut through the constable's protest. "I have been collecting my Tuesday tonic from this establishment for twenty years, young man, and I don't intend to stop because of some ridiculous misunderstanding."

Clara set down her ledger and moved to the window overlooking the street. Mrs. Penfield stood on the doorstep, umbrella clutched like a weapon, her steel-gray curls trembling with indignation beneath her modest hat. The constable—poor man—maintained his position in the doorway but had clearly met his match.

"Madam, I cannot allow anyone to enter during an active investigation—"

"My rheumatism cannot wait for your investigation to conclude!" Mrs. Penfield rapped her umbrella against the doorframe for emphasis. "Besides, I was at tea with your superior's mother just yesterday. I'm certain Chief Inspector Holloway would be distressed to hear his mother's dear friend was denied her necessary medicinal preparation."

Clara bit back a smile. Mrs. Penfield wielded social connections like a general deploying troops.

"Mrs. Penfield," Clara called down, opening the window despite the morning chill. "I'll be right down."

The widow looked up, triumph brightening her face. "There you are, my dear! This young man seems to think police orders supersede medical necessity."

As Clara descended the stairs to intervene, another voice joined the doorstep standoff.

"Is there a problem, Constable?"

Dr. Morris approached from the street, medical bag in hand. Clara stiffened instinctively at his arrival, recalling his dismissive tone from yesterday's interrogation.

Fletcher straightened. "Dr. Morris, sir. Just explaining to this lady that Miss Wetherly's shop is closed during the investigation."

To Clara's surprise, Morris glanced at Mrs. Penfield with what appeared to be genuine concern. "Ah, Mrs. Penfield, isn't it? I believe we met at the parish social last month. Your rheumatism troubling you again?"

"Indeed it is," she confirmed. "And Miss Wetherly's willow bark compound is the only thing that provides relief."

Morris nodded thoughtfully. "The poor woman clearly needs her tonic, Constable. Medical necessity, I'd say." He turned to Clara with a professionally polite nod that held none of yesterday's accusation. "Traditional botanical remedies have their place, particularly for such complaints."

Clara's eyebrows rose involuntarily. Had Dr. Morris just acknowledged the efficacy of her remedies?

Fletcher looked between them, clearly uncomfortable

contradicting a physician. "Inspector Redgrave's orders were quite clear..."

"I'll take full responsibility," Morris said, checking his pocket watch. "I've just examined our victim's body again and need to continue to the Yard. Please inform the Inspector I authorized this on medical grounds." With a curt nod to Clara and a gentler one to Mrs. Penfield, he continued down the street.

"Fifteen minutes only," Fletcher finally relented, stepping aside to allow Mrs. Penfield entry. "And I'll be right here watching."

Clara ushered Mrs. Penfield upstairs to her private sitting room, away from the constable's attentive ears. Marmalade, who had been dozing on the windowsill, raised his head to observe Dr. Morris's retreating figure, whiskers twitching forward with unusual interest.

"Well," Mrs. Penfield declared, settling into the overstuffed chair that had been Genevieve's favorite, "that was fortunate. I didn't realize Dr. Morris could be reasonable. He always seemed rather full of himself at church socials."

"Indeed," Clara replied, puzzled by the doctor's unexpected support. She moved to prepare tea, finding comfort in the familiar ritual. "Though I suspect he simply enjoys overriding Constable Fletcher's authority."

The sitting room remained exactly as her grandmother had left it—botanical prints in aged frames, the worn velvet chair, shelves of books on herbology and medicine.

Mrs. Penfield removed her gloves, watching Clara prepare the tea. "You look pale, my dear. Are you eating properly?"

"As well as can be expected under house arrest," Clara replied with a wry smile. "But I suspect you didn't battle the constable merely to inquire after my diet."

"Certainly not." Mrs. Penfield leaned forward, lowering her voice despite their privacy. "Well then, my dear. The entire neighborhood is talking, and for once, I've been listening rather than contributing."

Clara poured the tea into her grandmother's delicate cups. "And what exactly is being said?"

"Oh, the usual nonsense when something like this happens. Half believe you wouldn't harm a spider in your garden, the other half suddenly 'always suspected something odd' about your botanical preparations." Mrs. Penfield waved a dismissive hand. "People with no imagination finding drama where they can."

"And the more substantive conversations?" Clara prompted.

Mrs. Penfield's eyes gleamed at being taken seriously. "Lord Blackstone himself was seen visiting three shops on this block last week. Not sending representatives—himself! First time in twenty years he's deigned to leave Mayfair for Bloomsbury."

Clara nearly spilled the tea she was pouring. "Lord Blackstone? Personally?"

"Indeed. Making offers well above market value, from what I understand." Mrs. Penfield accepted her cup. "Meanwhile, that new developer—Halston—has men practically living in the neighborhood, approaching everyone who hasn't already sold."

"The competition seems unusually fierce for ordinary storefronts," Clara observed.

"That's just it!" Mrs. Penfield leaned forward conspiratorially. "They're saying there's railway plans, dear. Coming right through this part of Bloomsbury."

"Railway plans?" Clara's mind raced. "That would explain the property values..."

"Precisely. And that Barrett fellow was seen arguing quite publicly with Blackstone's solicitor outside the registry office just days before his death. Voices raised, threats exchanged—most undignified."

Clara placed her cup carefully on its saucer. "What sort of threats?"

"Something about 'breach of loyalty' and 'contractual obligations.' The solicitor accused Barrett of working both sides." Mrs. Penfield smiled thinly. "Which, I've since learned, he was. Mrs. Jenkins's son works as a clerk at the land registry office. Says Barrett filed paperwork for both Blackstone and Halston in the same week."

Clara absorbed this information. Barrett had been playing both developers against each other—a dangerous game.

"There's more," Mrs. Penfield continued, clearly enjoying her role. "Lord Blackstone seems particularly determined to acquire this block. His man told Mrs. Jenkins he 'always finishes what his family starts.' Seemed rather ominous, if you ask me."

"Did Barrett approach other shops besides mine?" Clara asked.

"Oh yes. He visited every building on the block." Mrs. Penfield sipped her tea. "Several people mentioned his hands were trembling—had been getting worse over weeks. Mr. Finch at the tobacconist thought he might have a drinking problem."

"Did anyone else notice his request for unusual herbs or medicines?"

"As a matter of fact, yes. He asked Dr. Morris about treatments for tremors at the pharmacy last week. Morris suggested Bromide of Potassium." Mrs. Penfield raised an eyebrow. "The doctor seemed rather impressed by your grandmother's work, by the way. Mentioned at the church social that Genevieve Hawthorne had 'remarkable insight for someone without formal training.' High praise from a physician, wouldn't you say?"

Clara found that difficult to reconcile with Morris's condescending manner yesterday, but people often showed different faces in different company.

"Mrs. Penfield," Clara said carefully, "I need your help. I cannot leave this shop, but I need to understand what's happening."

The widow straightened, her expression suddenly serious. "Whatever you need, my dear."

"I need information about both developers—their plans, their representatives, their methods. Who they're pressuring, what they're offering." Clara leaned forward. "And I need to know why Barrett was consulting both sides."

"A neighborhood investigation?" Mrs. Penfield's eyes sparkled with excitement. "Who should I speak with?"

Clara outlined her plan—which neighbors to visit, what questions to ask discreetly, and how to report back without arousing suspicion. Mrs. Penfield absorbed every detail with the precision of a military commander receiving orders.

When the fifteen minutes elapsed, Constable Fletcher knocked firmly on the door. Mrs. Penfield departed with her tonic and a conspiratorial smile, promising to return with information.

Alone again, Clara moved to the window, watching Mrs. Penfield's determined stride down the street. The neighborhood would yield its secrets to that woman more effectively than any police interrogation.

A sudden chill swept through the room. Behind her, Marmalade's fur stood on end, his ears flattening as his attention fixed on an empty corner. Clara had felt this particular cold many times since her grandmother's death—a presence both familiar and comforting.

"I know you're trying to help," she murmured to the empty room.

The air shimmered slightly in response. A book tumbled

from the upper shelf—a volume Clara didn't recognize. She moved to retrieve it, finding an old city planning document her grandmother had apparently saved. It fell open to a yellowed map of Bloomsbury, with proposed railway lines sketched across entire blocks.

The date at the bottom read 1841.

Clara studied the map with growing astonishment. This wasn't a new development scheme—it was a revival of plans abandoned fifteen years ago. Her street was marked with an asterisk, and her grandmother's precise handwriting noted in the margin: "B's first attempt."

Tucked between the pages, she found a newspaper clipping:

BLOOMSBURY RAILWAY EXTENSION *DELAYED*

Lord William Blackstone expressed disappointment as the Railway Commission delayed approval for the proposed Bloomsbury expansion. The controversial plan, which would have required extensive property acquisition in the historic neighborhood, has been postponed indefinitely due to funding concerns and resident opposition.

The date: May 17, 1842.

CLARA SAT HEAVILY in her grandmother's chair, pieces falling into place. This wasn't simply about current property values—it was the continuation of the Blackstone family's long-abandoned railway plan. Her shop wasn't just valuable real estate; it was the final obstacle to a scheme fifteen years in the making.

"This is about more than just my shop, isn't it, Grandmother?" she whispered.

The candle on her desk flared and danced brightly, as if in

confirmation.

As evening fell, Clara stood at her bedroom window, peering through a gap in the curtains. The gaslights had been lit, casting pools of murky illumination along the otherwise darkened street. In one such pool stood a tall figure she recognized immediately—Inspector Redgrave, his collar turned up against the mist, watching her shop with unwavering attention.

Their eyes met briefly across the distance. He made no move to hide his presence, nor did she retreat from his gaze. There was something oddly comforting about his vigilance, despite her frustration at being his primary suspect.

Movement further down the street caught her attention—another figure, this one more elegantly dressed, with the unmistakable bearing of wealth and privilege. The man stood in shadow, but his silhouette suggested the refined posture of aristocracy. As Clara watched, he turned toward her window, then quickly disappeared into the fog when he realized she'd spotted him.

She stepped back from the window, heart pounding. Had that been Lord Blackstone himself? Monitoring the property he'd sought for so long?

Clara moved to her writing desk and began methodically recording everything she'd learned. She created a list of suspects, with Blackstone and Halston at the top, elaborating their motives and connections to Barrett. She noted Barrett's trembling condition and unusual behavior, his double-dealings between developers, and the railway plans that provided motive for murder.

At the bottom of her list, almost as an afterthought, she wrote "Dr. Morris – Arrogant but seemingly uninvolved. Unusually knowledgeable about poisons. Contradictory behavior regarding botanical remedies."

She tucked the paper behind a loose panel in her dresser,

creating a makeshift investigation board hidden from prying eyes. The railway map and newspaper clipping joined her notes, along with a sketch of Barrett she'd made from memory, annotated with his symptoms.

Periodically, she checked the window. Redgrave remained at his post, unwavering. The second watcher did not return.

As she prepared for bed, Clara took one final glance outside. Redgrave stood in the same spot, his breath visible in the cold night air. His dedication to duty was remarkable, if misguided in its focus on her.

"Blackstone wants this property enough to kill for it," she murmured to herself. "But did he act directly, or employ someone versed in noxious botanicals?"

MARMALADE'S OBSERVATIONS – *Entry No. 2*

Three nights now, the tall man with silver buttons has watched our shop.

He stands in shadow where the gas lamp cannot reach him, trying to become part of the darkness itself. Humans are so obvious, even when they think themselves concealed.

His fingers tap rhythms against his coat. Not impatience—calculations. I recognize the pattern of a mind assembling pieces.

Clara doesn't see him. She's too busy sorting through papers at the worktable, pausing sometimes to speak to empty corners. Tonight, she found a receipt hidden behind the counter—surprise in her eyes, triumph in her voice.

"It's here, Grandmother," she whispered. "Exactly where you said it would be."

No one had spoken. No one had moved the papers. Yet she is certain.

Humans create meaning from coincidence. Perhaps that's their magic.

The silver-button man watches longer each night. His eyes track movements in our windows. Sometimes, they linger on Clara herself.

Not a predator's gaze. Something different. Something curious.

There's another watcher too. Smaller, quicker. Hidden better. I catch his scent sometimes—ink and money and something sharper beneath. He doesn't watch to protect. He watches to harm.

And a third—the one who smells of medicine and secrets. He passes by too often for coincidence, pausing to study our windows, his fingers lightly tracing the stonework as if measuring our defenses.

I stretched and padded to the window, placing one paw against the glass.

The silver-button man stiffened. Our eyes met across the street.

He knows I see him now.

Good. We understand each other.

six

Clara woke with a start, Marmalade's considerable weight pressing on her ribcage like a judgment. The cat blinked at her once—slow and solemn—before leaping from the bed in a fluid arc.

"Message received," she muttered, rubbing her eyes.

She'd slept poorly. Not that she expected anything else. Images from the day before drifted through her mind like fog: Barrett's blue-tinged lips, the glint of her own label on that amber jar, the sharp click of Redgrave's boot heels across her floorboards. Even sleep had offered no reprieve—only feverish dreams where her grandmother whispered warnings she couldn't understand.

The sun had barely broken the rooftops, but Clara welcomed the gray morning. Anything to anchor herself in routine.

She rose, dressed, and twisted her hair back with practiced hands, then moved to the washstand to splash cold water on her face.

Downstairs, voices drifted up—Constable Fletcher's, uncertain as always, and another she recognized immediately.

"...most irregular, but Inspector Redgrave allowed brief visits for business matters—under supervision."

"I should think so." The clipped reply carried a note of patronizing authority. "I'm not here for tinctures or botanical remedies. I'm here to discuss Miss Wetherly's account."

Clara descended the stairs, tightening the sash of her wrapper as she went. Mr. Pinkett stood in the center of her shuttered shop, hat in hand, every inch the concerned banker. Fletcher hovered uncomfortably by the door.

"Miss Wetherly," Pinkett offered a perfunctory bow, twisting his hat brim between his fingers. "I apologize for the hour, but I hoped to speak before the day became... complicated."

"You've a gift for understatement, Mr. Pinkett." Clara gestured toward the staircase. "We may speak upstairs. Constable Fletcher, you're welcome to listen from the landing —Inspector Redgrave's orders, I believe?"

Fletcher shifted his weight, evidently relieved to avoid taking a position. Pinkett offered a gracious, false smile and followed Clara up the narrow stairs.

She gestured toward the sitting room chair her grand-mother had once favored. He settled into it without invita-tion, the leather creaking beneath his bulk as he placed a worn leather folio across his lap.

"I'll be direct, Miss Wetherly," he said, extracting a paper with practiced efficiency. "Given recent events and your shop's forced closure, the bank has reviewed your loan's terms."

"I've never missed a payment."

"Indeed," Pinkett's lips curved into what might have passed for a sympathetic smile on a more genuine counte-nance. "Your record is impeccable. However, this loan was originally secured by your grandmother against the property itself. That arrangement remains binding."

Clara blinked. "I wasn't told the building was collateral."

"It's not uncommon for such details to be overlooked in family transitions. The deed is still in Genevieve Hawthorne's name. That complicates matters."

He laid the document on the table between them.

"The bank is prepared to offer a short-term extension—at a revised interest rate, of course. Alternatively, there are generous offers on the table from both Halston and Blackstone. A sale would satisfy the debt in full."

Clara picked up the document. The revised terms were extortionate.

"You said the deed is still in my grandmother's name?"

Pinkett inclined his head, a small gesture of affected regret. "Technically, yes. Which may cast doubt on your legal claim, should you wish to contest any transfer of ownership."

Her eyes narrowed. "Curious that didn't come up when I signed the loan transfer."

Pinkett's smile remained fixed, like a porcelain mask. "An oversight, I'm sure. The bank merely wishes to protect its investment."

Marmalade chose that moment to slink into the room and leap onto the windowsill with a disdainful flick of his tail. He studied Pinkett with the cold calculation of a predator assessing prey.

"I'll leave the documents with you," Pinkett rose, brushing imaginary dust from his waistcoat. "Three days to decide. After that... Well. The bank does have a responsibility to act in its best interest."

Clara didn't reply. She watched him descend the stairs, speaking low to Fletcher before departing into the morning fog.

Only when the door closed behind him did she move.

She crossed to the desk, where her grandmother's old files remained tucked away. Marmalade gave a short, approving chirp as she opened the bottom drawer.

The folder was there. Labeled in Genevieve's hand: "Ownership".

Inside, a properly recorded deed, notarized and stamped, naming Clara Wetherly as sole proprietor of 519 Bellrose Lane. Dated two years before Genevieve's death. No mention of any lien.

So Pinkett had lied.

Whether he assumed she was too grief-addled or too busy to check didn't matter. He had deliberately misled her—and stood in her shop pretending concern.

She set the folder down carefully and crossed to the window.

On the street below, two figures lingered near the curb. One was Pinkett. The other, tall and impeccably dressed in a dark coat with a silver-tipped cane, bore the unmistakable air of titled wealth. Clara recognized him instantly from the old Gazette illustrations her grandmother had saved—Lord William Blackstone, every inch as patrician as described, from the polished top hat to the calculating tilt of his chin.

She watched them confer. Pinkett handed over a folded document—her extension terms, no doubt—before tipping his hat and vanishing into the fog.

So. They wanted the property. Badly.

She turned from the window just in time to see another figure emerge from the mist.

Inspector Redgrave approached from the far end of Bellrose Lane, his stride brisk, coat trailing behind him in the wind. Clara remained motionless behind the lace curtain, noting the sharp line of his shoulders, the way his gaze scanned the street as if cataloging potential threats.

A knock on the doorframe startled her. Fletcher's voice followed: "Miss Wetherly? Inspector Redgrave is downstairs."

She took a breath, tucked the deed beneath a stack of innocuous papers, and descended.

Redgrave stood at the counter, raindrops glistening on his greatcoat, his expression carved from stone. He did not offer a greeting.

"You said you refused Barrett henbane."

"I did."

"What precisely did you give him?"

"A calming blend," Clara replied, her voice as measured as if discussing the weather. "Lemon balm, valerian root, skullcap —nothing he couldn't have obtained at any reputable apothecary. And certainly nothing toxic."

"And yet, he ended up dead behind your shop with a compound Dr. Morris identified—aconite, belladonna, and something akin to thorn apple. A precise formulation. Not something stumbled into by mistake."

"A deadly combination."

"Clearly, Miss Wetherly."

Clara folded her arms across her chest, the woolen sleeves of her dress rustling in the silence. "What exactly are you asking me, Inspector? Because my answer will not change. No, I did not give Mr. Barrett any combination of those botanicals, neither would I ever administer such a thing—to him or to anyone else. Even the most modest country dispenser of simples knows better than to mix aconite with belladonna. The interaction alone is erratic—if not fatal. And adding thorn apple? That's not a remedy; that's a death wish in a bottle. I may deal in poisons, yes—but only in the same way a surgeon deals in knives: with intention, training, and restraint. Whoever prepared that mixture wasn't seeking balance or relief. They meant to kill. So you see, inspector I could have murdered a man in this manner, but I surely did not do so. And I have absolutely no motive whatsoever."

She paused, watching a flicker of something—perhaps respect—cross his face. "But I know someone who might. In fact, I can name several."

Redgrave's brow arched upward, a hairline fracture in his professional mask.

"I believe," Clara continued, moving toward the counter with deliberate precision, "that Mr. Barrett was here under false pretenses. He was assessing the property. I believe his death was part of a coordinated attempt to force me to sell my building."

Redgrave regarded her with calculated skepticism. "That's quite a theory."

Clara reached beneath the counter and withdrew the newspaper clipping she'd unearthed the night before.

"My grandmother saved this. It's from a proposed railway expansion. Fifteen years ago. Every other business on this block has sold. Mine hasn't. Barrett called it the 'final holdout.'"

"I recall." Redgrave examined the yellowed paper, his gloved fingers tracing the faded illustration of rail lines. "And you think this ties to his death?"

"I think it gives someone motive to frame me."

"That is quite a theory."

"Theory or not, who stands to benefit from Mr. Barrett's death, that I cannot say, but I know who benefits from my disgrace. From my shop being closed, or my being forced to sell--or if I am imprisoned for say... murder, what would happen to my property, Inspector Redgrave?"

"It would be seized of course... "

"And sold at auction."

"You're suggesting murder. Conspiracy. Fraud."

"I'm suggesting someone benefits greatly from my disgrace."

Redgrave looked up, the lamplight catching the green flecks in his hazel eyes as uncertainty briefly shadowed his features. "Do you have proof?"

"Of course not, but I shall. Clearing my name has become my highest priority as I am sure you understand, inspector."

"Clearing your name?"

"Yes, Inspector. There are others with far stronger motives than mine."

"Is that so?"

"Quite. Lord Blackstone, for one."

His shoulders stiffened ever so slightly. "Lord Blackstone?"

"He's made more than one offer on this building, all of which I've refused. My grandmother turned him away years ago, and now his development company is trying again—with new tactics. Then there's Halston. Another suitor I declined. And finally, Mr. Pinkett."

"Pinkett? The banker?" Redgrave folded his arms, his great-coat still damp from the morning fog. "What's your accusation, Miss Wetherly—that your banker murdered a man in your alley?"

"I'm saying, Inspector, that Mr. Pinkett was in my shop this morning with a proposal to extend my loans—at rates so high they could only be intended to force me into selling. He claimed the deed was still in my grandmother's name and that there was a loan against the property that a sale would satisfy."

Redgrave pivoted sharply toward Fletcher, who seemed to shrink beneath his gaze. "You allowed him in?"

"He said it was permitted for business purposes, sir..."

Clara lifted her chin, her posture as straight as a hawthorn stem. "And after our conversation, I watched him speak with Lord Blackstone through the front window. Pinkett handed him something. A folded paper. Perhaps the terms he'd just pressed upon me."

"Those are serious implications."

"And they are backed by fact. I checked my records, Inspector. The deed is in my name—transferred two years before my grandmother's passing. There is no lien. No

outstanding debt. Pinkett lied. He was attempting to intimidate me into selling. And if he's working with Blackstone,
then they both had motive to frame me."

Redgrave regarded her in silence, his expression unreadable save for the slight narrowing of his eyes. Then: "That's
quite a tale, Miss Wetherly."

She met his gaze unflinchingly, like foxglove standing tall
against the wind. "It's the truth."

"But why would they want to kill Mr. Barrett?"

"Mrs. Penfield said that Mr. Barrett was seen arguing with
two men the day before he died. Perhaps--"

Redgrave's attention snapped back to her with sudden
intensity. "Mrs. Penfield? She was here, too?"

Clara nodded once, a small gesture of defiance. "She came
for her tonic, yes. And shared some rather useful
information."

He turned toward Fletcher, whose ears had reddened
noticeably. "I ordered no visitors."

"Dr. Morris said it was acceptable," Fletcher offered
weakly.

Redgrave's jaw tightened, a muscle flickering beneath the
skin. He turned back to Clara. "Enough. You will leave the
investigating to me."

Clara arched a brow, the ghost of amusement playing at the
corners of her mouth. "And if you investigate the wrong people?"

"This is not a game, Miss Wetherly. It is a criminal investigation. You are not a detective. You are a suspect. And I will
not have you tampering with witnesses or evidence while
under house order."

"So, you expect me to sit idly by while my name is dragged
through the mud and my life dismantled, piece by piece?"

"Yes," he replied, each word crisp as autumn frost. "And
Constable Fletcher will ensure that you do."

Clara's lips pressed together, trapping the protest that rose in her throat like steam from a kettle. Instead, she offered a brittle smile.

"Very well, Inspector. I wouldn't dream of interfering."

Redgrave studied her face a moment longer, his eyes lingering on hers as if searching for the lie beneath her words.Then he collected his coat. "No more visitors. No more interference. Do I make myself clear?"

"Crystal," Clara said sweetly.

He didn't seem convinced. But he left.

The moment the door closed behind him, Clara turned to Marmalade, who was now sitting atop the shelf by the back window.

"What do you think, old friend? Time to sit quietly and hope justice finds its way through the fog?"

Marmalade blinked slowly.

"No, I didn't think so."

She crossed to the desk and slipped the deed into a hidden compartment behind the drawer lining. Then she moved to the back of the shop, to the narrow staircase that wound down behind the alley-facing storeroom door.

Fletcher's silhouette was visible through the frosted glass of the front window, arms crossed, already bored.

Clara opened the back door with deliberate care, just wide enough to admit her without sound, then slipped down the stairs, boots barely touching the treads.

She paused at the mouth of the alley. Fog pressed close, but it carried with it the faint scent of pipe smoke and brick dust.

Barrett had been seen arguing with Blackstone's solicitor outside the registry offices.

If she could find out why, perhaps she could uncover what he knew—and why it got him killed.

She pulled her hood up, skirt lifted just enough to clear the puddles and vanished into the mist.

seven

The fog that blanketed London that morning was a mercy. Clara kept to the edges of the street, her boots selecting each cobblestone with deliberate care as she wove through the awakening city. Carts rattled past, their drivers' faces obscured in the gray haze. Perfect weather for secrets and lies.

She paused at the corner of Bloomsbury Street, studying the fresh chalk markings that adorned the buildings like ghostly prophecies. White lines delineating a future that had no place for her shop. No place for her.

"Penny for the Times, miss?" A newspaper boy materialized from the mist, cap pulled low, papers tucked beneath one thin arm.

"Not today, thank you."

"Heard about that business on Bellrose Lane?" the boy persisted, shifting from one foot to the other. "They say a woman who sells them botanical preparations poisoned a man right in her shop. Flowers and leaves and such—my mum says it's all well and good for headaches, but some folk use 'em for darker purposes."

Clara felt her shoulders stiffen beneath her woolen cloak. "Do they indeed?"

"Oh yes, miss. All sorts of talk 'round the neighborhood." The boy leaned forward, his voice dropping to a conspiratorial whisper. "Funny thing is, there was another lady here yesterday asking all about the railway plans and that very same shop. Said she was writing a story. Wanted to know about property values and such."

Clara reached into her reticule and fished a penny from her pocket. "Perhaps I'll take that paper after all."

The transaction complete, Clara tucked the newspaper away and turned—only to find herself staring directly into a pair of unblinking amber eyes. Marmalade sat in the middle of the pavement, his tail wrapped around his paws with regal precision.

"You cannot be here," she whispered urgently, glancing back toward Bellrose Lane. "How did you even—"

The cat merely blinked, then rose and trotted ahead of her as if leading the way.

"I suppose you've decided to become my accomplice?" Clara muttered, gathering her skirts as she followed. "Though I'd dearly love to know how you managed to escape past Fletcher and then track me through half of Bloomsbury. Do you have accomplices of your own?"

Marmalade's only reply was to suddenly dart sideways, directly between the legs of a passing gentleman. The man stumbled, caught himself against a lamppost, then spotted Clara.

"Good morning, madam," he said with a curt nod, adjusting his hat. "Do keep your pet on a lead. Most inconvenient when they dash about."

"My apologies, sir. He's not usually so... adventurous."

But Marmalade had already disappeared around the corner, his orange tail raised like a battle flag.

Clara quickened her pace, her pulse fluttering against her throat like a caged bird. If Fletcher discovered her absence, or worse, if Redgrave learned she had defied his direct orders, the suspicion against her would only strengthen. But she had no choice. With her reputation, her livelihood, and possibly her freedom at stake, she could not afford to sit idly by while others determined her fate.

By the time Clara reached the Registry Office, her feline companion was nowhere to be seen. She adjusted her bonnet and smoothed the front of her dress before ascending the stone steps with all the confidence she could muster. Inside, the vaulted entrance hall echoed with the precise sounds of official London—the scratch of nibbed pens, the thud of document stamps, the hushed murmur of civil servants going about the business of recording everything and everyone.

The cavernous room smelled of ink and dust and the particular mustiness of aging paper. Rows of high desks lined the walls, where clerks meticulously entered transactions into massive ledgers. At the center, beneath an impressive domed ceiling, stood a circular counter where the public could submit their queries and documents, each transaction requiring a precise arrangement of official stamps and seals.

Clara approached the central desk, her rehearsed inquiry poised on her lips, when a tremendous crash erupted from the far side of the room. A tower of carefully stacked papers cascaded to the floor, followed by the outraged cry of a clerk.

"A cat! There's a cat loose in the Registry!"

Clara pressed her lips together, turning discreetly away as several clerks abandoned their posts to chase the blur of orange fur darting between desks. Taking advantage of the distraction, she slipped toward a side counter where a young woman with wire-rimmed spectacles was meticulously entering data in a massive ledger.

"Miss Collins?"

The woman looked up, her severe expression yielding immediately to recognition."Miss Wetherly! Goodness, what are you doing here? Mother was just saying how terribly worried she is about you!"

Clara felt her tension ease at the unexpected sight of a friendly face. Harriet Collins had grown from the awkward, bookish girl who accompanied her mother to Hawthorne & Wetherly into a poised young woman—one of the few female clerks in the Registry Office.

"It's good to see you, Harriet. I hadn't realized you were working here now."

Harriet glanced furtively at her male colleagues, then lowered her voice. "Three years this May. I'd have visited the shop, but Father doesn't approve of Mother's 'botanical nonsense,' as he calls it." She squeezed Clara's hand briefly."Though Mother would never have managed her arthritis without your special tincture. She still speaks of you whenever Father is out of earshot. They've hired several of us women recently with all the property transactions from these new developments. The men don't like it, but they need hands to process the paperwork."

"I'm glad to hear it helped," Clara replied, leaning closer until the brim of her bonnet nearly touched Harriet's spectacles. "Harriet, I need your discretion. I'm in rather a difficult position."

"The entire neighborhood is talking about what happened," Harriet whispered, her eyes magnified behind her lenses. "Mother says it's absolute nonsense—you helping people for years only to suddenly turn poisoner? Ridiculous!"

"I'm grateful for her confidence. Unfortunately, Inspector Redgrave of Scotland Yard doesn't share it."

Harriet cast a quick glance around the room, where clerks still attempted to corner Marmalade among the filing cabinets. "What can I do? Mother would never forgive me if I didn't help."

"I need to see the property records filed by Silas Barrett. Particularly those concerning Bellrose Lane."

Recognition brightened Harriet's eyes. "That dreadful man? He was just here two days ago, looking sickly and irritable. Always so dismissive of the female clerks, with those trembling hands of his constantly rearranging his papers." She closed her ledger with quiet determination. "Come with me—I know exactly where those files are kept."

Harriet led Clara through a door marked 'Authorized Personnel Only' and down a narrow corridor lined with filing cabinets. She unlocked a side room with a small brass key.

"Property assessments are organized by district and date," she explained, striking a match to light a wall lamp. "Each must be stamped and registered with the proper tax authorities. Barrett's would be here, with the recent Bloomsbury evaluations."

"You know your way around impressively well," Clara observed.

Harriet's lips curved in a slight smile. "The men may tolerate our presence because of the increased workload with all these development projects, but they still expect us to fetch their files. I've memorized the entire system out of spite."

As Harriet began pulling folders, a familiar rustle drew Clara's attention. Impossibly, Marmalade sat atop a stack of documents on the center table, looking thoroughly pleased with himself.

"Is that your... assistant?" Harriet asked, adjusting her spectacles as if to confirm what she was seeing. "He looks remarkably qualified."

"He's something," Clara replied dryly. "Though qualification is debatable."

Marmalade merely blinked, then deliberately placed one paw atop a folder nearly hidden beneath others.

Harriet spread the documents across the table's polished surface, her brow furrowing as she compared them. "This is unusual. These are both Barrett's assessments of the same properties, but the valuations are entirely different."

Clara leaned forward, examining the precise columns of figures. One set listed each property on Bellrose Lane with modest valuations—below market price, certainly well below what Blackstone Development had offered. The other showed the same properties with valuations nearly triple the first set.

"The lower valuations were submitted to Blackstone Development," Harriet noted, tapping the authorization stamp with her fingernail. "The higher ones to Halston Properties."

"He was playing them against each other," Clara murmured, the pieces falling into place. "Telling Blackstone the properties weren't worth their investment, while convincing Halston they were undervalued opportunities."

She examined Barrett's signature across both documents. The earlier Blackstone report showed his precise, measured handwriting. The later Halston assessment revealed a subtle but unmistakable trembling in the stroke.

"His handwriting changes dramatically between these documents," Clara observed, tracing the air above the signatures. "His condition must have been worsening."

Harriet adjusted her spectacles, scrutinizing the signatures more closely. "Speaking of his condition, you'll never guess what I overheard. Two days before he died, Barrett was arguing quite heatedly with a medical gentleman in the corridor."

"A physician?" Clara asked, her attention sharpening like a blade against a whetstone.

"Indeed. One of those scientific types from Scotland Yard, I believe. And that wasn't his only quarrel that day. He later had words with Mr. Caruthers—Lord Blackstone's solicitor. Raised voices about 'contractual obligations' and 'breach of trust.' Most inappropriate for a government office."

Clara's mind raced like autumn leaves in a gale. Barrett had been consulting a medical expert. The same expert who might now be examining his body and declaring him poisoned by botanical preparations.

Before she could pursue this thought, the unmistakable sound of boot heels on stone echoed from the corridor—a precise, measured stride she immediately recognized.

"Inspector Redgrave," she whispered, her voice barely disturbing the air.

Harriet reacted with surprising swiftness, sweeping the documents into a drawer with practiced efficiency. "Side door. Through the administrative section."

Clara hesitated, glancing at the partial evidence they'd uncovered.

"Go," Harriet urged, already moving toward the files. "I'll transcribe the important details tonight. Mother knows where to find you."

As if sensing the urgency, Marmalade leapt from the table directly toward a clerk entering with a stack of files. The man's shout of surprise was punctuated by the crash of an overturned inkwell, its contents spreading across his trousers in a spectacular stain.

"I didn't think cats could look so satisfied with themselves," Harriet whispered, her eyes widening behind her spectacles, "but yours has mastered the expression."

Clara slipped through the side door as Redgrave's voice reached her ears—clipped, authoritative, asking about property assessments. She hurried through a maze of smaller offices and out a service entrance that deposited her in a narrow alley behind the Registry building.

She was halfway down the passage when a figure stepped into her path, silhouetted against the fog. Marmalade materialized at her feet, arching his back and emitting a low growl.

"I expressly forbade you from investigating, Miss Wetherly."

Inspector Redgrave stood like an unyielding sentinel, his greatcoat settling around him like dark wings, his expression as forbidding as January frost.

Clara lifted her chin, refusing to be cowed. "And what brings you to the Registry Office, Inspector? Surely you didn't follow me."

"I am conducting my investigation, Miss Wetherly. A concept you seem unfamiliar with."

"Conducting your investigation at the precise registry office I happen to be visiting? What a remarkable coincidence," Clara continued, holding his gaze steadily. "One might almost think you had taken my suggestions about Barrett's property dealings seriously."

Redgrave's face remained impassive, though a muscle twitched almost imperceptibly along his jaw. "I follow evidence, Miss Wetherly, not suggestions."

"And what evidence led you here today, Inspector? The same evidence I mentioned to you yesterday, perhaps?"

"What I'm pursuing is not your concern."

"Curious. I would think proving my innocence would be precisely your concern, Inspector."

"Your innocence," he replied, each syllable crisp as new linen, "would be better served by cooperation rather than sneaking past my constable to tamper with evidence."

"I've tampered with nothing. I'm simply trying to understand why a man who asked me for henbane ended up dead behind my shop with a poison mixture bearing my label."

A raindrop struck Clara's cheek, cold as accusation, followed quickly by another. The skies had darkened while they were inside, clouds gathering like conspirators. Redgrave glanced upward, then grudgingly gestured toward an awning extending from the back of a neighboring building.

They moved beneath it just as the rain became a downpour, Marmalade stalking irritably between them, his tail twitching with disdain for the weather.

"What were you looking for in Barrett's records?" Redgrave asked, his voice lowered though no less commanding.

Clara considered her response, weighing truth against advantage. "I wanted to understand his interest in my property."

"And?"

"And I discovered he wasn't being entirely honest with his employers." She brushed a droplet from her sleeve with deliberate composure. "He submitted two very different valuations of the same properties. One set for Blackstone, showing the buildings weren't worth the investment. Another for Halston, showing they were valuable opportunities."

Redgrave's eyes narrowed slightly, the green flecks in his hazel irises catching the dim light—a tell, Clara realized, that she'd surprised him. "You're suggesting Barrett was working against Blackstone's interests while in their employ?"

"I'm suggesting Barrett was working for his own interests, Inspector. Playing both sides to maximize his profit."

"That's a serious accusation."

"One supported by evidence in the Registry files," Clara replied, standing her ground like wisteria against stone. "I wonder if Blackstone discovered his duplicity. That would certainly provide motive for murder."

"As would refusing to sell a property that was the final obstacle to a lucrative development."

Clara held his gaze, unflinching as primrose in frost. "A

curious coincidence, don't you think? Barrett first visits my shop asking for henbane—which I refused to provide—and then appears dead in my alley."

"Coincidences often appear in criminal investigations."

"As do connections others miss," Clara countered, her voice gaining quiet strength. "Barrett's handwriting shows a progressive tremor. He was clearly unwell and seeking treatment. Might that not be relevant to how he died?"

Something flickered in Redgrave's expression—a momentary fracture in his professional mask. Before he could respond, Marmalade broke the tension by stretching up to bat repeatedly at Redgrave's pocket watch chain.

"Your cat appears to have criminal tendencies," Redgrave observed, the faintest hint of wry humor softening his voice.

"You've already established I associate with questionable characters, Inspector," Clara replied, the corner of her mouth lifting slightly. "Why should my cat be any different?"

The rain gentled to a misting caress, and Clara stepped back toward the alley. "I should return before my absence is discovered."

"You're deliberately withholding information pertinent to a murder investigation," Redgrave said, all trace of humor vanishing like morning dew.

"And you're deliberately ignoring evidence that points away from me. We each have our priorities, it seems."

He moved closer, the considerable difference in their heights forcing her to tilt her face upward to maintain his gaze. "Stay out of this investigation, Miss Wetherly. I won't warn you again."

Clara stood her ground, feeling the heat of his proximity despite the damp chill. "Then we understand each other perfectly, Inspector."

They parted without further words, Clara slipping back into the maze of fog-shrouded streets, heart pounding.

Marmalade stayed with her until they reached Bellrose Lane, then vanished into the mist as suddenly as he had appeared.

Clara ascended the back staircase to her shop, grateful to find Constable Fletcher still stationed at the front entrance, apparently unaware of her absence. She removed her damp shawl and was about to light the lamp when she noticed a slip of paper on the floor, just inside the door.

She retrieved it with cautious fingers, tilting the cream-colored note toward the window to read the precise, block lettering:

BARRETT KNEW TOO MUCH. SO DO YOU.

Her fingers tightened on the paper, crinkling its edges. Someone had been in her shop while she was gone—someone who had managed to slip past Constable Fletcher at the front door. Her gaze swept across the room, cataloging jars and drawers for any sign of disturbance. Who would have such access? Blackstone's men? Halston? Or someone with official authority who wouldn't be questioned? The threat was clear, but rather than frightening her, it awakened a fierce resolve. Whoever left this message had inadvertently confirmed she was asking the right questions.

As she moved farther into the room, she noticed The Gilded Leaf lying open on her worktable, though she was certain she had closed it that morning. The page displayed illustrations of several medicinal flowers, with her grandmother's flowing script beneath a drawing of marigold: "Watch the gardener who prunes too eagerly—often he removes more than weeds."

Marmalade appeared on the table beside the book with a silent leap, his orange bulk settling next to the open page as he calmly began washing his paws.

"You impossible creature," Clara murmured, running one finger along his spine. "Where were you hiding all this time?"

The cat paused mid-lick, his amber eyes focusing on something just beyond Clara's shoulder. She felt it then—the subtle drop in temperature, the faint scent of lavender water.

Clara didn't turn, but she felt her grandmother's presence as surely as the floorboards beneath her feet. "I'll find the truth, Grandmother," she whispered. "I promise you that."

eight

M

MY SHOP WAS VIOLATED TODAY.

Strange hands touched my things. Rude fingers rifled through Clara's papers. They disturbed the ordered peace of our domain.

I watched from atop the cabinet. They wore official clothes, these intruders, but didn't move with official purpose. They were searching for something specific.

Clara stood still as stone, hands folded before her, polite words masking fury. The silver-button man—Redgrave, she calls him—watched his men with careful eyes, occasionally glancing toward Clara with something like apology.

They found nothing, of course. The important things are well hidden.

The leather-bound book that smells of Clara's grand-mother remained untouched, though one man reached for it. I hissed, and his hand withdrew. Some boundaries even police respect.

After they left, Clara sank into her chair and pressed her hands to her face. Her shoulders trembled. I curled into her lap and watched as drops fell between her fingers.

"They think I'm a murderess, Marmalade," she whispered.

I purred reassurance against her fingers. Ridiculous notion. Clara heals; she doesn't harm. Even mice she shoos outside rather than allowing me my rightful hunt.

Something moved then—the edge of the book shifting slightly across the table. Clara didn't notice, busy with her tears. But I saw.

The room grew colder. The scent of lavender water—her grandmother's scent—drifted briefly past.

I watched the empty space beside the book.

We are not alone in this shop. We never have been.

And whatever watches with me knows Clara is in danger.

THE POUNDING on the shop door came precisely at eight o'clock. Clara set down her teacup, smoothed her apron, and crossed to the entrance where Constable Fletcher's silhouette was visible through the frosted glass.

"Miss Wetherly," he called, his tone formal. "Inspector Redgrave requires entry."

She opened the door to find not just Fletcher and Redgrave, but two additional constables and a thin, scholarly-looking man carrying a small case. The inspector removed his hat, his expression grave.

"Miss Wetherly. I have a magistrate's order to conduct a thorough examination of your premises." He produced an official-looking document bearing several seals. "Dr. Morris has completed his assessment of Mr. Barrett's remains."

Clara's throat tightened. "And what has he determined?"

"Death by poisoning from a botanical compound. Primarily monkshood, with traces of other herbs." Redgrave's gaze was steady. "The jar found beside the body bears fragments of a label with handwriting resembling your own."

"I see." Clara stepped aside. "You'll find my stock precisely as it should be, Inspector. I've nothing to hide."

"Mr. Jenkins here is from Apothecaries' Hall. He'll be examining your botanical specimens."

The search began methodically, though with far less finesse than Clara would have preferred. Jenkins examined her herb drawers with particular interest, while the constables rifled through her correspondence and ledgers. Throughout it all, Clara remained behind her counter, hands clasped before her, maintaining the dignity her grandmother would have expected.

From his perch atop the highest cabinet, Marmalade watched the proceedings with evident displeasure, his tail lashing whenever anyone approached Clara's most treasured possessions.

"Inspector," Jenkins called after nearly an hour. "The monkshood drawer."

Redgrave approached as Jenkins gestured to the partially filled drawer.

"How much should be here, Miss Wetherly?" Redgrave asked.

"Three ounces, as noted in my inventory ledger," Clara replied. "I use small amounts for legitimate tinctures. Primarily for neuralgic conditions."

Jenkins produced a small brass scale and weighed the contents. "Approximately one ounce present, Inspector. Two-thirds missing."

"My dispensary records account for every preparation," Clara said. "Each patient, each remedy, each ingredient is documented."

"We'll need to see those records."

Clara retrieved her dispensary ledger from beneath the counter and placed it before him. He began examining the neat entries, turning pages with methodical precision.

"Several neuralgic preparations in the past month," he noted. "Mrs. Hargrove, Mr. Wilson... These account for perhaps half an ounce, by your own documentation."

"I prepared additional tinctures for my regular stock. Those would be recorded in my inventory logs rather than the dispensary ledger."

"Convenient," Jenkins scoffed softly.

"It's standard practice," Clara countered. "Any reputable dispenser of botanical remedies maintains separate records for stock preparations versus individual prescriptions."

Redgrave continued examining her records while Jenkins turned his attention to her preparation area.

"Simple equipment," he observed. "Traditional methods. Though adequate for basic extraction of plant compounds."

"My grandmother taught me traditional botanical applications. My customers value time-tested remedies."

"Including monkshood?" Jenkins asked pointedly.

"In proper dilution, for appropriate cases, yes." Clara met his gaze. "As physicians have done for centuries."

The search continued methodically, with each corner of the shop examined. Constable Fletcher was dispatched to check her living quarters upstairs, while the others concentrated on the shop itself.

"Inspector," called one of the constables. "The bottles."

Redgrave crossed to where the man stood before a cabinet containing Clara's stock of empty bottles.

"Standard amber bottles," the constable explained, holding one up. "Similar to the one found with Barrett's body."

"Those are clear glass, not amber," Clara corrected. "I

would never store monkshood preparations in clear bottles. Light degrades the compounds."

"You're quite certain of this?" Redgrave raised an eyebrow.

"Absolutely. Potent preparations like monkshood tinctures are only ever stored in blue glass bottles, marked with a distinctive red seal." She gestured to a separate cabinet. "Those are kept separate from my standard remedies precisely because of their potency."

The constable opened the blue glass cabinet. "Twenty-four blue bottles, sir. All present according to her inventory."

Redgrave frowned slightly. "Then the bottle found with Barrett..."

"Could not have come from my monkshood preparations," Clara finished. "Though the jar itself might have been taken from my shop, its contents were not prepared by me."

Redgrave made a note in his small book. "Constable, check her expense ledgers for purchases of both bottle types."

The man dutifully examined Clara's records. "Three dozen clear glass purchased in January from Simmons Glassworks. Two dozen amber bottles purchased in December. Two dozen blue bottles purchased last autumn."

"And how many amber bottles remain in stock?"

"Twenty-one, sir."

"According to your dispensary records," Redgrave said, "you've dispensed three preparations in amber bottles since December."

"That's correct. They're used only for light-sensitive but non-toxic preparations like chamomile and valerian compounds."

"Which means none are missing. Yet the bottle found with Barrett was amber glass, not blue or clear."

Clara's fingers gripped the edge of the counter. "Anyone could have taken a bottle from my shop. Anyone with access."

"And who has such access, Miss Wetherly?"

"Regular customers. Delivery boys. I cannot watch every bottle every moment, Inspector."

Redgrave's expression remained professionally neutral, but something in his eyes suggested he wasn't entirely satisfied with the mounting evidence. He turned to the constable examining her correspondence.

"Anything of note, Richards?"

"Nothing connecting to Barrett directly, sir. Though there are several letters from the Metropolitan Merchant Bank regarding her business loan." The constable held up the most recent. "Final notice dated last week."

Clara felt heat rising in her cheeks. "My financial arrangements are hardly relevant to your investigation."

"On the contrary," Redgrave said. "Financial pressure provides excellent motive, particularly when the victim was attempting to acquire your property."

The search continued for another hour, each discovery seeming to tighten the noose around Clara's neck. The evidence, while circumstantial, was undeniably damning: missing monkshood that matched the poison, financial pressure from the bank, Barrett's clear interest in her property.

Finally, Redgrave signaled his men to conclude their examination. "We've seen enough for now. Richards, prepare the inventory of items we're taking as evidence."

As the constables gathered their findings, the bell above the door jangled. Mrs. Penfield entered, her expression morphing from pleasant anticipation to outrage as she surveyed the scene.

"Inspector Redgrave! What on earth is happening here?" she demanded, bypassing the constable who attempted to intercept her.

"Mrs. Penfield." Redgrave acknowledged her with a slight nod. "We're conducting an official investigation."

"By turning poor Clara's shop inside out?" Mrs. Penfield huffed. "I expected better judgment from you, Inspector."

"We follow the evidence, madam."

"And what evidence could possibly implicate Clara Wetherly? The girl who stayed up three nights straight tending cholera victims when your fine medical establishment had abandoned hope?" Mrs. Penfield positioned herself between Clara and the officials. "You're wasting valuable time here while the real culprit walks free."

"I appreciate your concern, Mrs. Penfield, but we must be thorough."

"Thorough!" she exclaimed. "While your time would be better spent investigating those developers and their associates. There's more happening in this neighborhood than meets the eye, Inspector."

Clara placed a gentle hand on Mrs. Penfield's arm. "It's all right. Inspector Redgrave is only doing his duty."

Mrs. Penfield sniffed but relented. "I'll return tomorrow, dear. When perhaps wiser heads will have prevailed." She fixed Redgrave with a final, withering look before departing.

After Mrs. Penfield left, Redgrave finished his instructions to the constables. They would take samples of Clara's monkshood, copies of her ledger entries, and examples of her bottles for comparison.

"The shop remains closed," Redgrave said. "Constable Fletcher will continue his post outside."

As his men prepared to leave, Redgrave lingered at the counter. "The evidence against you is substantial, Miss Wetherly," he said quietly. "The poison matches herbs from your shop. A significant quantity of monkshood is unaccounted for. You had both means and motive."

"Yet something troubles you," Clara observed.

Redgrave met her gaze, his expression betraying nothing. "I follow evidence, not impressions."

"Even when those impressions suggest the evidence may be too perfect? Too convenient?"

A moment of silence stretched between them. "Good day, Miss Wetherly," he finally replied, placing his hat on his head. "I suggest you use this time to consider your situation carefully."

After they departed, Clara sank into her chair, the emotional strain overwhelming her. She pressed her hands to her face, tears slipping between her fingers. The indignity of the search, the violation of her grandmother's sacred space, the mounting evidence against her—it was almost too much to bear.

She allowed herself this moment of weakness, knowing she would need her strength for what came next. Gradually, her tears subsided, replaced by a fierce determination. Someone had gone to extraordinary lengths to implicate her in Barrett's death. She needed to understand why—and who stood to benefit.

Clara began restoring order to her shop, carefully returning herbs to their proper drawers, reorganizing her ledgers, and setting her preparation area to rights. As she knelt to retrieve a small bowl that had rolled beneath her workbench during the search, her fingers brushed something metallic near her herb storage area.

She drew it out—a silver cufflink, its surface etched with an intricate oak leaf pattern. It certainly wasn't hers, nor did it appear to be something one of Redgrave's constables would wear. It must have fallen from someone's sleeve while they examined her herbs.

Clara turned it over in her palm, noting its quality. The silver was genuine, the craftsmanship fine—belonging to someone of means rather than a working man. She placed it on her desk, making a mental note to ask Fletcher if it belonged to any of the officers.

As she continued cleaning, her mind worked through what she had learned at the Registry Office yesterday—Barrett had been creating different property valuations for Blackstone and Halston, essentially playing both developers against each other. If someone had discovered his deception, it could certainly provide motive for murder.

The bell rang again, and Clara looked up to find Constable Fletcher at the door.

"Miss Wetherly, Mr. Pinkett from the Metropolitan Merchant Bank to see you."

Clara quickly tucked the cufflink into her pocket. "Send him in, please."

Pinkett entered, his round face set in an expression of practiced concern. "Miss Wetherly, I've just heard about this dreadful police search. Most distressing." He removed his hat, revealing thinning hair carefully combed over his scalp. "I came as soon as I could."

"How thoughtful," Clara said, her tone neutral. "Though I imagine your concern is primarily for the bank's investment rather than my welfare."

"You do me an injustice," Pinkett replied, settling his considerable bulk into the chair opposite her desk. "I've always held your grandmother in the highest regard. Her business acumen was remarkable for a woman of her generation."

Clara studied his face, noting the slight sheen of perspiration despite the cool day. "What brings you here, Mr. Pinkett? I doubt it's merely to express sympathy."

He sighed heavily. "Directness was always a Wetherly trait. Very well. The bank's directors have reviewed your loan status in light of recent developments." He placed his leather portfolio on the desk. "I regret to inform you that they've authorized me to call in the note."

"On what grounds?" Clara demanded.

"Criminal investigation creates unacceptable financial

risk." Pinkett opened his portfolio, withdrawing several documents. "The standard terms allow for accelerated repayment under such circumstances."

"This is hardly standard, Mr. Pinkett. My shop has been closed for days due to this investigation. How am I expected to generate income to repay the loan?"

"That is precisely the directors' concern." He adjusted his spectacles. "However, I've negotiated a small concession. If you can provide fifty pounds by tomorrow afternoon, I can arrange a thirty-day extension."

Clara stared at him in disbelief. "Fifty pounds? You know that's impossible."

"Not entirely," Pinkett replied, his voice dropping. "I understand Blackstone Development maintains their offer to purchase your property. They would certainly advance enough to clear your debt."

"How convenient for everyone involved," Clara observed coldly. "Except me."

"Business is rarely convenient, Miss Wetherly. Merely necessary." Pinkett gathered his papers. "I'll return tomorrow at two o'clock. Either with the payment or the sale documents."

As he rose to leave, Clara noticed something—his right cuff showed a single silver cufflink with an oak leaf pattern. The match to the one she had found beneath her workbench was conspicuously absent.

"Good day, Miss Wetherly," Pinkett said with a slight bow. "I do hope you'll consider the bank's offer carefully. These difficult circumstances needn't result in your complete financial ruin."

After he departed, Clara retrieved the cufflink from her pocket, examining it with renewed interest. The intricate oak leaf pattern matched the one on Pinkett's wrist exactly. Which meant he had been in her herb storage area recently—though he had never mentioned visiting the shop before today.

She turned the silver piece over in her hand, a cold certainty settling in her chest. Pinkett had access to her herbs. Pinkett stood to benefit from Barrett's death and Clara's ruin.

Clara moved to her small writing desk and began documenting her thoughts, connecting what she knew:

1. Barrett worked for both Blackstone and Halston, creating different property valuations for each
2. Pinkett was pressuring her about her loan and insisting she sell to Blackstone
3. Pinkett's cufflink was found near her herb storage, suggesting he had access to her monkshood
4. He had never mentioned visiting her shop before today

The pieces were beginning to align into a pattern she couldn't ignore. But suspicion wasn't proof, and the cufflink alone wouldn't convince Redgrave to shift his focus from her to Pinkett.

She needed more—concrete evidence of Pinkett's movements, details of his connections to Barrett and the developers, confirmation that he had visited her shop when she wasn't present.

As Clara was considering her next steps, a knock came at the door. It was Constable Fletcher again.

"Miss Wetherly, Inspector Redgrave asked me to inform you of a change in arrangements."

Clara set down her pen. "What sort of change?"

"I'm being reassigned, miss. Budget constraints at the Yard —too many constables tied up in surveillance duties with the Paddington case."

"You mean I'm no longer to be watched?" Clara asked, unable to hide her surprise.

"Inspector says you're not to leave town, and the shop remains closed to business. But they can't spare a man for round-the-clock surveillance."

"I see," Clara said, keeping her tone neutral despite the surge of hope this development inspired. "When does this change take effect?"

"Immediately, miss. I'm to report to Paddington Station within the hour." He hesitated. "The Inspector wanted me to remind you that interfering with the investigation would result in immediate arrest."

"Of course. Please thank Inspector Redgrave for the... consideration."

After Fletcher departed, Clara could hardly believe her good fortune. Without police surveillance, she would be free to pursue her own investigation—beginning with the cufflink and its connection to Pinkett.

She placed the silver cufflink in a small envelope and tucked it into a secure drawer in her desk. Tomorrow, she would begin gathering evidence, starting with her network of neighborhood allies. If anyone knew Pinkett's habits and connections, it would be the women of Bloomsbury who noticed everything while society pretended they noticed nothing.

As darkness fell outside her window, Clara felt a strange calm replacing her earlier distress. For the first time since finding Barrett's body, she had something tangible to pursue —a path that might lead away from her and toward the true killer.

She had no way of knowing that this path would lead her to another body—and deeper danger than she could possibly imagine.

nine

"He's been skimming from Blackstone's accounts for years," Mrs. Jenkins announced, setting her teacup down with enough force to rattle the saucer. "My Herbert delivered pastries to their offices last Tuesday and overheard Pinkett discussing what he called 'Barrett's unfortunate error in judgment.' Said it with such venom, Clara, like the man had personally offended him."

Clara's sitting room had never accommodated so many visitors at once. What had begun as Mrs. Penfield's solitary return visit had transformed, within hours, into what could only be described as a council of war. Five of Bloomsbury's most observant women perched on every available surface—the worn settee, the reading chair, even the small trunk beneath the window. The morning light spilled across their determined faces as they shared intelligence like generals planning a campaign.

"That doesn't necessarily implicate him in murder," Clara noted, though she slipped Mrs. Jenkins's revelation into her mental ledger alongside the silver cufflink now hidden in her desk. "Though it does suggest he knew more about Barrett's activities than he admitted."

"It's the timing that troubles me," said Mrs. Winters from her place near the hearth. The dressmaker's thin fingers never stopped moving, stitching invisible seams as she spoke. "Pinkett examined your shop at least once when you were absent. I saw him myself, ten days ago, slipping in through the back while that young delivery boy distracted Fletcher with questions about becoming a constable."

"And you didn't mention this to me?" Clara asked, unable to hide her shock.

Mrs. Winters had the grace to blush, her needle pausing mid-stitch. "In hindsight, perhaps I should have done, but you know, dear, I thought at the time..." She hesitated, color deepening in her lined cheeks. "Well, I wondered if perhaps you were meeting the gentleman in secret, if you understand my meaning."

Clara felt heat flood her own face as she understood the implication all too well. "Mrs. Winters! I assure you—"

"No need to explain, dear," the dressmaker hurried on. "A woman alone must be practical sometimes. It wasn't my place to judge."

"But you are certain it was Mr. Pinkett?" Clara pressed, steering the conversation back to the matter at hand.

"Absolutely certain," Mrs. Winters replied. "That waistcoat of his—with the brass buttons—is unmistakable. As is that peculiar way he has of checking his pocket watch every few minutes, as though time might escape him if he doesn't keep it under observation."

Clara made another notation. Pinkett had access to her shop. Pinkett's cufflink was found near her herb storage. Pinkett had been heard discussing Barrett in terms suggesting personal resentment. The pattern was forming with disturbing clarity.

"We need proof, not just suspicion," Clara said. "Inspector Redgrave has already decided I'm the most likely culprit. He won't shift his focus without compelling evidence."

Miss Harriet Collins, who had arrived breathless from the Registry Office during her midday break, produced a small packet from her reticule. "Perhaps these might help." She handed the papers to Clara. "The copies I promised. Barrett's conflicting property assessments for Blackstone and Halston. I've added something else—the signature page of a third report I found this morning."

Clara unfolded the documents, spreading them on the small table. The women gathered closer, a rustle of skirts and soft exclamations as they examined the evidence.

"Look at the dates," Harriet pointed out. "The first assessment for Blackstone shows artificially low values, dated three months ago. The second, for Halston, shows much higher values, dated six weeks ago. But this third document—filed just two days before Barrett's death—contains something odd."

Clara studied the signature page Harriet indicated. Barrett's trembling hand had signed a final assessment, this one bearing Mr. Pinkett's countersignature as a witness.

"A bank representative countersigning a developer's property assessment?" Clara frowned. "Is that standard practice?"

"Not in my experience at the Registry," Harriet said. "I couldn't access the full document—it's been marked confidential by order of Lord Blackstone himself. But the fact that it exists, with Pinkett involved..." She let the implication hang in the air.

Mrs. Penfield leaned forward, her voice lowering despite the privacy of Clara's sitting room. "George Pinkett dines at the Empire Club every evening at eight o'clock. Never varies his schedule—creature of rigid habits, that man. My late husband was a member, and the porter still tells me everything for a few coins at Christmas." She smiled with the satisfaction of a chess player announcing checkmate. "Tonight, he's meeting with Lord Blackstone and his solicitor."

Clara felt a quiet thrill of possibility. "If I could somehow overhear their conversation..."

"Impossible," Mrs. Jenkins declared. "It's a gentlemen's club. No women permitted beyond the reception area."

"The service entrance," Mrs. Winters suggested, her needle gleaming in the sunlight. "My nephew works in the kitchens. The staff corridor passes directly behind the private dining rooms. Thin walls—he says the servers hear everything."

"Your nephew might risk his position," Clara cautioned.

Mrs. Winters' mouth curved in a slight smile. "Timothy owes me several favors involving a young lady his mother doesn't approve of. He'll help."

The women continued planning well into the afternoon, each contributing some piece of knowledge about Pinkett's habits, associations, or movements. Clara documented everything methodically, the familiar practice of recording herbal measurements now applied to building a case against a potential murderer.

As the gathering dispersed, Mrs. Penfield lingered behind. She watched Clara organizing her notes with an expression of maternal concern.

"You understand the risk you're taking," she said quietly. "If Pinkett is indeed Barrett's killer, following him could place you in considerable danger."

"I understand," Clara said, meeting the older woman's gaze steadily. "But I have little choice. Each day my shop remains closed is another day closer to financial ruin."

Mrs. Penfield sighed, patting Clara's hand. "Your grandmother was always proud of your determination, even when it worried her. She would understand your reasons, even if she might caution more prudence."

"She taught me that some risks are necessary," Clara said, a slight smile softening her features. "Though I'm certain she would have found a more elegant solution than skulking about gentlemen's clubs."

"Genevieve always did have a particular elegance about her methods," Mrs. Penfield agreed with a quiet laugh. "I remember how she handled that dreadful customs inspector who tried to confiscate her imported botanical specimens. The poor man left thinking she had done him a favor!"

After Mrs. Penfield departed, Clara returned to her preparations. The afternoon light began to fade as she considered her next steps. She had gathered many pieces but couldn't yet see the complete picture they formed. Whatever Pinkett's involvement, she needed proof that Redgrave couldn't ignore.

As twilight settled over Bloomsbury, Clara prepared for her evening expedition. She chose her darkest dress, a navy wool that would blend into shadows, and a charcoal gray shawl that could be drawn across her face if necessary. Practical boots replaced her usual indoor slippers.

Her preparations felt simultaneously foreign and familiar —like following the steps of a procedure she'd only read about. In a small pocket sewn into her skirt, she placed a tiny vial of chamomile tincture—not for any practical purpose, but its familiar scent had always steadied her nerves in difficult moments.

As she pinned her hair in a modest knot that wouldn't attract attention, Clara caught movement in the mirror—not her own reflection, but a silvery shimmer behind her, like moonlight on disturbed water. The temperature in the room dropped perceptibly. In the mirror, she could see her breath forming small clouds in the suddenly chilled air.

"I'm being careful," she murmured, addressing the empty room. "But I must do this."

The candle on her dressing table flared suddenly higher, then settled back to its normal flame. Clara considered the phenomenon with the practical mind her grandmother had nurtured—perhaps a draft, or simply the candle guttering as it sometimes did. Yet some part of her wondered.

A soft scratching at her bedroom door announced Marmalade, who entered with his usual air of ownership. He circled her feet once, then leapt to the windowsill, his amber eyes fixed on the darkening street below.

"You can't come along," Clara told him, stroking his orange fur. "But I appreciate the concern."

The cat merely blinked slowly, his tail twitching against the window glass. In the street beyond, the lamplighter moved from post to post, his long pole brightening the gathering gloom. Soon it would be eight o'clock, and Pinkett would arrive at the Empire Club for his meeting with Blackstone.

Clara checked her small pocket watch—a gift from her grandmother upon completing her botanical training. Time to depart if she wanted to arrive before Pinkett and position herself appropriately.

She descended the back stairs silently, grateful that Fletcher's reassignment meant no one watched her movements. The evening air carried the particular blend of coal smoke and approaching rain that defined London nights. As she slipped into the shadows behind her shop, Clara felt a curious blend of terror and exhilaration.

For all her preparations, she could not possibly anticipate what waited at the Empire Club—or how this night would transform her understanding of Barrett's murder. She only knew that every instinct and every piece of evidence urged her forward into the gathering darkness.

· · ·

CLARA SLIPPED through the fog-softened streets of Bloomsbury like a shadow. Her navy wool dress absorbed what little light filtered through the evening mist, and her charcoal shawl, drawn partially across her face, obscured her features from casual observation. The cobblestones glistened beneath the occasional gas lamp, still slick from an earlier shower.

Eight chimes echoed from a distant church bell as she approached the Empire Club. The imposing Georgian facade stood four stories tall, its windows glowing with the warm light of crystal chandeliers and polished brass fixtures. A steady stream of carriages deposited well-dressed gentlemen at the marble steps, each man disappearing through the heavy oak doors into London's temple of masculine privilege.

Clara positioned herself across the street, partially concealed by the awning of a bookseller's shop closed for the evening. Her grandmother's pocket watch ticked steadily in her palm as she waited, its familiar weight reassuring against her fingers. According to Mrs. Penfield's intelligence, George Pinkett never varied his schedule—eight o'clock precisely at the Empire.

True to prediction, a carriage pulled up at three minutes past eight. Pinkett emerged, his considerable bulk straining the seams of his waistcoat as he paid the driver. Clara noted his customary brass buttons gleaming in the lamplight. He ascended the steps with the self-importance of a minor official granted access to superior circles.

"Now for the difficult part," Clara murmured to herself, slipping the watch back into her pocket.

She circled around to the service entrance Mrs. Winters had described, finding it exactly as promised—a narrow passage between the club and neighboring building leading to a plain wooden door. A young man in kitchen whites stood smoking in the shadows, his face brightening when he spotted her.

"Miss Wetherly?" he asked, dropping his cigarette and grinding it beneath his heel. "Aunt Margaret said you'd be coming. I'm Timothy."

"Thank you for helping," Clara replied, keeping her voice low. "Your aunt speaks highly of you."

"This way, quickly." He gestured toward the door. "Staff changes in ten minutes. You can slip in with the confusion."

Timothy led her through a bustling kitchen where no one spared them a second glance, then along a narrow service corridor that ran behind several private dining rooms. The passage was dimly lit, smelling of cigar smoke and roast beef that seeped through the walls.

"Third door is where he always dines," Timothy whispered, pointing to a small serving hatch. "Blackstone's private room. I've got to get back to the kitchens, but stay as long as you need. No one checks this corridor after the main courses are served."

"You've been most helpful," Clara said, pressing a coin into his palm.

"Aunt Margaret said you were being framed," Timothy replied, pocketing the money. "Hope you catch whoever's really responsible."

With that, he disappeared back toward the kitchens, leaving Clara alone in the shadowed passage. She moved closer to the serving hatch, its small wooden panel slightly ajar. Through the narrow opening, she could hear the murmur of conversation accompanied by the clink of crystal and silver.

"—absolutely essential we complete the acquisitions by month's end." The voice was cultured, authoritative—Lord Blackstone, she presumed. "The railway commission meets the following week. Properties not secured by then will cost us double once the plans become public."

"I've accelerated pressure on the Wetherly woman," Pinkett replied, his tone deferential. "The business loan is being called due immediately. Without income from her shop, she'll have no choice but to sell."

"She still refuses the direct offers?" Blackstone asked.

"Stubbornly so," Pinkett confirmed. "Just like her grandmother. That family has a most inconvenient sense of legacy."

The clink of glasses punctuated their conversation, followed by the scrape of cutlery against fine china. Clara strained to catch every word, her breath shallow to avoid detection.

"And what of our other matter?" Blackstone's voice lowered slightly. "Has that been resolved to your satisfaction?"

A pause. "I am meeting with him tonight at my office," Pinkett replied carefully. "I will give you a full report in the morning."

"Can he be trusted after that business with Barrett?"

Clara's heart quickened. She pressed closer to the hatch.

"He's taken care of that problem quite effectively, wouldn't you say?" Pinkett answered, a note of smug satisfaction in his voice.

"At considerable cost to our discretion," Blackstone observed coldly. "Barrett's death has drawn unnecessary attention."

"A regrettable necessity," Pinkett replied. "His duplicity with Halston could have cost us everything. The property valuations alone—"

"Yes, yes," Blackstone interrupted. "What's done is done. Though I'm not convinced this continuing arrangement is wise. One incident may be overlooked. Two becomes a pattern."

"The Wetherly situation requires resolution," Pinkett insisted. "We've come too far to allow sentiment about an old shop to derail everything."

"Just ensure this is handled with greater subtlety," Blackstone said, his tone suggesting the topic was closed. "Now, about the northern parcels..."

The conversation shifted to property acquisitions in another neighborhood, details Clara recognized as unrelated to her situation. She stepped back from the hatch, mind racing to process what she'd overheard. Pinkett and Blackstone clearly knew about Barrett's death—not just as a tragic event, but as a "problem" that had been "taken care of." And now Pinkett was meeting someone tonight, presumably the same someone who had "handled" Barrett.

She needed to witness that meeting.

Clara slipped back through the kitchen during a bustling dinner service, her presence barely registered among the hurrying staff. Outside, the evening fog had thickened, reducing the gas lamps to hazy orbs of yellow light suspended in the darkness. Perfect cover for what she needed to do next.

The Metropolitan Merchant Bank stood three streets away from the Empire Club, its imposing stone facade now dark save for a single lamp burning in an upper window—Pinkett's office, she presumed. Clara found a sheltered doorway across the street that afforded a clear view of the bank's entrance while keeping her hidden in shadow.

The cold seeped through her woolen dress as she waited, the pocket watch ticking away nearly forty minutes before a carriage deposited Pinkett at the bank's steps. He fumbled with his keys, eventually swinging open the heavy door and disappearing inside. Moments later, the ground floor lamps flickered to life.

Clara settled deeper into her hiding place. Whoever Pinkett was meeting would arrive soon, and she needed to see who it was—needed evidence that would convince Inspector Redgrave to look beyond her to the true conspiracy surrounding Barrett's death.

The fog swirled and thickened, occasionally obscuring her view entirely before reluctantly parting again. Nearly fifteen minutes later, a figure emerged from the mist, approaching the bank with purposeful strides. Clara strained to make out details—a well-dressed gentleman of medium height, wearing a top hat and carrying a small leather case. He paused at the bank entrance, consulting a pocket watch that caught the lamplight, revealing a distinctive emblem on its case—a caduceus, the medical symbol of intertwined serpents around a staff. Clara's breath caught at the sight, certain she had seen that emblem before, though she couldn't immediately place where.

The visitor rapped on the door, was admitted by Pinkett himself, and disappeared inside. Clara counted to one hundred, giving them time to settle into their meeting, then crossed the street. The bank's ground floor featured tall windows, most with curtains drawn, but one—slightly ajar—offered a partial view of an interior staircase. If she could reach the alley alongside the building, perhaps she might find a better vantage point to observe the meeting upstairs.

The narrow passage between the bank and neighboring tobacconist smelled of damp stone and abandoned refuse. Clara pressed close to the wall, careful to avoid the deeper puddles that would betray her presence with splashing sounds. A faint light spilled from a small window high above—Pinkett's office, judging by its position. She needed to get closer, needed to see who he was meeting.

An abandoned crate provided the elevation she required. Clara carefully positioned it beneath the window, tested its stability, then gathered her skirts and stepped up. The makeshift platform wobbled slightly but held her weight. Through the window, she could see a portion of Pinkett's office—a bookcase filled with ledgers, the corner of an ornate desk, and a chair where Pinkett himself sat in profile, speaking animatedly to someone just out of her line of sight.

The banker's face appeared flushed, his usual pomposity replaced by what looked like agitation. He gestured emphatically, though Clara could hear nothing through the thick glass. Something about his manner suggested not a business meeting but a confrontation. As she watched, Pinkett reached for a cup on his desk, raised it to his lips, and drank.

The effect was almost immediate. His hand flew to his throat. The cup clattered to the desk, liquid spilling across papers. Pinkett rose halfway, then collapsed forward, his body convulsing briefly before going terrifyingly still. Unlike Barrett's bluish lips, Pinkett's face had turned an alarming shade of gray, his eyes dilated unnaturally wide—a different poison entirely from what had killed Barrett, Clara noted with detachment even in her shock.

A gasp escaped her lips before she could suppress it.

The figure who had been speaking with Pinkett moved into view—gloved hands carefully retrieving the cup, methodically wiping it clean with a handkerchief, then replacing it precisely on the desk. The care taken suggested someone familiar with removing evidence, someone with medical knowledge of what authorities might look for. The visitor turned toward the window, and though the face remained in shadow, Clara felt the shock of recognition pass between them. She had been seen.

The crate shifted beneath her weight as she scrambled down, her skirts tangling around her ankles. Behind her, the window creaked open. Clara abandoned stealth for speed, racing down the alley toward the street, heart pounding in her ears. Footsteps followed—measured, unhurried, confident.

She emerged onto the main thoroughfare, nearly colliding with a passing lamplighter who steadied her with a concerned "Careful there, Miss!" before continuing on his rounds. Clara glanced back to see a dark figure exit the alley, pause to adjust hat and gloves, then turn sharply in the opposite direction.

"Wait!" Clara called out, but the figure was already disappearing into the fog.

Clara pursued, her practical boots slapping against wet cobblestones. The killer—for surely that's what she had witnessed—moved with precise knowledge of the neighborhood, turning down one narrow passage, then another. The fog thickened with each turn, until Clara found herself alone on an unfamiliar street, the echo of distant footsteps fading into silence.

She had lost them.

For several moments, Clara stood motionless, gathering her wits. Pinkett was dead. She had witnessed his murder. And the killer had seen her face clearly enough to recognize her again.

She needed to alert the authorities, but how? Running through the streets shouting "murder" would likely result in her own arrest rather than a proper investigation. She needed to be strategic, even now.

A red police box stood at the corner where two larger streets intersected. Clara hurried to it, broke the glass with her elbow (wincing at the sharp pain), and pulled the whistle within. Its shrill cry cut through the fog, summoning help while allowing her to remain anonymous for a precious few minutes—time enough to consider how to explain her presence.

It took less than five minutes for the first constables to arrive, followed shortly by additional officers. Clara approached them with the composure her grandmother had instilled in her through years of practice.

"There's been a murder," she stated calmly to the sergeant who appeared to be in charge. "Mr. George Pinkett, at the

Metropolitan Merchant Bank. I witnessed it through the
window."

"And you are, Miss...?" the officer asked, clearly suspicious
of a well-dressed woman alone on the streets at night.

"Clara Wetherly," she replied, seeing no benefit in deception. "I was returning from visiting a friend when I noticed
unusual activity at the bank. Mr. Pinkett appeared to collapse
after drinking something."

It wasn't the complete truth, but it wasn't entirely a lie
either. She would reveal the full details to Inspector Redgrave,
who would inevitably be summoned once her name was
mentioned. The officers escorted her back to the bank, where
they forced entry with commendable efficiency. Clara
remained silent as they discovered Pinkett's body in his office,
exactly as she had described.

The police constables had barely secured the scene when
the doorway darkened with a familiar silhouette. Inspector
Redgrave entered, his greatcoat still beaded with moisture
from the fog outside. He strode purposefully into the room,
barking orders to his men until his gaze fell upon Clara
standing near Pinkett's desk. He froze mid-stride.

The color drained from his face, replaced by a darkening
flush that crept from collar to hairline. His eyes, usually so
carefully controlled, widened with genuine shock before
narrowing to dangerous slits.

"Miss. Wetherly." Her name emerged as a low growl, each
syllable sharp with barely contained fury.

Clara lifted her chin, refusing to be cowed despite the knot
of apprehension tightening in her stomach. The sheer rage
emanating from the inspector would have sent most women
reaching for their smelling salts, but Clara stood her ground,
one hand still resting on the desk where Pinkett's teacup sat
with its suspicious residue.

Redgrave's mouth opened, then closed, as if even his

considerable vocabulary failed before this new development. Around them, the constables grew suddenly preoccupied with their duties, casting sidelong glances at the brewing storm centered in the banker's office.

When he finally spoke again, his voice was terrifyingly quiet, each word precise as a surgeon's knife.

"Of all the preposterous, reckless—" He stopped, drawing a sharp breath between clenched teeth. "Step away from the body. Now."

The final word echoed in the sudden silence of the room. Clara realized every officer had frozen, watching the tableau with the breathless anticipation of theatergoers at a particularly dramatic scene.

She had prepared explanations, evidence, and arguments, but they withered before the raw intensity of Redgrave's fury. Tomorrow there would be time for words. Tonight, there was only the terrible knowledge reflected in his eyes: whatever innocence he might have believed she possessed had now been irrevocably called into question.

ten

"What," Inspector Redgrave enunciated with terrifying precision, "were you thinking?"

The banker's office had cleared of all but two constables who studiously examined the far corners of the room, desperately pretending not to listen. Clara stood her ground beside Pinkett's desk, the dead man's presence between them like an accusation neither could ignore.

"I was thinking," Clara said, "that while the authorities were busy searching my botanical drawers for evidence of crimes I didn't commit, someone else was murdering the men connected to Barrett's death."

A muscle twitched in Redgrave's jaw. "So you took it upon yourself to prowl through London at night, alone, following a man who has now become the second victim in this case?"

"I took it upon myself to pursue evidence other than that which conveniently appeared at my doorstep," Clara countered. Her composure was remarkable given the circumstances, though internally she recognized the recklessness of her actions with growing clarity. "And in doing so, I witnessed Mr. Pinkett's murder."

Redgrave stared at her for a long moment before turning to his men. "Leave us."

The constables exchanged uncertain glances.

"Now," he added, his tone brooking no argument.

When the door closed behind them, Redgrave removed his hat and ran a hand through his dark hair, revealing the silver at his temples that made him appear older than his years. The gesture was so unexpected—so human—that Clara momentarily forgot her defensive posture.

"Tell me everything," he said, his voice lower now. "From the beginning."

Clara hesitated, weighing how much to reveal. "I discovered evidence suggesting Mr. Pinkett had access to my shop when I wasn't present."

"What evidence?"

She reached into her pocket and withdrew the silver cufflink, placing it carefully on the desk between them. "This was found beneath my workbench near the botanical storage after your search of my premises. I noticed this evening that Mr. Pinkett wears—wore—an identical mate on his right cuff."

Redgrave picked up the cufflink, examining the intricate oak leaf pattern. "This is hardly conclusive, Miss Wetherly."

"It became more so when Mrs. Winters, the dressmaker next door, informed me she had witnessed Pinkett entering my shop through the back door while I was absent, ten days before Barrett's murder."

The inspector's expression didn't change, but something shifted in his eyes—the faintest flicker of doubt. "Continue."

Clara outlined what she had learned: Pinkett's connection to Blackstone Development, his aggressive efforts to force her to sell, his unusual countersignature on Barrett's final property assessment.

"I needed to understand his involvement," she explained.

"So when I learned he was meeting Lord Blackstone at the Empire Club this evening—"

"You decided to eavesdrop on a private conversation between a peer of the realm and a banker," Redgrave finished, his tone sharpening again. "Did it occur to you that such actions might be considered illegal?"

"Did it occur to you that murder is considerably more illegal than eavesdropping?" Clara returned, her patience fraying. "Lord Blackstone and Mr. Pinkett discussed Barrett's death not as a tragic event, but as a 'problem' that had been 'taken care of.' Blackstone expressed concern about the attention it had drawn, and Pinkett assured him the 'Wetherly situation' would be resolved."

Redgrave paced the small office, his footsteps measured and precise. "What you're suggesting—accusing a peer of the realm—"

"I am recounting a conversation I overheard," Clara interrupted, "in which Lord Blackstone expressed knowledge of Barrett's murder as a deliberate act. He then expressed concern about a 'second incident' creating a 'pattern.' Hours later, Mr. Pinkett is dead from what appears to be poison."

"And you followed Pinkett from the club to witness this second incident?"

"I followed him because he mentioned meeting someone at his office tonight—someone connected to Barrett's death. I needed to see who it was."

Redgrave halted his pacing, turning to face her directly. "Did you?"

"Not clearly," Clara admitted. "A well-dressed gentleman of medium height, wearing a top hat. He carried a small leather case." She hesitated. "There was one distinctive detail— a pocket watch with a medical emblem on its case. A caduceus."

Something imperceptible shifted in Redgrave's expression

—a tightening around the eyes, a slight paling beneath his tan. It was gone almost instantly, replaced by his usual professional mask, but Clara had caught it nonetheless.

"You recognize that description," she said, not a question but a statement.

"I know several medical men who might fit such a vague description," he replied, his tone deliberately neutral.

"This one," Clara pressed, "slipped something into Pinkett's tea that killed him within moments of consumption. The symptoms were different from Barrett's—no blue lips, but rather a grayish pallor and dilated pupils. A different poison entirely, suggesting someone with extensive knowledge of toxic compounds."

Redgrave was silent for a long moment, studying her with an intensity that might have unnerved a less determined woman. "Did he see your face, Miss Wetherly?"

The question struck her with unexpected force. Until that moment, she hadn't fully processed the implications of being seen by the killer.

"Yes," she admitted, her voice softer now. "I was watching through the window. When Pinkett collapsed, I... I gasped. The killer looked directly toward me before I fled."

Something dangerous flashed across Redgrave's features. "So not only did you witness a murder, but the murderer witnessed you witnessing it."

"I believe so, yes."

"Have you any comprehension," Redgrave said with deceptive softness, "of the danger you have placed yourself in? A killer who has now dispatched two men has seen your face and knows you can identify him."

Clara lifted her chin slightly. "I'm aware of the risk."

"No," Redgrave countered, collecting his hat from the desk, "I don't believe you are." He consulted his pocket watch

briefly. "It's nearly midnight. I'm escorting you home immediately."

"That's hardly necessary—"

"It is not a request, Miss Wetherly." The words were
clipped, final. "I have a murder scene to process and a killer to
apprehend. I cannot do either effectively if I'm wondering
whether you've become the third victim."

The fog had thickened further as they stepped out of the
bank, transforming London's familiar landscape into a ghostly
labyrinth. Redgrave's hand settled at Clara's elbow, his touch
firm but not unkind as he guided her through the misty
streets. Neither spoke for several minutes, the silence between
them taut with unspoken thoughts.

"Your theory about Barrett is intriguing," Redgrave said
suddenly, his voice low. "The progression of his symptoms
over time suggests a more complex poisoning than I initially
considered."

Clara glanced up at him, surprised by this concession. "His
handwriting shows a progressive tremor that worsened over
weeks. That's consistent with certain types of botanical poisoning—small doses that accumulate in the system."

"Creating a condition that might appear as natural illness,"
Redgrave mused, "until the final, fatal dose."

"Precisely," Clara agreed. "I believe Barrett was being
slowly poisoned before he ever came to my shop. His request
for henbane was genuine—he was seeking relief from symptoms that were deliberately induced."

Redgrave slowed his pace slightly. "What makes you so
certain?"

"The pattern of his deterioration. The timing of his symptoms aligning with regular medical consultations—"

"Medical consultations?" Redgrave interrupted sharply.

"According to registry clerk Miss Collins, Barrett was seen
arguing with a medical gentleman from Scotland Yard two

days before his death." Clara watched Redgrave's reaction carefully. "In the corridor outside the property office."

The inspector's expression remained unreadable, but his grip on her elbow tightened fractionally. "That connection warrants investigation."

"As does the pocket watch with the caduceus emblem," Clara added.

They had reached Bellrose Lane, the familiar silhouette of Hawthorne & Wetherly emerging from the fog like a ship from stormy seas. The shop windows were dark, the street deserted save for a stray cat slinking along the opposite wall.

Redgrave accompanied Clara to her door, waiting as she retrieved her key and unlocked it. "Bar your doors and windows," he instructed. "Don't admit anyone until morning —not even if they claim to come from the police."

"You believe I'm in immediate danger?" Clara asked, the reality of her situation finally settling into her bones with a cold certainty.

"I believe," Redgrave replied carefully, "that you have witnessed two murders connected to your property and Barrett's poisoning. Until I determine the extent of those connections, yes, you are in danger." He hesitated, then added with unexpected gentleness, "Be careful, Miss Wetherly. There are forces at work here beyond a simple property dispute."

"I'm beginning to understand that," Clara said softly.

Redgrave touched the brim of his hat in a brief salute. "Lock the door behind me. I'll return in the morning with any developments from the bank."

Clara watched him disappear into the fog before securing the door as instructed. The familiar confines of her shop, usually so comforting, now seemed filled with shadows and unfamiliar angles. She lit a single lamp, keeping the flame low to avoid broadcasting her presence to anyone watching from the street.

The events of the night replayed in her mind as she moved through her nightly routine, each moment gaining new significance with repetition. Pinkett's conversation with Blackstone. The mysterious visitor with the medical pocket watch. The instantaneous effects of the poison—so different from Barrett's symptoms, yet administered with similar precision.

Two murders, both connected to Blackstone Development and the railway plans. Two victims who had known about Barrett's duplicity. And now Clara herself, a witness who could potentially identify the killer.

As she prepared for bed, the weight of her discoveries pressed upon her like a physical presence. She checked the windows twice, tested each lock, and placed her grandmother's small pistol on the bedside table before extinguishing the lamp.

Sleep, when it finally came, was fitful and haunted by dreams of pocket watches ticking away the seconds of her life.

MARMALADE'S OBSERVATIONS – Entry No. 4

The second watcher came inside tonight.

I knew his scent immediately—ink and medicine and poison. He moved with purpose through the darkness, pausing beneath the window near the preparation table. His tools gleamed faintly in the moonlight—thin metal implements that worked expertly at the latch until it surrendered with a soft click.

Clara was asleep upstairs. The silver-button man had left hours ago after another of their conversations that circle like cats before settling.

The intruder slipped through the window with barely a sound, movements precise as a surgeon's. He moved carefully through the shop, examining drawers, opening cabinets. Not stealing—searching. His fingers lingered on Clara's account books, on the letters from the bank, on the deed to the building.

Then he approached the tea counter. From his pocket came a small vial. Dark liquid dripped into the tea canister Clara prepares each morning.

I watched from the banister, calculating distance. Timing. Purpose.

He replaced the lid with a satisfied smile. Turned toward the window. Would have escaped cleanly.

But some things cannot be permitted.

I leapt, a perfect arc of orange intention. Landed on the counter with deliberate clumsiness. My tail—purely by accident, you understand—swept across the surface.

The poisoned canister fell. Shattered. Contents scattered across the floorboards.

The man swore, lurched toward me. I arched, hissed warning. He hesitated.

Upstairs, floorboards creaked. Clara, awakened.

The man glanced up, then at the broken evidence of his crime. Made his choice. Fled through the window as Clara's footsteps reached the stairs.

She found only me and the broken canister, innocently licking my paw beside the wreckage.

"Marmalade," she scolded, "what have you done?"

If only she knew. But some heroics must go unrecognized.

I purred and wound between her ankles, keeping her from touching the scattered leaves. Tomorrow, she would prepare fresh tea.

And live another day because her guardian has excellent timing and a conveniently clumsy tail.

Clara stood amid the wreckage of her tea canister the following morning, surveying the scattered leaves with bleary-eyed confusion. The precious Ceylon blend—an indulgence she rarely permitted herself—lay ruined across the floorboards, intermingled with fragments of porcelain.

"I don't understand how you managed this," she muttered to Marmalade, who sat washing his face with elaborate unconcern. "The canister was pushed all the way back against the wall."

The cat merely blinked at her, then returned to his grooming with redoubled focus.

Clara knelt to gather the larger fragments, careful not to cut her fingers on the shards. As she worked, a peculiar scent caught her attention—an undertone beneath the familiar Ceylon aroma, something bitter and acrid that didn't belong among the tea leaves.

She lifted a pinch to her nose, inhaling cautiously, her botanical training immediately registering something amiss. The bitterness reminded her of certain physic roots, but with a sharper mineral edge she couldn't immediately identify —not unlike the crude arsenic compounds sometimes used for vermin control, yet more refined.

Clara gathered a small sample into a clean envelope, sealing it carefully. The rest she swept into the dustbin, ensuring not a leaf remained that might accidentally find its way into a cup.

As Clara washed her hands in the basin, her gaze fell upon the window latch near her preparation table. Though she distinctly remembered checking it twice before retiring, it now stood slightly ajar—the old iron mechanism showing fresh scratches around its edge where a thin tool had been inserted to manipulate it from outside.

"Clever," she murmured, examining the marks. The window had always been troublesome, its fittings worn from decades of use. Her grandmother had mentioned having it repaired, but like many small tasks, it had been postponed in favor of more pressing concerns. Now that negligence had nearly proven fatal.

She closed the window firmly, making a mental note to have a locksmith attend to it immediately. No matter how carefully she secured the doors, her shop contained a dozen such vulnerabilities—aging windows, the cellar grate, even the chimney flue. All potential entries for someone determined enough to gain access.

A cold certainty settled in her stomach as she dried her hands. Someone had entered her shop in the night. Someone had tampered with her tea. And Marmalade's nocturnal clumsiness, far from being an annoyance, had potentially saved her life.

She stroked the cat's orange fur with newfound appreciation. "It seems I owe you my thanks rather than my scolding."

Marmalade purred in response, rubbing his head against her hand with unusual affection.

eleven

Morning light filtered through the window, casting a pale glow across Clara's worktable as she meticulously assembled her evidence. The previous night's attempt on her life—for she was now certain that's what the tampered tea represented—had crystallized her resolve. No longer content to merely defend herself against suspicion, she would actively pursue the truth behind Barrett's death and its connection to the railway development.

She arranged Barrett's documents chronologically, securing them with string in a neat portfolio. From her pocket watch chain, she removed the small glass vial that normally held emergency tincture, now containing the suspicious residue from her tea. Her grandmother's voice echoed in memory: Evidence, properly presented, becomes undeniable.

The street outside remained quiet as Clara donned her most respectable walking outfit—the navy wool dress with minimal embellishment and a sensible bonnet. Practical garments that would allow her to traverse London without drawing undue attention, yet formal enough to convey seriousness of purpose at Scotland Yard.

As she opened her door, she was startled to find a young constable standing at attention outside her shop.

"Good morning, Miss Wetherly," he said, touching his hat respectfully. "Constable Thomas, assigned by Inspector Redgrave to keep watch on your premises."

"When were you posted here, Constable?" Clara asked, noting his fresh appearance and alert manner.

"Just this morning, Miss. The Inspector gave the orders first thing—said it was in light of recent events."

Clara nodded, processing this information. "Did you happen to notice any unusual activity around the shop in the early hours? Any visitors or disturbances?"

"I'm afraid I wouldn't know, Miss. I only arrived at six bells." The young officer shifted uncomfortably. "Has there been trouble in the night?"

"Perhaps," Clara replied, considering that whoever had tampered with her tea had come and gone unobserved. "I have urgent business with Inspector Redgrave concerning evidence in Mr. Pinkett's murder. You're welcome to accompany me to Scotland Yard, or I can proceed alone."

The young officer hesitated, uncertainty furrowing his brow. "I'm to keep watch on the shop, Miss."

"Then the shop will be vacant while you do so," Clara answered, tucking her portfolio securely under one arm. "Unless you believe the furniture requires supervision more than the proprietor requires protection?"

His mouth opened, then closed in confusion.

"I'm certain the Inspector would prefer you accompany me," Clara added more gently, "considering recent events."

Constable Thomas sighed with the resignation of a man outmaneuvered. "Please wait a moment while I secure the premises, Miss."

. . .

SCOTLAND YARD BUSTLED with morning activity when they arrived—constables coming and going, clerks hurrying between offices with stacks of papers, and the occasional well-dressed gentleman conferring in hushed tones. The imposing Gothic building seemed designed to intimidate, its corridors a labyrinth of male authority from which females were largely excluded.

Clara observed how conversation quieted as she passed, officers glancing sideways at the unusual sight of a woman who was neither criminal nor grieving relative. The weight of their collective judgment pressed against her like a physical force, yet she kept her spine straight, her portfolio clutched like a shield.

Constable Thomas led her to Redgrave's office, knocking sharply on the oak door.

"Enter," came the clipped response.

The inspector's office was precisely as Clara had imagined it would be—austere, methodical, and revealing in its spartan functionality. Unlike the cluttered spaces favored by most men of authority, Redgrave maintained a space of almost military precision. His desk stood centered beneath the window, allowing light to fall across its surface without casting the occupant's face in shadow—an interrogator's arrangement that permitted him to read expressions while concealing his own.

The walls held no decorative flourishes save for an anatomical sketch of the human circulatory system and several carefully framed maps of London districts. A single bookshelf contained leather-bound volumes on criminal law, medical jurisprudence, and—Clara noted with interest—three botanical reference texts, their spines more worn than the others.

Behind his desk hung a small, unassuming landscape painting—a country estate visible through morning mist, the artist's style suggesting it dated from the previous century.

Family home, perhaps, though the frame was simple, almost deliberately understated. It seemed at odds with the functional nature of everything else in the room, a personal touch he had permitted himself despite his otherwise methodical environment.

Redgrave glanced up from a document, his expression shifting from irritation to surprise as he registered Clara's presence.

"Miss Wetherly," he said, rising with automatic courtesy. "I believe my instructions were quite clear regarding your remaining indoors."

"They were perfectly clear, Inspector," Clara replied, placing her portfolio on his desk. "As was the attempt to poison me last night."

Redgrave stiffened, his gaze flicking briefly to Constable Thomas before returning to Clara. "Explain."

"Someone entered my shop in the night," Clara stated calmly. "They tampered with my tea supply, adding a substance with a distinctive bitter aroma consistent with certain mineral toxins. I've brought a sample." She removed the small vial from her pocket, placing it carefully beside the portfolio. "Had my cat not knocked the canister to the floor, I would likely be your third victim."

Constable Thomas shifted uncomfortably by the door. Redgrave's expression darkened as he gestured to a straight-backed chair opposite his desk.

"Sit down, Miss Wetherly. Thomas, return to your post. Send word if you observe anything unusual."

When the door closed behind the constable, Redgrave remained standing, studying Clara with an intensity that might have unnerved a less determined woman.

"You handled a potentially poisonous substance without protection," he observed, his tone caught between accusation and grudging admiration.

"I handled it with the same care I apply to all potentially harmful compounds," Clara corrected. "My grandmother ensured I understood proper techniques for examining unknown substances without exposure."

Redgrave finally sat, his posture rigid as he reached for the vial. He held it to the light without opening it, examining the dark residue clinging to the glass.

"And you're certain this was deliberately added to your tea?"

"Absolutely certain," Clara affirmed. "The tea was Ceylon, which has a distinctive aroma. This carried an underlying bitterness consistent with crude arsenic preparations, though more refined in composition."

"You're remarkably knowledgeable about poisons, Miss Wetherly," Redgrave observed, returning the vial to his desk.

"I'm knowledgeable about substances that affect the human body, Inspector. Their designation as medicine or poison often depends merely on dosage and intent." Clara met his gaze directly. "Just as Barrett's trembling hands suggest a possible poisoning, rather than a natural condition."

Redgrave's expression remained neutral, though something flickered behind his eyes—interest, perhaps. "You mentioned Barrett's hands. What evidence supports this theory?"

Clara opened her portfolio, spreading the documents in a neat chronological arrangement across his desk. "These are copies of Barrett's property assessments from the Registry Office, spanning the three months before his death. Notice the progression in his handwriting."

Redgrave leaned forward, studying the documents with careful attention. The earliest showed Barrett's signature as firm and precise—each letter meticulously formed. The middle documents revealed a subtle but unmistakable wavering in the strokes. By the final assessment, dated two days before his death, the signature had deteriorated significantly, the letters trembling and disconnected.

"A progressive tremor," Redgrave murmured, almost to himself. "Worsening over time."

"Which could suggest poisoning administered in small doses," Clara proposed. "Particularly preparations containing certain toxic compounds that accumulate in the system."

"Or it could indicate a legitimate medical condition," Redgrave countered, his gaze lifting to meet hers. "Essential tremor, nervous exhaustion, or several other natural ailments can present with similar symptoms."

"I was initially inclined to believe it was a natural ailment," Clara admitted. "Until he appeared dead behind my shop with a poison jar bearing my label."

The moment stretched between them—an unexpected bridge of shared understanding. For the first time, Clara felt not the weight of his suspicion but the spark of intellectual recognition.

"These assessments are dated at regular intervals," Redgrave observed, returning to the documents. "Have you any evidence linking the deterioration to outside influence?"

"Not yet," Clara said honestly. "But I believe the progression suggests something beyond natural decline. The tremor's acceleration in the final weeks before his death seems suspicious, particularly when combined with his request for henbane—which my grandmother's notes indicate can interact fatally with certain other compounds."

Redgrave rose abruptly, moving to the window where the morning light outlined his silhouette against the glass.

"What you're suggesting would require someone with considerable botanical knowledge," he said, his back to her. "And access to Barrett over an extended period."

"Yes," Clara agreed. "Someone he trusted. Someone whose recommendations he followed without question." She paused deliberately. "Or someone whose orders he couldn't refuse."

Redgrave turned, brow furrowed. "Meaning?"

"Lord Blackstone," Clara stated firmly. "Barrett was working for him. They were seen arguing publicly just days before Barrett's death. Blackstone stands to make a fortune once the railway plans are approved—plans that required acquiring my property to complete. And now, after Barrett's death, I find my tea poisoned."

A muscle tensed in Redgrave's jaw. "Accusing a peer of the realm is not something to be undertaken lightly, Miss Wetherly."

"And yet murder is not something to be overlooked because of a title," Clara countered. "Have you questioned Lord Blackstone about his connection to Barrett? Or his conversation with Pinkett at the Empire Club the night Pinkett was murdered?"

"You are venturing into dangerous territory," Redgrave warned, his tone cooler now. "The investigation is proceeding according to proper channels."

Clara leaned forward, her frustration evident. "Proper channels that conveniently avoid aristocratic drawing rooms? Barrett and Pinkett are dead. Someone tried to poison me. All three of us connected to property that Lord Blackstone desperately wants to acquire. Yet you seem remarkably reluctant to consider him a suspect."

"I consider all evidence, Miss Wetherly." Redgrave's voice had taken on a clipped formality that hadn't been present moments before. "But evidence must be substantial to justify questioning someone of Lord Blackstone's standing."

"Substantial?" Clara echoed incredulously. "Two men are dead! How many more bodies must accumulate before aristocratic 'standing' becomes irrelevant?"

Redgrave's expression had closed entirely now, the brief

connection between them severed. "You've constructed an intriguing theory, I'll grant you that. But theories require proof, and proof requires proper examination." He gestured to the vial. "I'll have this tested."

"By whom?" Clara asked, unable to keep the edge from her voice. "Someone who will approach the evidence without preconceived notions about my guilt?"

"Scotland Yard employs several examiners, Miss Wetherly," Redgrave replied, his tone cooling. "Procedures will be followed."

Clara gathered her documents, sensing she had reached the limits of Redgrave's receptiveness for the moment. "Will you at least concede it's possible I'm not your killer, Inspector?"

He studied her for a long moment, his expression softening almost imperceptibly. "I follow evidence, Miss Wetherly, not possibilities. But..." he hesitated, as if weighing his words carefully, "your observations about Barrett's progressive symptoms are...medically sound."

Something in his phrasing caught Clara's attention. "You have medical knowledge beyond police requirements."

It wasn't a question, but Redgrave answered nonetheless, his voice lower, almost distant. "I was engaged to a physician's daughter once. I found myself...educated in certain matters by proximity." He straightened, the brief window into his past closing as quickly as it had opened. "It was a lifetime ago."

Before Clara could respond to this unexpected revelation, a sharp knock interrupted them. The door opened to reveal a familiar figure—Dr. Morris, immaculately dressed as always, a leather case tucked under one arm.

"Inspector, I have the preliminary findings on—" He stopped, noticing Clara. "Miss Wetherly. An unexpected pleasure."

Clara inclined her head slightly, noting the perfect composure with which he masked his surprise. "Dr. Morris."

"Miss Wetherly has brought evidence potentially related to our investigation," Redgrave explained, his professional manner instantly restored. "Including possible contamination of her tea supply."

"Indeed?" Morris raised an eyebrow, his gaze falling to the vial on Redgrave's desk. "How fortunate you discovered it before consumption."

"Yes," Clara replied evenly. "Quite fortunate."

"Well, I shan't interrupt your discussion," Morris said smoothly, placing a sealed document on Redgrave's desk. "My findings on Pinkett's autopsy, Inspector. Most illuminating. We can discuss them at your convenience." With a cordial nod to Clara, he excused himself, the door closing behind him with a definitive click.

Clara gathered her portfolio, sensing the interview had reached its natural conclusion. "Will you inform me of the results when my tea sample is tested?"

"If the results prove pertinent to your safety, yes," Redgrave answered, his careful phrasing revealing the boundaries of what he considered her right to know.

As Clara prepared to depart, a young woman appeared at the office door—Harriet Collins from the Registry Office, her wire-rimmed spectacles slightly askew as if she had hurried.

"Inspector Redgrave," she said, slightly breathless. "I've brought the additional registry documents you requested concerning Barrett's property assessments." Her gaze fell on Clara, brightening with recognition. "Oh! Miss Wetherly. I didn't expect to find you here."

"Miss Collins," Clara acknowledged with genuine pleasure. "What a fortunate coincidence."

"Hardly coincidence," Harriet replied with a small smile. "I've been combing through registry files since our conversation. There's a pattern to Barrett's property dealings that seemed suspicious, so I brought everything to Inspector Redgrave."

Redgrave accepted the documents with a nod. "Thank you, Miss Collins. Your assistance is appreciated."

"I found something else that might interest you both," Harriet continued, lowering her voice slightly. "Barrett was seen arguing with Mr. Pinkett at the bank just days before his death. Quite heated, according to the clerk who witnessed it. Something about 'conflicting valuations' and 'divided loyalties.'"

Clara and Redgrave exchanged a glance, the significance of this connection impossible to ignore.

"Miss Collins," Redgrave said carefully, "I'd appreciate your discretion regarding these observations."

"Of course, Inspector," Harriet replied, straightening her spectacles. "I've worked at the Registry long enough to understand the value of discretion."

After Harriet departed, Clara remained standing before Redgrave's desk, the weight of this new information settling between them.

"Two victims, connected through property valuations and confrontation," she said quietly. "Both connected to Lord Blackstone."

"Circumstantial," Redgrave replied, though with less conviction than before. "But worth investigating."

Clara moved toward the door, pausing with her hand on the latch. "You said you were engaged to a physician's daughter once."

Redgrave stiffened almost imperceptibly. "It was not relevant to our discussion."

"And yet you mentioned it," Clara observed. "Was she... is she...?"

"She died," Redgrave said simply, his fingers tightening

almost imperceptibly, a flash of pain crossing his eyes so quickly Clara might have imagined it, gone before she could interpret its meaning. "That's all you need to know." He shuffled papers on his desk, a clear dismissal. "Good day, Miss Wetherly. Constable Thomas will escort you home."

Clara knew better than to press further, recognizing the carefully constructed wall he had raised. Yet as she departed, she carried with her not just the echo of that brief personal revelation, but the certainty that Inspector Redgrave understood more about poisoning cases than his official position might suggest—and a growing suspicion about his reluctance to investigate Lord Blackstone.

THE WALK home passed in tense silence, Clara's frustration mounting with each step. Constable Thomas maintained a respectful distance, but Clara could feel his curious glances.

"He won't pursue Lord Blackstone, will he?" she finally asked, unable to contain her thoughts any longer.

Thomas looked startled by the direct question. "I couldn't say, Miss. The Inspector conducts his investigations as he sees fit."

"Even when the evidence points directly to the aristocracy?"

The constable hesitated, clearly uncomfortable with the direction of the conversation. "The Inspector is... thorough, Miss. He follows where the evidence leads."

"Unless it leads to certain drawing rooms," Clara murmured.

Thomas frowned slightly. "Inspector Redgrave isn't one to be intimidated by social standing, Miss. If anything, he's harder on those of his own class."

Clara stopped walking, turning to face the young officer. "His own class?"

Thomas looked as though he immediately regretted his words. "I only meant—that is—I shouldn't have spoken out of turn, Miss."

"No, please," Clara pressed. "I'm trying to understand the inspector's hesitation."

Thomas shifted uncomfortably, glancing around before lowering his voice. "It's not common knowledge, Miss, and he doesn't speak of it, but the Inspector comes from... well, a titled family. Third son of the Earl of Redgrave, he is. Left that life behind years ago, after some trouble. I've only heard whispers about it."

The revelation struck Clara with unexpected force. The landscape painting in his office—not just any country estate, but his family home. His formal diction, his posture, his automatic adherence to certain social courtesies—all markers of aristocratic upbringing she should have recognized.

"And you believe this makes him harder on the aristocracy?" she asked, her voice carefully neutral.

"The other constables say he holds the nobility to a higher standard than most," Thomas replied. "Something about accountability and privilege. But he's also careful—requires absolute proof before making accusations." He straightened, clearly uncomfortable with gossiping about his superior. "That's just idle talk around the station, Miss. I shouldn't have mentioned it."

As they approached Hawthorne & Wetherly, Clara found herself studying the neighboring shops—Mrs. Winters' dressmaking establishment, Jenkins' former tobacco shop now bearing a "SOLD" sign, the small bookbinder where Mr. Peterson had practiced his craft for thirty years before selling to Blackstone Development just last month.

"It seems I'm the last holdout on the block," she remarked to Constable Thomas.

The young officer glanced around, nodding. "Yes, Miss. I

heard Blackstone's been buying everything in sight. Offering good money too."

"And yet some things aren't measured in pounds and shillings, Constable," Clara replied. "My grandmother built this shop from nothing. Three generations of Wetherly women have served this community. That legacy can't be assessed on a property valuation."

Thomas nodded respectfully. "My own grandmother kept a small medicinal garden. Used to say the right plant in the right hands was worth more than any doctor's visit."

"Your grandmother sounds like a wise woman," Clara said with a small smile.

"That she was, Miss." He looked uncomfortable for a moment. "If you don't mind my asking... why not sell? With the prices they're offering, you could open a finer shop in a better neighborhood."

Clara paused, considering how to explain something so fundamental to her being. "This isn't merely a shop, Constable. It's my heritage. Every floorboard, every shelf—they hold memories. My grandmother's voice still echoes in these walls. Some connections can't be replicated, no matter how fine the new establishment might be."

The constable performed a thorough inspection of the premises before declaring it secure, promising to maintain his watch from his post across the street.

"Thank you, Constable," Clara said, genuinely appreciative of his diligence. "Would you care for some tea? I've a fresh tin of Darjeeling that remains mercifully untampered with."

"Most kind, Miss, but I must maintain my position," Thomas replied, touching his hat respectfully before resuming his post.

Inside, Clara removed her bonnet and gloves, the familiar surroundings bringing momentary comfort after the tension of her Scotland Yard visit. She moved automatically to prepare a cup of tea, then hesitated, the memory of last night's discovery still fresh. Instead, she filled the kettle with fresh water, selecting a new tin of Darjeeling from her private stock—one she kept sealed in her personal quarters rather than the shop.

As the water heated, Clara conducted her own inspection of the shop, her senses alert for any sign of disturbance. At first glance, everything appeared in order—the counter clean, the drawers closed, her ledgers stacked neatly beside the register.

Yet something felt subtly wrong.

She paused, allowing her awareness to expand beyond conscious observation, the way her grandmother had taught her. Listen to the shop, Genevieve would say. It speaks in its own language.

The sensation intensified—a whispered warning without words. Clara moved carefully through the space, her fingers trailing lightly across surfaces, noting minute discrepancies. The dried lavender bundles hanging from the ceiling had been disturbed, their arrangement slightly altered. The third drawer in her storage cabinet stood not fully closed, though she distinctly remembered securing it. And most tellingly, The Gilded Leaf had been moved—still on its stand, but angled differently, the pressed violet bookmark now between different pages than where she had left it.

Someone had searched her shop again, with such meticulous care that only her intimate knowledge of its order revealed the intrusion.

Clara opened The Gilded Leaf to the page now marked by the violet—an entry on distinctive botanical poisons and their manifestations in the human body. Her grandmother's precise handwriting detailed symptoms of various compounds, with particular attention to monkshood and its interactions with other substances.

The kettle's whistle startled her from her contemplation.

As she prepared her tea, Clara found herself contemplating the growing connections between Barrett's death, Pinkett's murder, and the relentless pressure to acquire her property.

The revelation about Redgrave's aristocratic background cast his reluctance to pursue Lord Blackstone in a new light. Was he protecting a fellow peer? Or was his insistence on substantial evidence before making accusations against the nobility merely the caution of a man who understood the consequences of challenging such power?

She carried her cup to the window, watching Constable Thomas faithfully maintaining his vigil across the street. The young officer represented Redgrave's protection—official, visible, and undoubtedly well-intentioned. Yet Clara couldn't shake the certainty that the greater danger came not from obvious threats, but from someone moving freely through the circles of authority, someone whose position placed them above suspicion.

As darkness began to fall over Bloomsbury, Clara decided to visit Mrs. Winters to inquire about any neighborhood gossip regarding Barrett's final days. She informed Constable Thomas of her intention, and despite his protests about the hour, insisted it was merely a few doors down.

She had barely stepped into the street when the clatter of hooves and the rumble of wheels accelerated suddenly. Clara looked up to see a carriage bearing down on her at alarming speed, the driver's face obscured by shadow. Before she could react, a strong hand grasped her arm, yanking her back onto the pavement as the carriage swerved deliberately toward where she had stood, wheels scraping the curb.

"Good God!" Constable Thomas exclaimed, his grip still firm on her arm. "That was no accident! He drove straight at you!"

Clara's heart hammered against her ribs as she watched the

unmarked carriage disappear around the corner, its lamps swaying wildly in the gathering dusk.

"Are you hurt, Miss?" Thomas asked, his young face pale with alarm.

"No," she managed, though her voice sounded distant to her own ears. "Thanks to your quick action."

Thomas insisted on escorting her back to her shop, all thoughts of visiting Mrs. Winters abandoned. As Clara locked her door, her hands trembling slightly, Marmalade appeared on the windowsill, his amber eyes fixed on something beyond the glass—something Clara herself could not see.

"We're being watched," she murmured, more to herself than to Marmalade. "And whoever is watching has decided I'm too dangerous to ignore."

The cat blinked slowly, as if in agreement, then turned his vigilant gaze back to the London night.

twelve

The fog had thickened by the time Constable Thomas escorted Clara back to her shop, his young face still pale with the shock of what they'd witnessed. The carriage that had nearly struck her had disappeared into the London night, leaving only the memory of deliberate malice and the scrape of wheels against the curb.

"I'll need to check every room, Miss," Thomas insisted as Clara unlocked the door. "Someone who'd try to run you down with a carriage mightn't hesitate to break in while you were out."

Clara nodded, grateful for his diligence despite the intrusion on her privacy. "Of course, Constable."

By lamplight, they moved through the narrow corridors of Hawthorne & Wetherly, the constable methodically examining each corner, closet, and shadow. The shop felt different tonight—the familiar shelves of botanical remedies and tinctures no longer offering their usual comfort but instead seeming to conceal potential dangers in their darkened recesses.

"All secure, Miss," Thomas declared finally, returning to

the front room where Clara waited. "Though I'll need to report this incident to Inspector Redgrave immediately. I shouldn't leave you alone, but—"

"You have your duty," Clara finished for him. "I understand. The shop is locked, and I have my grandmother's pistol." She gestured to the small weapon she'd retrieved from her desk drawer. "I'm not entirely helpless, Constable."

Thomas looked doubtful but nodded. "I'll return at first light, Miss Wetherly. Keep your doors locked and windows secured. And perhaps..." he hesitated, glancing at the pistol, "best keep that close at hand."

After the constable departed, Clara secured the door behind him and extinguished all lamps save one. She carried it upstairs to her bedroom, where Marmalade already occupied the center of her pillow, his orange bulk sprawled in proprietary slumber. She gently shifted him aside, placing her grandmother's pistol on the bedside table before changing into her nightdress.

Sleep proved elusive. Each creak of the old building's timbers startled her to alertness, each distant rattle of passing wheels tensed her muscles for flight. When exhaustion finally claimed her, her dreams were fragmented—shattered glass, pounding hooves, a pocket watch with a serpent emblem swinging like a pendulum.

Morning arrived with Marmalade's insistent paw batting at her face. Clara attempted to roll away, but the cat was unrelenting, headbutting her shoulder, pulling at her blankets, and finally emitting a yowl of frustration that jolted her fully awake.

"What on earth has gotten into you?" she muttered, pushing herself upright.

The cat leapt from the bed and paced before her closed bedroom door, looking back at her with imperious expectation. When Clara didn't immediately follow, he returned to the bed, nipped at her sleeve, then repeated his journey to the door.

"Very well," Clara sighed, reaching for her dressing gown. "Though I hope whatever crisis demands my attention warrants this disruption."

She followed Marmalade down the narrow stairs, the cat bounding ahead with an urgency she couldn't fathom. In the shop below, morning light filtered through the windows, casting long shadows across the worn floorboards. Marmalade sat precisely centered atop a cream-colored envelope that had been slipped beneath the door—an envelope Clara was certain hadn't been there when she'd locked up the previous night.

Clara approached cautiously, noting the heavy stock and gold embossing before she even touched it. Marmalade rose and stepped aside, as if having completed an assignment, then sat watching as she lifted the envelope and broke its ornate seal.

The letterhead read "Halston Properties, Ltd." in elegant copperplate script. The contents were equally precise:

MISS CLARA WETHERLY,

Regarding the property at 12 Bellrose Lane, trading as "Hawthorne & Wetherly,"

In light of the unfortunate events plaguing the neighborhood, Halston Properties wishes to offer you a path forward that should prove considerably more advantageous than the one chosen by your neighbors.

We hereby offer the sum of £3,200 for your property and business—a figure exceeding market value by no less than 75%. This exceptional offer reflects both the strategic location of your establishment and our desire to conclude this transaction expeditiously.

Unlike our competitors, we understand the value of legacy

and tradition. Should you accept, we would be amenable to preserving the Hawthorne & Wetherly name on the premises, albeit in a modified capacity.

Given recent circumstances, we strongly urge you to consider this offer without delay.

Yours faithfully,

James Halston

CLARA SANK into her grandmother's chair, the letter trembling slightly in her hands. Three thousand two hundred pounds—an astronomical sum that would allow her to establish a new shop in any neighborhood of London, with ample funds remaining to live comfortably for years. A lifetime of financial security offered in exchange for the walls that had witnessed three generations of Wetherly women.

For the first time since Barrett's body had appeared in her alley, genuine doubt crept into Clara's mind. Was her stubborn refusal to sell merely prideful folly? People were dying. She herself had nearly been crushed beneath carriage wheels. How many more would suffer before this ended?

She traced her fingers along the worn edge of the counter, feeling the smooth depression where her grandmother's hand had rested in precisely the same spot for decades. Each drawer, each shelf, each crack in the floorboards held memories no amount of money could purchase—her first successful tincture preparation under Genevieve's watchful eye; the midnight hours preparing remedies during the cholera outbreak when doctors had abandoned hope; the quiet evenings learning to read tea leaves by lamplight.

"You'd never surrender to threats, would you, Grandmother?" she murmured aloud, her voice barely disturbing the morning quiet.

On the shelf above the preparation table, a teacup rattled

in its saucer, though nothing had touched it. Clara froze, watching as the delicate porcelain settled back into stillness. A coincidence, most likely—the vibration of a passing cart, perhaps, or the settling of the old building's foundation.

Yet as Clara folded Halston's letter and tucked it into her pocket, a sense of clarity replaced her doubt. Whatever dangers might come, whatever threats might materialize, this shop was more than brick and timber. It was her heritage, and she would not surrender it—not to Blackstone, not to Halston, not to fear itself.

Marmalade, apparently satisfied with her decision, hopped onto the counter and began his morning ablutions as if nothing of significance had occurred.

"We've had quite enough drama for one morning, I think," Clara told him, reaching for her kettle. "And someone managed to deliver this while Constable Thomas was away reporting to Inspector Redgrave." She glanced toward the window, suddenly aware that whoever had slipped the envelope beneath her door had done so within the last few hours—and had managed to avoid the notice of any night watchmen.

She was measuring tea leaves into the pot when a sharp knock interrupted her thoughts. Through the glass, she could see Constable Thomas's uniform, and beside him, the taller figure of Inspector Redgrave, his dark coat still beaded with morning dew.

"Good morning, Miss Wetherly," Redgrave said when she opened the door. His gaze swept over her quickly, assessing. "Constable Thomas reported the incident last night. Are you unharmed?"

"Quite unharmed, though not for lack of trying on the driver's part," Clara replied, gesturing them inside. "And now it seems I've received a rather interesting proposition."

She handed Redgrave the letter from Halston. The inspector read it quickly, his expression revealing nothing.

"Interesting timing," he observed, returning the letter. "Halston has shown no previous interest in your property, to my knowledge."

"Perhaps Blackstone's public interest made him reconsider," Clara suggested. "Or perhaps recent events have made me seem a more... willing seller."

Redgrave's eyes narrowed slightly. "This offer was delivered overnight?"

"Sometime after Constable Thomas departed to report to you," Clara confirmed. "Apparently, my shop has become quite the nocturnal thoroughfare."

"I don't like it, sir," Thomas interjected. "First the carriage tries to run Miss Wetherly down, then this letter appears while she's unguarded. It feels coordinated."

"Indeed." Redgrave turned to examine the street outside the window. "This pattern of escalation concerns me, Miss Wetherly. I'm assigning a second constable to evening patrol of your street."

"I appreciate the precaution, Inspector," Clara said, "though I wonder if such resources might be better spent investigating the deaths of Mr. Barrett and Mr. Pinkett."

"Rest assured, those investigations continue," Redgrave replied, turning back to face her. "In fact, I interviewed Lord Blackstone yesterday evening regarding Mr. Pinkett's murder."

Clara's interest sharpened. "And?"

"He has a solid alibi. He was at his gentleman's club with no fewer than six witnesses during the time of Pinkett's death."

Clara noted the subtle shift in Redgrave's manner—less accusatory than in their earlier encounters, more protective, though still maintaining professional distance. "And have you questioned Mr. Halston as well?" she asked.

"Investigations continue in multiple directions," Redgrave replied carefully, neither confirming nor denying.

Clara realized with mild surprise that he was taking her

theories more seriously than his initial dismissiveness had suggested. "I see," she said.

After the inspector and constable departed to examine the scene where the carriage had nearly struck her, Clara sent a message to Mrs. Penfield requesting a visit. If anyone could provide information about Barrett's final days and Halston's activities, it would be the widow with her extensive network of neighborhood intelligence.

Mrs. Penfield arrived within the hour, bringing not only her formidable gossip but also a basket of shortbread that Clara suspected was as much excuse as offering.

"Attempted murder in broad daylight!" she exclaimed, settling her substantial frame into the shop's most comfortable chair. "And now Halston extends an offer! The audacity! Though I must say, my dear, the sum is rather considerable."

"Indeed," Clara agreed, preparing tea for them both. "Though I wonder what makes my property suddenly so valuable to both developers."

Mrs. Penfield leaned forward conspiratorially. "That's not all that's curious. I've been asking discreet questions about Mr. Barrett, as you requested. He'd been seeing a doctor regularly before his death—had been for weeks. His health was declining noticeably."

Clara paused in pouring the tea. "Did anyone mention what symptoms he displayed?"

"Mrs. Jenkins said he visited their tobacco shop the day before his death. His hands shook so badly he could barely sign their guest book." Mrs. Penfield accepted her cup with a nod of thanks. "And he was overheard complaining that the treatments were making him worse, not better."

"Did anyone mention which doctor Barrett consulted?" Clara asked, trying to keep her tone casual.

"A Harley Street physician, I believe. Very expensive. Barrett complained about the fees." Mrs. Penfield sipped her tea. "Though that wasn't his only complaint. He was apparently providing information to both developers—Blackstone and Halston. Made quite a profit playing them against each other, until..."

The unspoken "until he ended up dead in your alley" hung in the air between them.

"There's one other bit of gossip you might find interesting," Mrs. Penfield continued, reaching for a shortbread. "Miss Eleanor Blackstone—that's Lord Blackstone's secretary and distant cousin—has recently become engaged to a physician's cousin. Quite the social connection for a working secretary."

Clara found her interest piqued by this seemingly casual observation. "A physician's cousin? Do you know which physician?"

Mrs. Penfield shook her head. "The particular name escapes me, though I could certainly make inquiries. It struck me as interesting mainly because Miss Blackstone has always seemed so dedicated to her work—hardly the type to pursue romantic entanglements."

The afternoon sun streamed through the shop windows as they continued their conversation, casting a warm glow that belied the darker undercurrents of their discussion. Clara was just returning from the back room with a fresh pot of tea when a tremendous crash shattered the tranquility.

A brick smashed through the front window, sending glass shards spraying across the counter. Clara instinctively ducked, but not before glimpsing the paper wrapped around the projectile.

Constable Thomas rushed in from his post outside, his young face flushed with alarm. "Are you hurt, Miss Wetherly? Mrs. Penfield?"

"We're unharmed," Clara assured him, straightening carefully to avoid the broken glass. "Though I confess I'm growing rather weary of these dramatic interruptions."

She approached the brick cautiously. A note had been secured with twine, and beneath it, a newspaper clipping. The message was brief, printed in block letters: "BARRETT COULDN'T DECIDE. PINKETT COULDN'T DECIDE. WILL YOU?"

The newspaper clipping showed an announcement of Halston's recent successful Manchester development, the heading proclaiming "Halston Properties Transforms Derelict District Into Commercial Success."

Thomas insisted on searching the street immediately but found no trace of the brick-thrower. "This happened in broad daylight, Miss," he said upon returning, his expression troubled. "I was right outside and saw no one suspicious."

"We should notify Inspector Redgrave immediately," Clara said, wrapping the brick and note in clean paper. "This escalation suggests growing desperation."

Mrs. Penfield departed shortly thereafter, insisting that Clara remain vigilant and promising to discover more about Miss Blackstone's physician connection. Alone in the shop, Clara swept the broken glass with methodical precision, her mind processing the implications of the morning's events.

The brick incident, coming so soon after Halston's offer, suggested coordination rather than competition between the developers. Yet if they were working together, why the different approaches? And how did Barrett's declining health —his trembling hands and complaints about worsening treatments—fit into the picture?

Inspector Redgrave arrived within the hour, examining the broken window with grim attention. He took the brick, note, and clipping as evidence, his expression darkening as he read the threatening message.

"I've received the analysis of your tea sample," he said after completing his inspection. "Dr. Morris was quite thorough. There was no evidence of tampering or toxins."

Clara stared at him in disbelief. "That's impossible. I know what I smelled."

Redgrave studied her reaction, his head tilting slightly. "Could you describe it again? The exact nature of what you detected?"

"A distinctive bitterness beneath the tea's natural aroma," Clara explained, her certainty undiminished. "Similar to certain mineral compounds, but with a particular acrid quality I've encountered in specific toxic preparations. I've worked with botanical remedies my entire life, Inspector. I know when something isn't right."

She could see the doubt in his eyes, frustration rising within her. "Could someone else analyze the sample?" she asked. "Perhaps a different examiner might detect what Dr. Morris missed."

"You question the analysis," Redgrave observed, his tone neutral. "May I ask why?"

Clara hesitated, reluctant to voice suspicions without evidence. "It's not something I can explain clearly. Just... a feeling I can't shake."

"Police work requires evidence, Miss Wetherly, not feelings." His dismissal was automatic, practiced.

"Have you never had a feeling about a case you couldn't explain?" Clara challenged, meeting his gaze directly. "Something you knew was true before you could prove it?"

The question caught him off guard. A flicker of something —recognition, perhaps—crossed his face before he could mask it. The silence between them stretched, holding more meaning than either was prepared to acknowledge.

"Yes," he finally admitted, his voice lower than before. "I suppose I have had that particular experience."

Clara felt the subtle shift between them—not quite trust, but a bridge of understanding neither had anticipated.

"I'll send the sample to another examiner," Redgrave

conceded. "Though I warn you it will take time. The Yard's resources are limited."

"Thank you," Clara said simply.

After Redgrave departed, Clara sat at her small desk, attempting to organize the conflicting threads of evidence. The pocket watch with the medical emblem seen the night of Pinkett's murder. Barrett's declining health while under a doctor's care. The analysis finding nothing in tea she knew was tampered with. The newspaper clipping suggesting Halston's involvement. Miss Blackstone's engagement to a doctor's relative.

The pieces refused to form a coherent pattern. Were Blackstone and Halston working together, or against each other? And why the persistent medical connections that kept appearing at the edges of her investigation?

With growing frustration, Clara turned her attention to the amber bottle found with Barrett's body. If she could somehow trace its origins, perhaps she might establish a more direct connection between her shop and the murderer.

She retrieved her sales ledgers from beneath the counter, methodically checking every entry for amber bottles sold within the past six months. The precise handwriting—her own and occasionally Mrs. Hudson's when she had minded the shop—recorded each transaction with meticulous detail: date, customer, contents, price.

Nearly an hour into her search, Clara's finger froze above an entry from two months prior: "Amber bottle (4 oz.) sold to E. Phillips, assistant. 3s. 6d." A notation in the margin indicated the purchase had been made "on behalf of employer."

Clara frowned, searching her memory. She had no recollection of anyone named Phillips, which suggested Mrs. Hudson had handled the transaction during Clara's brief illness two months ago. The name tickled at the edge of her mind, though, producing a vague sense of recognition she couldn't quite place.

Then it came to her—Phillips, the young woman she had glimpsed at the police station, carrying documents for Dr. Morris. She had overheard a constable greet her: "Miss Phillips, the doctor's waiting in his office."

Clara sat back, the implication settling coldly in her stomach. If Morris's assistant had purchased a bottle from her shop two months ago—the same type found with Barrett's body— it created a connection she couldn't ignore. But it still didn't fully explain the broader pattern, or why Barrett had been killed.

The evening fell softly outside her window as Clara remained at her desk, the connections and contradictions swirling in her mind. Despite the fear that had briefly taken hold that morning, she felt a renewed determination hardening within her.

"I won't be driven from my home by threats, Grandmother," she said aloud to the empty shop. "Not when there are still so many questions unanswered."

She made a methodical list of what she knew and what she still needed to discover:

1. Why are both developers suddenly so interested in her property?
2. Why did Barrett's health deteriorate before his death?
3. What is the significance of the medical connection?
4. How did her bottle end up at the murder scene?

As night settled over Bloomsbury, Clara placed her grandmother's pistol on her bedside table with deliberate care.

Tomorrow she would begin investigating Eleanor Blackstone's connections, following this new thread wherever it might lead.

Outside her window, a figure watched from the shadows, then turned and disappeared into the fog-shrouded street.

Marmalade, from his perch on the windowsill, batted at the glass as if attempting to catch something only he could see, his tail lashing with feline frustration as the shadowy form vanished into the London night.

thirteen

Clara set out from her shop just after dawn, the early light casting long shadows across Bellrose Lane. Despite Constable Thomas's insistence on accompanying her, she had persuaded him that her business at the Registry Office required privacy—and that in daylight, with the streets filled with market-goers and early workers, she would be safe enough.

"It's barely three streets away," she had assured him. "And no one would attempt anything with half of Bloomsbury watching."

The constable had reluctantly agreed, though she noticed him adjusting his uniform coat as if preparing to follow at a discreet distance the moment she turned the corner.

The brick through her window yesterday had altered something fundamental in Clara's approach. No longer content to defend against accusations, she had determined to uncover the full truth—not just about Barrett's death, but about the seemingly desperate interest in her modest shop. The threatening note had mentioned both Barrett and Pinkett, suggesting the same hand orchestrated both deaths.

The Registry Office stood like a monument to bureau-cratic authority, its Portland stone facade imposing against the morning sky. Inside, the cavernous entrance hall echoed with the precise sounds of official London—the scratch of pens, the thud of document stamps, the hushed murmur of civil servants going about the business of recording everything and everyone of consequence.

Clara made her way to the side desk where Harriet Collins sat, her wire-rimmed spectacles catching the light as she bent over a massive ledger.

"Miss Collins," Clara greeted softly.

Harriet looked up, her professional expression immedi-ately warming. "Miss Wetherly! I was hoping you might come today." She glanced around the hall before lowering her voice. "I've found something you should see."

"Something related to Barrett's property assessments?" Clara asked.

"More significant than that." Harriet closed her ledger with deliberate care. "Come with me."

She led Clara through a maze of corridors to a small docu-ment room where maps and plans were stored. After checking that they were alone, Harriet unrolled a large diagram across the central table.

"This was filed three days ago," she explained, securing the corners with brass weights. "Planning permission for the new Metropolitan Railway extension."

Clara studied the detailed map showing proposed railway lines cutting through Bloomsbury. Her eyes traced the familiar streets until they found Bellrose Lane—where a large rectangular structure had been drawn directly atop her shop and the surrounding buildings.

"The proposed Bloomsbury Station," Harriet explained, her finger tapping the precise location. "Your shop sits exactly where the main entrance would be."

Clara's breath caught as understanding dawned. "This is why both developers wanted my property so desperately."

"Railway-adjacent property values increase tenfold overnight," Harriet confirmed. "But station-front properties? Those are worth a fortune."

Clara traced the station's outline with her fingertip, noting how it encompassed nearly the entire block. "Every shop on Bellrose Lane is included in this plan."

"Exactly," Harriet nodded. "But this isn't all I discovered." She withdrew a yellowed document from her portfolio. "I searched the historical records after our last conversation. Fifteen years ago, the Metropolitan Railway Commission proposed an almost identical plan."

Clara unfolded the aged document, finding a remarkably similar station drawn over the same location. "What happened to this proposal?"

"Abandoned after significant local opposition," Harriet replied. "And look at this notation in the margin."

In faded ink, someone had written: *G. Hawthorne petition successful. Route adjusted per commission decision, June 1842.*

"Genevieve Hawthorne," Clara breathed. "My grandmother organized the opposition."

"The railway was rerouted," Harriet confirmed. "And according to our archives, Lord Blackstone lost a considerable investment as a result."

"Which explains his family's persistent interest in our property," Clara said, pieces falling into place. "This isn't merely about a new development—it's the revival of plans Grandmother thwarted years ago."

"History repeating itself," Harriet agreed, "only more desperately this time."

Clara continued examining the documents, details catching her trained eye. "The new plans were filed by Blackstone Development, but there's a second signature here. The Medical Research Fund as co-investor?"

"Curious, isn't it?" Harriet adjusted her spectacles. "I inquired about that with Lord Blackstone's secretary when she came to review these files. She seemed unusually interested in the medical charity that owns adjacent properties."

"Miss Eleanor Blackstone was here?" Clara asked, suddenly alert.

"Yesterday afternoon," Harriet confirmed. "Quite insistent on examining these particular plans."

As they returned the documents to their proper storage, Clara thanked Harriet for her assistance. "You've taken considerable risk helping me."

Harriet smiled wryly. "The Registry values discretion above all—but not when it conceals murder. My position gives me access to patterns others might miss." She hesitated. "There's something else you should know. Barrett filed amendments to these plans just days before his death—amendments that would have required a new property evaluation and delayed approval by months."

This revelation settled like a stone in Clara's chest. Barrett hadn't merely been sowing discord between developers—he had actively threatened the entire railway project. "Thank you, Harriet. I'm indebted to you."

"Just be careful," Harriet warned. "Whoever killed Barrett and Pinkett clearly has significant influence."

As Clara emerged into the main hall, a familiar figure caught her attention—a slender woman in a well-tailored gray dress, her hair arranged in a precise chignon beneath a modest hat. Eleanor Blackstone stood at the central desk, passing documents to a clerk with the efficiency of someone accustomed to navigating bureaucratic channels.

Clara approached directly, noting how Eleanor stiffened upon recognizing her.

"Miss Blackstone," Clara greeted with deliberate pleasantness. "What a fortunate coincidence."

Eleanor's composure faltered only momentarily before her professional mask settled back into place. "Miss Wetherly. I wasn't aware you had business at the Registry."

"Property concerns," Clara replied with careful ambiguity. "I understand you were reviewing the railway plans yesterday."

"I'm not at liberty to discuss my employer's business associations," Eleanor responded, her gloved fingers tightening slightly around her portfolio.

"I'm not inquiring about Lord Blackstone's business," Clara clarified, "but rather about the Medical Research Fund's involvement in the project."

Eleanor visibly stiffened. "I don't know what you're implying."

"I'm not implying anything," Clara answered smoothly. "Merely seeking to understand why a medical charity would co-invest in a railway development—particularly one that requires my shop's removal."

"The Fund's investments are diverse," Eleanor replied, her tone cooling further. "Lord Blackstone is known for forming advantageous partnerships."

Clara noted the expensive brooch at Eleanor's collar—pearl and silver in an intricate pattern that suggested significant cost, well beyond a secretary's typical means. "I understand congratulations are in order regarding your engagement."

Eleanor's hand moved instinctively to her brooch. "Thank you," she replied stiffly.

A registry clerk approached, nodding respectfully to Eleanor. "Miss Blackstone, will your fiancé be joining you at the medical charity dinner this evening?"

Eleanor quickly excused herself, hurrying toward the exit without introducing the clerk to Clara. The brief exchange, while superficially cordial, had revealed Eleanor's discomfort when questioned about the medical connection.

Clara left the Registry with her mind whirling, the railway plans explaining so much yet raising even more questions. Rather than returning directly to her shop, she made her way to Mrs. Winters' dressmaking establishment a few doors down from Hawthorne & Wetherly.

The bell above the door chimed softly as Clara entered. The shop smelled of fabric sizing and steam, with bolts of material arrayed along the walls and a large cutting table dominating the center of the room. Mrs. Winters looked up from her work, her thin fingers stilling on the delicate lace she was attaching to a bodice.

"Clara, my dear," she greeted, setting aside her needle. "I heard about the brick. Outrageous! Are you quite all right?"

"I'm unharmed," Clara assured her, "though rather determined to understand what's happening in our neighborhood." She closed the distance between them, lowering her voice. "Mrs. Winters, you mentioned seeing Barrett visit shops on the block before his death. Did he behave strangely during these visits?"

The dressmaker glanced toward the back room where her assistant was pressing a waistcoat, then gestured Clara closer. "His last visit was most peculiar," she confided. "His hands trembled so badly he could hardly hold my measuring tape when I asked him to mark a hemline. Kept looking over his shoulder, as if expecting someone to appear at any moment."

"When was this?" Clara asked.

"Three days before they found him," Mrs. Winters replied. "And the strangest thing—he dropped an envelope when leaving. I tried to return it, but he'd already disappeared around the corner."

"What did you do with it?" Clara asked, anticipation quickening her pulse.

Mrs. Winters moved to her desk, withdrawing a small drawer. "I kept it, meaning to return it if he came back." She handed Clara a cream-colored envelope, slightly creased along one edge. "I never had the chance."

Clara opened it carefully. Inside was a printed notice from a Harley Street physician—a prescription for a "calming tonic" to address "nervous tremors and anxiety." The prescription was signed with a flowing initial: "M."

"Did Barrett mention anything about his health during these visits?" Clara asked.

"He looked increasingly unwell," Mrs. Winters replied. "His complexion was sallow, and when I inquired, he muttered something about 'useless treatments' and 'money wasted on doctors.'"

Clara carefully folded the prescription and tucked it into her pocket. "Did he mention anything about the railway plans?"

Mrs. Winters raised an eyebrow. "So you've discovered that particular secret? Yes, there was considerable talk about it. The medical charity has been buying everything they can near the proposed railway—quite the coincidence, wouldn't you say?"

"Medical charity?" Clara repeated, the connection strengthening. "You mean the Medical Research Fund?"

"That's the one. Established by some Harley Street physicians to advance medical science—or so they claim. Though it seems their true interest lies in property development rather than healing the sick."

Clara thanked Mrs. Winters for her insights and was preparing to leave when the dressmaker called her back. "Be cautious, my dear. Barrett wasn't the only one asking questions about that railway. Mr. Pinkett was remarkably interested in who was buying what—and now they're both gone."

The warning followed Clara as she stepped back into the street, the morning's discoveries forming a pattern she couldn't ignore. The railway plans explained both developers' interest in her property, but the medical connection—the prescription signed "M," Eleanor's engagement to a physician's relative, the Medical Research Fund's involvement in the railway—suggested something more complex than simple property speculation.

As Clara turned the corner toward Bellrose Lane, a slight figure detached itself from the shadows of a doorway. She tensed momentarily before recognizing the anxious demeanor of a young man she'd glimpsed near Barrett's usual haunts.

"Miss Wetherly," he called softly, approaching with obvious reluctance. "A moment, please."

Clara regarded him warily. "I'm afraid you have the advantage, sir."

"Thomas Finch, ma'am," he replied with a quick, nervous bow. "I was Mr. Barrett's assistant at the property office. I've been... well, I've been watching for you."

"Mr. Finch," Clara acknowledged, now understanding his connection to the case. "What business do you have with me?"

"I need to speak with you—privately," he said, fidgeting with his hat brim. "About Barrett. About what he discovered. About why he died."

Clara hesitated, assessing the young man's demeanor. His clothes were rumpled, his collar frayed at the edges, suggesting recent hardship. Fear, not malice, seemed to drive his nervous energy.

"We can speak at my shop," Clara offered.

"No!" Finch's reaction was immediate. "Too dangerous. They're watching your shop."

"Who is watching, Mr. Finch?"

"Everyone," he replied cryptically. "Blackstone's men. Halston's men. Others."

Clara studied him more carefully, noting the shadows

beneath his eyes, the slight tremor in his hands reminiscent of Barrett's symptoms. "Are you in danger as well?"

He nodded, swallowing hard. "Barrett discovered the railway plan independently. He realized how valuable your property is—far more valuable than either developer was admitting. He was extorting both of them for higher payments."

"And they discovered his double-dealing," Clara surmised.

"Worse than that," Finch continued, his voice barely audible. "He found financial records showing how much certain parties stood to gain once the railway was approved. He threatened to expose the entire scheme unless he received a percentage."

"Which parties, Mr. Finch?"

His eyes darted around again. "Blackstone and Halston despised each other, but both wanted Barrett silenced. There were others involved too—investors with significant influence."

"Medical investors?" Clara pressed.

Finch's eyes widened. "How did you—" He stopped himself, glancing over his shoulder. "I have documents—Barrett's records. Proof of the entire conspiracy." He withdrew a small key from his waistcoat. "In a lockbox at my lodgings. But I can't return there. They're watching."

"Who is 'they,' Mr. Finch?" Clara insisted.

"I'll explain everything," he promised, pocketing the key. "But not here. Meet me tonight at eight o'clock, behind St. Mary's Chapel. I'll bring the documents."

"Why are you telling me this?" Clara asked, suspicion mingling with curiosity.

"Because you refused to sell," Finch replied, his gaze finally meeting hers directly. "Barrett said anyone who stood up to both Blackstone and Halston must have courage. And because you're next on their list unless the truth comes out."

With that ominous declaration, he melted back into the crowd, leaving Clara standing on the corner with the weight of his revelations pressing against her chest.

By the time she returned to her shop, Constable Thomas was pacing anxiously outside. "Miss Wetherly! I was about to send for Inspector Redgrave. You've been gone for hours."

"My apologies, Constable," Clara replied absently, her mind still processing Finch's words. "I had more business than anticipated."

Inside, she found Marmalade sprawled across her counter in a patch of sunlight, his orange bulk arranged with deliberate nonchalance. The cat opened one eye as she entered, then stretched with exaggerated indifference before padding across to inspect her pocket where Barrett's prescription lay hidden.

"Yes, I've found something interesting," Clara told him, scratching behind his ears. "Though I'm not entirely certain what it means."

She spent the afternoon organizing her discoveries, creating a timeline that connected Barrett's declining health with the railway plans and the Medical Research Fund's involvement. The prescription signed "M" provided the first tangible link between Barrett and a physician—a new thread in this increasingly tangled mystery.

As evening approached, Clara debated whether to inform Inspector Redgrave about her meeting with Finch. The young man's fear had seemed genuine, as had his belief that they were being watched. If she alerted Redgrave, would his official presence frighten Finch away? Or would it provide necessary protection?

In the end, she decided to meet Finch alone first. If his documents proved as significant as he claimed, she would immediately bring them to Redgrave. The risk seemed justified if it meant uncovering the truth behind Barrett's death—and potentially preventing her own.

She informed Constable Thomas she would be attending evening services at St. Mary's Chapel, a half-truth that allowed her to approach the meeting location without arousing suspicion. Thomas insisted on escorting her to the chapel doors, which she accepted with gracious thanks.

The evening air carried a faint mist that softened the gaslights along the street. St. Mary's bell tolled seven times as Clara entered the side door, nodding to the elderly verger who recognized her from previous visits. She slipped through the nave, past the few parishioners attending vespers, and exited through the small door leading to the garden cemetery behind the chapel.

Ancient headstones stood like silent sentinels in the gathering dusk, their inscriptions softened by decades of London weather and coal smoke. Clara positioned herself near the eastern wall where she would have a clear view of anyone approaching from the street.

Eight o'clock came and went. The chapel bell marked the half-hour, then nine. No sign of Thomas Finch.

A growing uneasiness settled in Clara's stomach. Had Finch lost his nerve? Or had something—or someone—prevented him from keeping their appointment?

When the clock struck half-past nine, Clara decided to return home. As she made her way toward the garden gate, a glint of metal caught her eye from behind a weathered memorial stone. She approached cautiously, pulse quickening.

A small brass key lay on the ground—identical to the one Finch had shown her. Beside it, a man's hat crushed flat, its band stained with what appeared, even in the dim light, to be blood.

Clara knelt, examining the scene without touching anything. The grass showed signs of a struggle—flattened in places, torn in others. A distinctive heel print pressed into the soft earth suggested someone had been dragged away.

Thomas Finch had arrived for their meeting—but someone else had found him first.

Clara examined the scene more carefully, noting a trail of disturbed grass leading toward the cemetery's east gate. Small droplets of what appeared to be blood marked the path at irregular intervals. Whatever had happened here had been violent and recent.

A man's life could be at stake. Clara had no time for hesitation or protocol.

She moved quickly through the chapel, startling an elderly caretaker as she emerged into the front vestibule. "I need a police officer immediately," she told him with such urgency that he merely pointed toward the street. "The station is three blocks north, miss."

Clara hurried through the darkening streets, her mind racing with possibilities. Finch had claimed to have documents proving a conspiracy between the developers. The same conspiracy that had already claimed Barrett and Pinkett. Now Finch himself was in danger—or worse. And Clara couldn't shake the sense that the initial "M" on Barrett's prescription represented a thread that connected everything.

The police station appeared ahead, its lanterns glowing through the evening mist. Clara gathered her courage as she climbed the steps. Redgrave wouldn't be pleased to see her involved once again, but a man's life outweighed her concerns about the inspector's disapproval.

As she reached for the door handle, a carriage pulled up sharply behind her. The door opened before the wheels had fully stopped, and Inspector Redgrave himself emerged, his face grim in the lamplight.

"Miss Wetherly," he acknowledged with visible surprise. "What brings you to my doorstep at this hour?"

"Violence at St. Mary's Cemetery," Clara replied without preamble. "Thomas Finch—Barrett's assistant—arranged to meet me with evidence about the murders. He never arrived. I found signs of a struggle, blood, and this." She held out her handkerchief containing the brass key.

Redgrave's expression shifted from surprise to sharp attention. "When did this happen?"

"Within the hour," Clara replied. "Inspector, he claimed to have documents proving a conspiracy involving both developers and medical investors. Documents that might explain Barrett's death—and now his own disappearance."

"Come inside," Redgrave said, holding the station door open. "I need every detail, Miss Wetherly, and I need it now."

As Clara followed him into the station, she realized that whatever barriers had stood between them were momentarily set aside. For the first time since Barrett's body had appeared in her alley, she and the inspector were finally working toward the same goal.

fourteen

"**A**nd you're certain this is the key Finch showed you?" Inspector Redgrave asked, examining the small brass key Clara had placed on his desk. The lamp cast deep shadows across his face, emphasizing the furrow between his brows as he regarded both the evidence and Clara with careful attention.

The Scotland Yard interview room felt stifling despite the late hour, its walls a drab institutional green that had likely witnessed countless confessions and accusations over the years. Clara sat primly in the wooden chair across from Redgrave, her posture betraying none of the fatigue that pulled at her limbs after the night's alarming discovery.

"Absolutely certain," she replied. "It has the distinctive notch in the teeth that I observed when he showed it to me earlier today. And the hat was unmistakably his—the same one Mr. Finch wore when we spoke this afternoon."

Redgrave made a notation, his handwriting precise and economical. "And he mentioned specific documents? Evidence of some conspiracy between the developers?"

"He claimed to have proof that both Blackstone and

Halston wanted Barrett silenced." Clara hesitated, deciding how much to reveal. "He also mentioned investors with significant influence."

"Did he specify who these investors might be?" Redgrave's pen hovered above the paper, his attention sharpening.

"No, but he was frightened—genuinely frightened. Said they were watching him, watching me." Clara met Redgrave's gaze directly. "His fear was not performative, Inspector. And now he's missing, possibly injured or worse."

Redgrave set down his pen, leaning back slightly in his chair. The lamplight caught the silver at his temples as he studied her with an expression she couldn't quite decipher—not quite suspicion anymore, but something more complex.

"You should have informed Constable Thomas immediately," he said finally. "Meeting Finch alone was reckless, Miss Wetherly."

"If I had arrived with police in tow, Mr. Finch would have disappeared before we ever saw him," Clara countered. "His fear of official involvement was palpable."

"And yet someone found him regardless." Redgrave sighed, a brief crack in his professional demeanor. "We'll need to examine the scene immediately," he said, rising from his chair and reaching for his coat. "Evidence may already be compromised by the elements, and if Finch is injured, every moment counts."

"I'm coming with you," Clara stated, rising as well.

Redgrave's brow furrowed. "Absolutely not. This is police business, Miss Wetherly, and potentially dangerous."

"I'm the only one who knows precisely where Finch intended to meet me," Clara countered. "Every minute you spend searching the cemetery without my guidance is a minute wasted."

"I can take a detailed description—"

"In the dark? With nothing but lantern light?" Clara interrupted, her tone firm but not confrontational. "A description won't show you the exact memorial stone, the precise spot where I waited. And I've already demonstrated my observational skills are... valuable to your investigation."

"Your observational skills nearly got you run down by a carriage," Redgrave retorted, though without his earlier sharpness.

"An event which, you'll note, I observed with particular clarity," Clara replied, the barest hint of a smile touching her lips.

Redgrave's jaw tightened momentarily, clearly torn between procedure and practicality. A flicker of something—perhaps reluctant amusement—crossed his features before being swiftly mastered.

"You will remain with the officers at all times," he said, his voice leaving no room for negotiation. "And you will follow my instructions without question. Is that clear?"

"Transparently," Clara replied, already adjusting her shawl.

Redgrave turned to the constable in the doorway. "Assemble two men with lanterns. We're proceeding to St. Mary's Chapel immediately."

Within minutes, they were heading into the night, constables bearing bull's-eye lanterns to illuminate their way through London's foggy streets.

THE GRAVEYARD LOOKED ENTIRELY different by lantern light, the beams casting long, macabre shadows across the weathered tombstones. What had seemed merely somber in daylight now held an air of foreboding, the mist curling around ancient monuments like restless spirits.

"This way," Clara directed, leading Redgrave toward the eastern wall where she had waited for Finch. The damp hem of her dress caught against the overgrown grass as she moved between graves with practiced care.

Two constables followed at a discreet distance, their lanterns creating overlapping pools of light that pushed back the darkness. Clara indicated the memorial stone behind which she had found the key and hat. "There, behind that angel monument."

Redgrave knelt, his movements precise as he examined the ground without disturbing potential evidence. "Boot prints," he observed. "Several sets. And here—" he pointed to a darkened patch on the grass, "—blood, I believe."

"Fresh, too," Clara noted, observing how it had not yet fully soaked into the earth despite the night's dampness.

"You have a disturbingly practiced eye for such matters, Miss Wetherly," Redgrave remarked, glancing up at her.

"When one works with plants, Inspector, one becomes familiar with the properties of all manner of substances," she replied. "Blood, like most organic materials, behaves according to predictable patterns."

"Is there anything you haven't studied?" There was a note in his voice that might almost have been admiration, had it not been so carefully guarded.

"The proper appreciation of cricket," Clara answered with perfect seriousness. "I find it utterly incomprehensible."

The corner of Redgrave's mouth twitched briefly before he returned to his examination. "Significant signs of struggle," he observed, pointing to the disrupted earth and broken twigs. "And drag marks leading toward the gate. He was carried away."

"But alive, I think," Clara said. "The blood pattern suggests injury, not mortal wounding."

"Again with the disturbing expertise," Redgrave murmured, rising to his feet. "Did Finch mention where this lockbox might be kept?"

"His lodgings," Clara replied. "Though he said he couldn't return there because 'they' were watching."

Redgrave exchanged a glance with the senior constable. "And we have no idea where these lodgings might be."

"Perhaps Barrett's office would have an address for his assistant?" Clara suggested.

Redgrave regarded her with that same expression of reluctant appreciation she had glimpsed earlier. "A reasonable suggestion," he acknowledged. "Constable Wilson," he called to the younger officer, "have Myers continue examining the scene. We're proceeding to Barrett's former office."

The development firm's offices occupied the second floor of a respectable building near the Strand. Despite the late hour, a clerk was already at his desk when they arrived, apparently unsurprised by the police presence.

"Inspector Redgrave," the young man greeted, rising from his chair. "Lord Blackstone mentioned you might return."

"Did he indeed?" Redgrave's tone revealed nothing. "We're seeking information about Thomas Finch, Mr. Barrett's assistant."

"Poor Finch," the clerk said, shaking his head. "Hasn't been seen since Mr. Barrett's unfortunate accident. We assumed he'd found other employment."

Clara noted the clerk's choice of words—"accident" rather than "murder"—but kept her observation to herself.

"We'll need his home address," Redgrave stated, more command than request.

The clerk hesitated. "I'm not certain I'm authorized to—"

"This is a police investigation into multiple deaths," Redgrave interrupted, his voice hardening. "Your authorization is irrelevant."

The clerk swallowed visibly, then turned to a large ledger. "Of course, Inspector. Just a moment."

As the clerk searched for the information, Clara took the opportunity to study the office. Maps of London neighborhoods lined the walls, many marked with red pins. One map in particular caught her attention—the Bloomsbury district with a precisely drawn rectangle over Bellrose Lane.

"The railway station," she murmured.

"I beg your pardon, Miss?" the clerk asked, looking up from his ledger.

"Nothing of consequence," Clara replied smoothly. "Have you found Mr. Finch's address?"

"Yes, here it is. 17 Markham Street, third floor rear. Though as I said, he hasn't been in since—"

"Thank you for your assistance," Redgrave cut him off, copying the address into his notebook. "Good day."

Outside, Clara matched Redgrave's brisk pace as they headed toward Markham Street. "He seemed rather nervous for a simple clerk," she observed.

"Indeed," Redgrave agreed. "And remarkably present at this late hour."

"You noticed that as well?"

"I notice a great many things, Miss Wetherly." His tone was dry but not unkind. "Including the map that caught your attention. The proposed railway station, I presume?"

"Precisely where my shop stands," Clara confirmed. "I've recently learned there were similar plans fifteen years ago that my grandmother helped defeat through community opposition."

Redgrave's step faltered almost imperceptibly. "Fifteen years? That would have been during the first railway expansion proposals under—"

"Lord Blackstone," Clara finished. "The same family, pursuing the same plan, requiring the same property."

Redgrave was silent for several paces, processing this information. "That creates a more personal motive than mere financial gain," he said finally.

"Precisely my thought," Clara agreed. "Though it doesn't explain all the connections that keep appearing."

"One mystery at a time, Miss Wetherly," Redgrave cautioned, though his expression had softened slightly. "Let's see what Mr. Finch's lodgings might reveal."

Markham Street proved to be a narrow, dingy lane flanked by lodging houses of dubious quality. Number 17 stood slightly apart from its neighbors, its brick facade stained with decades of London soot. The landlady—a corpulent woman with shrewd eyes and a suspicious nature—blocked their path in the narrow hallway.

"Police, are you? What's the boy done then?" she demanded, arms folded across her substantial bosom.

"Mr. Finch is not accused of any wrongdoing," Redgrave assured her. "We believe he may have information pertinent to our investigation."

"Haven't seen him in days," the landlady sniffed. "Rent's due tomorrow. If he's not back by then, his things go to the curb."

"We need to examine his rooms," Redgrave stated firmly. "Police business."

The landlady eyed Clara skeptically. "And who's she then? Don't look like no police to me."

Before Redgrave could respond, Clara smiled pleasantly. "I'm a botanical specialist consulting on the case, Mrs...?"

"Hatch," the woman supplied reluctantly. "Botanical specialist? What, like them garden ladies?"

"More like analyzing evidence requiring specialized knowledge," Clara replied, keeping her tone friendly but professional. "Mr. Finch may be in considerable danger, Mrs. Hatch. Your cooperation could save his life."

Something in Clara's demeanor—or perhaps the mention

of danger—softened the landlady's resistance. "Third floor rear," she said finally, producing a large ring of keys. "Mind you don't disturb the other lodgers. Respectable house, this is."

As they climbed the creaking stairs, Redgrave glanced sideways at Clara. "Botanical specialist?" he murmured, the ghost of amusement briefly crossing his features.

"It's not inaccurate," Clara replied with quiet dignity. "And considerably more effective than watching you debate legal jurisdiction with Mrs. Hatch for the next hour."

"I am capable of persuasion without debating legal distinctions, Miss Wetherly."

"Certainly. Just as I am capable of flight if given sufficient motivation, but neither seems the most efficient approach to our current situation."

The faintest suggestion of a smile tugged at the corner of Redgrave's mouth before his professional mask resumed its place.

Finch's room was small but meticulously organized—a single bed, a writing desk, a small bureau, and a washstand constituting the entirety of its furnishings. Unlike the haphazard bachelor quarters Clara had expected, every surface was ordered with almost compulsive precision. Books stood in perfect alignment on the narrow shelf, arranged by height. The bed was made with hospital corners, the thin blanket stretched drum-tight.

"Military background, perhaps?" Clara suggested, noting the precision.

"More likely institutional," Redgrave replied, examining the worn spines of the books. "Many orphanage boys develop such habits."

Clara approached the desk, where neat stacks of paper were arranged at precise angles. "He was certainly methodical."

Redgrave began a systematic search of the room, his movements efficient and practiced. Clara watched him locate a loose floorboard beneath the rug, revealing a small hollow containing a worn leather journal.

"Barrett's handwriting," Redgrave confirmed, leafing carefully through the pages. "Appears to be a record of property assessments and... personal appointments." He frowned slightly. "Medical appointments, primarily."

"May I?" Clara held out her hand.

After a moment's hesitation, Redgrave passed her the journal. Clara examined the entries with her practiced eye for detail, noting the pattern of Barrett's deteriorating script alongside notations about "treatments" and "worsening symptoms."

"His appointments with the doctor increased in frequency over the last month of his life," she observed. "And each time, he notes his condition deteriorated afterward."

"Suggesting incompetent treatment, perhaps," Redgrave mused.

"Or deliberate harm," Clara countered. "Look here—" she pointed to an entry dated one week before Barrett's death. "'Tremors worse after tonic. Dr. M insists continue.'"

Redgrave's expression sharpened. "Dr. M," he repeated, his voice carefully controlled. "A partial identification."

"Better than none," Clara replied, then withdrew the prescription notice from her pocket. "This may help complete it. This was dropped by Barrett during his last visit to Mrs. Winters. Note the signature."

Redgrave examined the prescription, his expression revealing nothing as he recognized the flowing "M" at the bottom. "An interesting coincidence," he acknowledged. "But still circumstantial at best."

Clara continued examining the room while Redgrave sought further hidden compartments. She paused at a small gap between the bureau and the wall, noticing a piece of paper that had fallen behind it. Carefully extracting it, she found herself holding a bank receipt.

"Inspector," she called softly. "Look at this."

The receipt documented a substantial transfer from the Medical Research Fund to an account in Barrett's name, dated two weeks before his death. Beneath it was a notation in Barrett's increasingly unsteady hand: "Final payment for property assessments. M.R.F. requires immediate results."

Redgrave took the receipt, studying it with intensity. "The Medical Research Fund," he murmured. "This creates a direct financial connection between Barrett and a medical charity."

"There's more," Clara said, having discovered several folded documents wedged beneath the mattress. "Financial records showing the Fund as a major investor in both development companies. Why would a medical charity invest so heavily in property speculation?"

Redgrave examined the documents, his expression growing increasingly troubled. "These suggest a level of coordination between supposedly competing developers."

"And look at this," Clara indicated a list of trustees at the bottom of one page. As she scanned the names, her finger stopped abruptly over one particular entry. "The Medical Research Fund is administered by a board of Harley Street physicians, with Dr. Malcolm Morris serving as treasurer."

Redgrave's reaction was subtle but unmistakable—a slight tightening around his eyes, a momentary stillness. "Dr. Morris," he repeated, his tone betraying nothing. "The Scotland Yard examiner."

Their eyes met across the small room, the significance of this discovery hanging in the air between them. Morris was not simply a Scotland Yard examiner—he was financially connected to both development companies through the

Medical Research Fund, and potentially to Barrett's deteriorating health through the mysterious "Dr. M" signature.

"This is... unexpected," Redgrave said carefully, though his
expression suggested he had immediately grasped the implications.

fifteen

"Inspector Redgrave!" The constable's breathless voice shattered the moment of realization, his urgent arrival suggesting the night's discoveries were far from complete.

"There's been a development. Thomas Finch has been found in an alley near Harley Street, sir. Alive, but only just."

"Condition?" Redgrave asked tersely.

"Serious head trauma, sir. He's at St. Thomas's Hospital under police guard."

"Conscious?"

"Intermittently, sir. The doctors aren't optimistic."

Redgrave gathered the documents they had discovered. "We'll continue this investigation at the hospital. Miss Wetherly, your involvement has been... unorthodox but valuable. However, I must insist you return to your shop. This matter has become increasingly dangerous."

"With respect, Inspector," Clara replied firmly, "I've already been targeted twice. My shop has been violated, my tea poisoned, and a carriage nearly crushed me in the street. I am safer in your company than alone."

A flicker of something—concern, perhaps—crossed Redgrave's face before he could master it. "Very well," he conceded after a moment's consideration. "But you will remain in the background at the hospital. This is still an official police investigation."

As they made their way downstairs, Clara noticed Mrs. Hatch watching them from her door with undisguised curiosity. "Find what you were looking for, did you?" the landlady called.

"Your assistance has been most helpful, Mrs. Hatch," Redgrave replied diplomatically.

"The boy in trouble, then?" she persisted.

"Mr. Finch has been injured," Clara answered before Redgrave could deflect the question. "If anyone comes asking about him or his belongings, it would be best not to mention our visit."

Mrs. Hatch's eyes widened slightly. "Injured, you say? Not by ordinary mischief, I'd wager." She lowered her voice. "Had a gentleman inquiring after him yesterday. Proper sort, medical type. Said he was Finch's doctor, checking on him."

Clara and Redgrave exchanged a glance. "Did this doctor leave his name?" Redgrave asked.

"Morris, I believe. Asked when Finch was last seen, who'd visited him. Very concerned about the boy's health, he seemed."

"Thank you, Mrs. Hatch," Redgrave said, pressing a coin into her palm. "Your discretion in this matter would be appreciated."

Outside, a light rain had begun to fall, beading on Clara's shawl as they walked toward the main thoroughfare to find a carriage. Neither spoke until they were seated in the relative privacy of a hansom, the rhythmic clop of the horse's hooves providing cover for their conversation.

"Dr. Morris has been rather busy for a medical examiner," Clara observed quietly.

"It seems so," Redgrave agreed, his expression guarded. "Though we must be careful not to leap to conclusions without sufficient evidence."

"The evidence is mounting, Inspector. Barrett's declining health while under medical care. The Medical Research Fund's involvement in property speculation. Morris inquiring about Finch just before the young man is found gravely injured."

"And yet," Redgrave countered, "the second analysis of your tea returned negative results, just like the first."

Clara stared at him, momentarily speechless. "When?"

"Late yesterday. I had the sample sent to an independent examiner as you requested. The report arrived just before you came to the station." Redgrave watched her reaction carefully. "They found no traces of any toxic compounds."

"That's impossible," Clara insisted, her voice steady despite her shock. "I know what I detected. I've worked with plants my entire life."

"I don't discount your expertise, Miss Wetherly," Redgrave replied, his tone measured. "But physical evidence must take precedence over sensory impression, however educated that impression might be."

Clara studied his face, noting the conflict behind his practiced neutrality. "Who had access to the sample between analyses?" she asked finally.

The question hung in the air like a challenge. Redgrave's expression stiffened almost imperceptibly. "Are you suggesting someone within Scotland Yard deliberately tampered with evidence?"

"I'm suggesting," Clara replied carefully, "that if the same person analyzed both samples, and if that person had reason to conceal the truth..."

She left the sentence unfinished, but its implication was clear. Redgrave turned to look out the carriage window, his profile sharp against the gray London day. When he spoke again, his voice was low, controlled, but with an edge that suggested suppressed emotion.

"There are men in every profession who place self-interest above duty, Miss Wetherly. Even in institutions meant to uphold justice."

Clara sensed there was more behind this statement than he was revealing—some personal knowledge that informed his reluctant consideration of corruption within his own ranks. But she knew better than to press him. Whatever darkness lay in Redgrave's past, he guarded it closely.

"Your attention to detail is... unexpectedly useful in this matter," he acknowledged after a moment. "I would be remiss to dismiss your observations merely because they challenge conventional wisdom."

Coming from Redgrave, this constituted high praise indeed. Clara inclined her head slightly in acknowledgment. "Then we are agreed that further investigation is warranted, regardless of the tea analysis."

"We are," Redgrave confirmed. "Though I must insist on proceeding carefully. If there is indeed corruption within Scotland Yard, we must be methodical in gathering evidence."

The hansom slowed as they approached St. Thomas's Hospital, its imposing Gothic facade rising like a monument to suffering and healing alike. As they descended, Redgrave offered Clara his hand—a small courtesy that nonetheless marked a significant evolution in their professional relationship.

"We'll speak with Finch if his condition permits," Redgrave explained as they entered the bustling hospital corridor. "If not, we'll need to—"

He stopped abruptly as a familiar figure emerged from a

side room—Dr. Malcolm Morris, medical bag in hand, deep in conversation with a hospital physician. The doctor looked up, surprise briefly crossing his features before his professional smile appeared.

"Inspector Redgrave," Morris greeted, approaching them with polished confidence. "Miss Wetherly. I wasn't expecting to find you here."

"Dr. Morris," Redgrave acknowledged neutrally. "I might say the same. This seems rather beyond your jurisdiction as medical examiner."

"Professional courtesy," Morris explained smoothly. "When I heard a witness in the Barrett case had been found injured, I naturally offered my expertise. Head trauma can be so tricky to assess properly."

Clara observed Morris carefully, noting how his gaze lingered briefly on the folder of documents in Redgrave's hand. "How fortunate that you were available," she remarked. "Have you been examining many patients at Harley Street recently?"

Something flashed in Morris's eyes—recognition, perhaps, that her question wasn't entirely innocent. "My private practice continues alongside my duties at Scotland Yard," he replied. "Though I'm curious what brings you into this investigation, Miss Wetherly. I believed Inspector Redgrave preferred to keep civilians at a distance."

"Miss Wetherly is assisting with certain specialized aspects of the case," Redgrave interjected before Clara could respond. "I'm sure you can appreciate the value of domain expertise in complex investigations."

"Botanical expertise, is it?" Morris's smile remained fixed, though his eyes had cooled considerably. "An unusual addition to a police investigation."

"Unusual circumstances occasionally demand unusual

methods," Clara replied, her tone pleasantly neutral while meeting his gaze directly.

"Indeed. Well, I won't keep you. Mr. Finch is in the third room on the left. Sadly, he's unlikely to be of much help. His injuries have rendered him largely incoherent."

As Morris departed with a slight bow, Clara noted how his gloved fingers tightened almost imperceptibly around the handle of his medical bag. Beside her, Redgrave's posture had subtly shifted to something more protective, his body angled slightly between her and the retreating physician.

"What a remarkable coincidence," Clara murmured as they continued down the corridor. "Dr. Morris happening to be available to examine the very witness who might connect him to Barrett's death."

"Coincidences do occur in investigations," Redgrave replied, though his tone suggested he found this one as troubling as she did.

They found Thomas Finch pale and still on the hospital bed, his head swathed in bandages, a uniformed constable sitting at attention beside him. The young man's breathing was shallow, his complexion waxy beneath livid bruises.

"He's been like this since they brought him in, sir," the constable reported. "Muttering now and then, but nothing sensible."

As they approached the bed, Finch's eyelids fluttered weakly. Clara moved closer, noticing a subtle change in his breathing as she came into his field of vision.

"Mr. Finch," she said softly. "It's Clara Wetherly. Can you hear me?"

His lips moved, forming words without sound. Clara leaned closer, straining to catch any coherent utterance.

"The doctor," Finch whispered, the words barely audible. "He knows... always watching Barrett... controlled everything."

Clara glanced at Redgrave, who had moved to the other side of the bed. "Did you hear that?" she asked.

Before Redgrave could respond, a nurse bustled into the room. "The patient needs rest," she announced firmly. "Dr. Morris has prescribed a sedative regimen to reduce brain pressure."

"We need a few more minutes with him," Redgrave countered, displaying his badge.

"I have my orders, Inspector," the nurse replied, producing a syringe from her apron pocket. "Doctor's orders take precedence in medical matters."

Clara noticed Finch's eyes widen at the sight of the syringe, his hand weakly reaching toward her in what appeared to be warning or alarm. Without thinking, she placed herself between the nurse and the patient.

"What exactly has Dr. Morris prescribed?" she asked, medical knowledge from her plant practice rising to the surface. "Morphine is contraindicated in cases of head trauma due to its effects on pupillary response and respiratory depression."

The nurse hesitated, clearly unprepared for such specific objection. "I... I'm simply following the doctor's orders."

"Perhaps we should consult the attending physician," Clara suggested, maintaining her position beside Finch. "I believe he would be most interested in a trauma patient receiving sedatives that might mask critical neurological symptoms."

Something in her authoritative tone made the nurse reconsider. "I'll speak with Dr. Harmon," she conceded, withdrawing with the syringe still in hand.

As soon as she departed, Redgrave turned to Clara with a mixture of surprise and approval. "That was... unexpectedly knowledgeable."

"Botanical expertise includes understanding medicinal

compounds and their effects," Clara replied, turning her attention back to Finch. "Mr. Finch, we found your documents. We know about the Medical Research Fund and its connection to both developers."

Finch's eyes focused briefly, recognition flickering across his features. "Barrett's book," he whispered. "Under floorboard... proof."

"We have it," Redgrave assured him. "Rest now. There will be a different constable at your door, with orders to admit no one without my explicit permission."

As they prepared to leave, Finch's fingers weakly caught Clara's sleeve. "Be careful," he managed. "He's everywhere... inside..."

With that final warning, his energy seemed to fade, eyes closing as exhaustion claimed him. Redgrave summoned a different officer to replace the constable, giving explicit instructions about who was permitted entry.

As they walked back through the hospital corridors, Clara glanced at the documents Redgrave carried. "We have evidence connecting Morris to the Medical Research Fund, and both to Barrett's declining health. What we still lack is proof that Morris deliberately poisoned Barrett or killed Pinkett."

"Or tampered with evidence within Scotland Yard," Redgrave added, his voice low enough that only she could hear. "If what you suspect about your tea sample is correct, we're dealing with corruption at institutional levels."

The implications hung between them as they stepped back into the rainy London afternoon. If Morris had access to evidence, influence over medical examinations, and connections to both victims, he represented a far more dangerous adversary than they had initially believed.

"What's our next step?" Clara asked as they descended the hospital steps.

Redgrave's expression was grimmer than she had yet seen

it. "We need to establish whether Dr. Morris was treating Barrett medically before his death. And we need to determine exactly what happened to your tea sample between analyses."

"Both avenues potentially lead to accusations against a respected Scotland Yard examiner," Clara observed. "Will your superiors support such an investigation?"

The question clearly struck a nerve. "My duty is to the truth, Miss Wetherly, regardless of where it leads or who it implicates."

As they reached the street, Clara noticed a black carriage parked across from the hospital entrance, its driver watching them with unusual attention. Redgrave followed her gaze, his hand moving instinctively toward his coat pocket.

"It seems our investigations haven't gone unnoticed," he observed quietly.

"Finch said 'he's everywhere... inside,'" Clara recalled. "If Morris has allies within Scotland Yard..."

"Then we must be exceedingly careful about whom we trust," Redgrave finished, flagging down a passing hansom. "I'm taking you home, Miss Wetherly. Lock your doors and admit no one. I have inquiries to make that I must handle alone."

"And if those inquiries endanger you?" Clara asked, surprising herself with her concern for his safety.

Something shifted in Redgrave's expression—a momentary softening that revealed the man beneath the inspector's formal exterior. "Then I would be grateful for your extraordinary powers of observation, should they become necessary."

As Clara entered the carriage, she realized their relationship had fundamentally changed. They were no longer investigator and suspect, but reluctant allies against a conspiracy that reached further than either had initially imagined.

The hansom pulled away, leaving Redgrave standing in the

rain, watching until it turned the corner and disappeared from view. Inside, Clara felt the weight of Finch's warning settling over her—the doctor knows... always watching... he's everywhere... inside.

If Morris had indeed orchestrated Barrett's slow poisoning while using his position to cover his tracks, what would he do when he realized they were closing in on the truth?

sixteen

M

THE HUMAN HAD FINALLY FALLEN asleep. Hours of organizing papers, muttering to herself, and staring at the rain had exhausted even Clara's stubborn determination. Her breathing had settled into that predictable rhythm that meant I could finally claim the center of the bed without negotiation.

The shop was unusually cold tonight. Something about the air felt wrong—too still, too expectant. I'd spent the evening prowling the perimeter, checking each window, each door, sensing a change in pressure that humans never notice before danger arrives.

I was halfway through my evening ablutions when I caught it—a scent that didn't belong. Not the usual London fog and coal smoke, but something sharper. Chemical. Deliberate.

Pawing aside the curtain, I watched as a figure moved

beneath the gaslight across the street. Tall, precise movements, familiar somehow. The silver gleam of a pocket watch caught the light as he checked the time with practiced efficiency.

The medical man. The one who smelled of herbs and secrets. The one whose scent lingered in Barrett's clothing and Finch's room.

I dropped to the floor as he glanced toward our window, instinct telling me to remain unseen. He wasn't alone. A second figure waited in the shadows—smaller, anonymous in a heavy coat, carrying something that sloshed faintly as he moved.

They separated at Clara's door. The medical man continuing down the street while his companion slipped into the narrow alley beside the shop.

I raced downstairs, paws silent on the worn steps, and positioned myself at the kitchen window. The acrid smell was stronger now. Through the glass, I saw the second man splashing turpentine along the back wall, beneath the window frames, around the doorway.

I recognized that smell from Clara's workroom, where she used it to clean her brushes and dissolve stubborn resins. But this was no cleaning—this was destruction being prepared with methodical care.

I was halfway up the stairs when I heard it—the soft whoosh of flame taking hold, the crack of wood protesting the sudden heat.

Clara still slept, unaware that death was climbing the walls outside.

Humans. So dull-sensed it's a miracle they've survived this long.

I leapt onto her bed, directly onto her chest, and dug my claws in—just enough to penetrate her nightdress without drawing blood. Desperate times, desperate measures.

She bolted upright, affronted. "Marmalade! What on earth—"

I had no time for her indignation. I meowed—not my usual dignified communication, but a harsh, urgent sound—then bounded to the door, looking back at her with what I hoped transmitted the appropriate level of emergency.

"What's gotten into you?" she muttered, then frowned, finally registering what I'd already known for precious minutes. "Do I smell smoke?"

I raced back, tugging at her sleeve with my teeth, then to the door again. Finally, her slower human senses caught up. The smoke was seeping beneath the bedroom door, and now she could hear the crackling from below.

"Fire!" Her voice caught as understanding dawned. She leapt from bed, snatching her dressing gown and—proving her intelligence despite being human—The Gilded Leaf from her bedside table.

The smoke thickened as we descended the stairs, black and choking. Clara pressed a damp cloth to her face, but I could see her struggling for breath. The main shop floor was already impassable, flames licking up the shelves, consuming generations of botanical knowledge with indifferent hunger.

Clara hesitated, her eyes fixed on her grandmother's cabinet. "The records—"

I bit her ankle. Not hard, but enough. There was no time for sentiment or hesitation. Already the stairs behind us were catching, the fire moving with unnatural speed. The turpentine was doing its work with brutal efficiency.

We needed another way out.

I pushed past her toward the small window in the back room—the one that opened onto the roof of the storage shed. It would be a tight fit for her, but Clara was slender, and the alternative was becoming increasingly deadly.

The window latch was stiff with age. Clara's fingers

fumbled with it as the smoke thickened around us. Finally, it gave way, and cold night air rushed in, momentarily clearing the choking darkness.

Clara looked back once more at the shop, tears cutting tracks through the soot on her cheeks. Then she lifted me, tucking me securely under one arm despite my dignity, and climbed awkwardly through the window.

The roof tiles were slick with rain, treacherous beneath her bare feet. I wriggled free—I'm perfectly capable of navigating rooftops without assistance, thank you very much—and led the way to where the shed roof met the neighbor's garden wall.

We'd barely cleared the wall when the upstairs windows shattered, belching flame and smoke into the night. Clara stood transfixed, clutching The Gilded Leaf to her chest, watching as her heritage, her livelihood, her home surrendered to the flames.

Behind us, neighbors were emerging, shouting for water, for help. In the distance, fire bells began to clang.

I smelled him before I saw him. The medical man stood across the street, partially concealed in shadow, watching Clara with the detached interest of a scientist observing an experiment. His companion was nowhere to be seen, already vanished into the night to collect his payment, no doubt.

The medical man's expression revealed nothing, but the slight adjustment of his gloves, the satisfied straightening of his shoulders—these told their own story. He believed he'd eliminated a threat. He believed Clara had lost everything.

He didn't realize what she'd saved—not just the book, but the evidence she'd hidden inside it. The prescription with his initial. The receipt with his name. The proof of his deception.

Nor did he know what burned in her eyes as she watched her shop collapse into embers. I recognized it, though—the same look her grandmother had worn when protecting what was hers. A look that promised justice and retribution in equal measure.

As the fire brigade arrived with their pumps and hoses, Clara finally tore her gaze from the ruins. Her eyes swept the street, pausing momentarily on the spot where the medical man had stood. But he had vanished, confident in his victory.

She didn't see what I saw—that this wasn't a victory at all. This was the moment Clara Wetherly truly became dangerous.

The inspector arrived minutes later, his coat hastily buttoned over nightclothes, his expression shifting from professional concern to something more visceral when he spotted Clara standing barefoot in her nightdress, soot-streaked and shivering.

I watched as he wrapped his coat around her shoulders, as his hand lingered briefly at her back, steadying her. I observed how his eyes hardened as he surveyed the deliberate destruction, how his posture shifted from investigator to protector.

Two hunters now, not one. Both with the scent of their prey.

Mrs. Penfield insisted Clara come to her home, fussing over her with blankets and tea. From my perch on the windowsill, I kept watch over the street below, ensuring the medical man did not return.

Clara sat silent, staring into the fire in Mrs. Penfield's grate. Her fingers moved absently through the pages of The Gilded Leaf, pausing occasionally on passages only she could see in the dim light.

The others believed she was in shock. I knew better.

I recognized the subtle changes in her breathing, the slight narrowing of her eyes, the almost imperceptible nod she gave to herself.

She was planning. The same methodical precision she used for her most complex botanical preparations was now being turned toward a different kind of recipe altogether.

I settled more comfortably on my perch. My human had survived. The evidence was safe. And tomorrow, Clara would begin to weave a trap for the man who thought he'd destroyed her.

Humans are so predictable in their underestimation of each other. But the medical man had made a grave miscalculation.

He'd assumed Clara's power resided in her shop. He didn't understand that her true inheritance—her grandmother's knowledge, determination, and quiet cunning—was carried within her, never within those fragile wooden walls.

I closed my eyes, purring softly. Morning would bring grief, yes. But it would also bring the beginning of the hunt.

And I, for one, was looking forward to it.

seventeen

Clara woke with a start, momentarily disoriented by unfamiliar surroundings. The bed beneath her was too soft, the ceiling above unfamiliar with its pattern of faded roses. Pale morning light filtered through lace curtains she didn't recognize, casting unfamiliar shadows across the coverlet.

For one blessed moment, confusion reigned—a brief suspension between sleep and memory.

Then the smell of smoke in her hair brought it all rushing back. The fire. Her shop. Everything lost in a single night of calculated destruction.

She closed her eyes again, drawing a ragged breath that caught painfully in her throat. Her chest felt tight, whether from smoke inhalation or grief, she couldn't determine. Perhaps both. Her fingers curled reflexively against the blanket, feeling the slight sting of burns she'd barely registered in the chaos of escape.

Mrs. Penfield's guest bedroom was meticulously maintained despite infrequent use, every surface adorned with delicate figurines and framed daguerreotypes of stern-faced

relatives. Even the washstand boasted a porcelain basin deco-
rated with hand-painted forget-me-nots and gold trim—a
stark contrast to Clara's own practical earthenware.

Forcing herself upright, Clara surveyed what remained of
her possessions: The Gilded Leaf rested on the bedside table,
its leather cover smoke-stained but intact. Beside it lay the few
documents she'd managed to save—the mysterious prescription with only an initial for signature, the registry papers
Harriet had provided, her notes on the financial connections
between the developers. Precious little salvaged from a lifetime
of work.

A soft weight landed on the bed as Marmalade appeared,
studying her with his usual penetrating stare. His orange fur
smelled of smoke, but he seemed otherwise unaffected by their
ordeal.

"I suppose I have you to thank for our survival," Clara
murmured, stroking his head. "Though gratitude seems inade-
quate under the circumstances."

The cat accepted this acknowledgment as his due, pressing
briefly against her hand before settling at the foot of the bed to
begin his morning ablutions.

Clara looked down at her borrowed nightgown, the lace at
its throat a delicate confinement she would never have chosen
for herself. Her own nightdress had been ruined—smoke-
blackened and torn during their escape across Mrs. Winters'
garden wall. Like so much else, it was now beyond recovery.

Rising on unsteady legs, she moved to the window and
pulled back the curtain. The morning was gray and sullen, rain
pattering steadily against the glass as if the skies themselves
mourned her loss. From Mrs. Penfield's second-floor window,
she could just make out the charred shell of Hawthorne &
Wetherly in the distance, its once-proud facade now a
blackened skeleton against the misty street.

Three generations of knowledge. The carefully cultivated

stock of herbs and tinctures. Her grandmother's collection of rare botanical specimens brought back from India by her seafaring grandfather. The ceiling beams worn smooth by decades of drying herbs. All gone.

For one treacherous moment, doubt crept into Clara's heart. Had her stubbornness been misplaced? If she had accepted one of the many generous offers for her property, she would now be comfortably situated elsewhere, her herbs and remedies intact, her livelihood secure. Instead, she stood amid the wreckage of her life, with nothing but a smoke-stained book and a handful of papers to show for her determination.

"Perhaps you were wrong, Grandmother," she whispered, pressing her forehead against the cool glass. "Perhaps some battles aren't worth fighting."

No answer came, of course. Only the steady patter of rain against the window and the distant sounds of Mrs. Penfield's maid preparing breakfast below. The silence pressed against her with unexpected weight.

A soft knock interrupted her thoughts.

"Clara, dear? Are you awake?" Mrs. Penfield's voice came muffled through the door. "I've brought tea and some breakfast. You must keep up your strength."

"Come in," Clara called, quickly wiping away the moisture that had gathered in her eyes.

Mrs. Penfield entered bearing a laden tray, her normally placid face creased with concern. She'd already dressed for the day in a dark blue morning dress with a lace collar that precisely matched the doilies arranged throughout her home.

"You look exhausted, my dear," she declared, setting the tray on a small table. "Hardly surprising after such a night. But tea remedies many ills, as your grandmother always said."

"Not all ills, I fear," Clara replied softly, returning to perch on the edge of the bed.

"No," Mrs. Penfield agreed, her usual chatter subdued.

"Not all." She poured steaming tea into a delicate cup. "Though you're alive, which is more than might have been without that remarkable cat of yours."

Marmalade, hearing himself discussed, paused in his washing to cast a smug glance their way.

"Mrs. Winters sent over one of her day dresses," Mrs. Penfield continued, gesturing to a modest navy wool laid out on a chair. "Not perhaps what you would choose, but service-able until more suitable arrangements can be made. And Miss Collins brought hairpins and a comb. The entire neighbor-hood has been most concerned."

Clara accepted the tea, its warmth seeping into her still-chilled hands. "Their kindness is appreciated."

"Kindness! It's the least anyone could do. Arson! In our neighborhood!" Mrs. Penfield's indignation momentarily overcame her restraint. "Inspector Redgrave was absolutely certain. Said the fire spread too quickly, burned too hot to be accidental. Turpentine, he believed." She lowered her voice dramatically. "Deliberate destruction, Clara."

"Yes," Clara agreed, the single word carrying the weight of her understanding. This was no random act of violence, but a calculated attempt to eliminate her—both physically and, failing that, through the destruction of her livelihood.

"The Inspector was most attentive," Mrs. Penfield contin-ued, her tone shifting subtly as she arranged toast and preserves on a plate. "Most attentive indeed. When he found you in your nightdress, standing barefoot in the rain... well! The concern on his face was quite remarkable for a man of his professional disposition."

Despite everything, Clara felt heat rise to her cheeks. "He was performing his duty, Mrs. Penfield. Nothing more."

"Hmm," her hostess replied, the single syllable laden with implication. "His 'duty' kept him at your side until nearly dawn, and his coat remains draped over my sitting room chair. Hardly standard procedure, I would imagine."

Clara chose not to engage with this line of discussion. "Has there been any word on how the investigation will proceed?"

"He promised to return this morning with further information," Mrs. Penfield replied, pouring herself a cup of tea and settling into a nearby chair. "Though I gather there's some resistance at Scotland Yard to pursuing certain avenues." She hesitated. "Clara, I don't wish to pry, but... do you know who might have done this?"

Clara considered her response carefully. Mrs. Penfield's gossip network had proven valuable, but caution was still warranted. "I have concerns about several possibilities," she admitted. "Connected to Barrett's death and the railway development."

Mrs. Penfield nodded, her expression unusually solemn. "Evil business, all of it. But you must remember, dear—while they've destroyed your shop, they haven't destroyed your knowledge." She tapped her temple significantly. "What's in here can't be burned away."

The simple wisdom of this observation struck Clara forcefully. Her hand moved automatically to The Gilded Leaf. "Nor what's preserved here," she murmured.

As she lifted the book, it fell open naturally between her hands, as if the pages themselves sought a specific place. Clara found herself looking at her grandmother's illustration of The Magician card—a figure standing between heaven and earth, one hand raised toward the sky, the other pointing downward. Around him, the tools of his power: cup, wand, pentacle, and sword.

Beneath the drawing, Genevieve's flowing script provided interpretation:

"The Magician stands at the crossroads of possibility. When he appears in times of loss, remember his message: 'As above, so below.' What seems destroyed in the material world may be transformed rather than ended. The Magician commands the elements through understanding, turning obstacle into opportunity. What appears to defeat you may become the instrument of victory."

Clara traced the words with her fingertip, finding unexpected resonance in these writings she had so often dismissed as mere superstition. Was this coincidence, or was Genevieve still guiding her, even now?

Her earlier moment of doubt dissolved, replaced by a quiet certainty. No, she had not been wrong to resist. The shop was more than brick and timber—it was the physical embodiment of her heritage, her knowledge, her place in the world. She would rebuild it, stone by stone if necessary.

She became aware of Mrs. Penfield watching her closely. "Your grandmother always said that book had a way of opening to precisely what was needed," the older woman observed. "I never quite believed it myself until the day after Mr. Penfield passed. I came to Genevieve for a sleeping draught, and as she reached for that very book, it fell open to a page about grief and restoration. The comfort I found there..." She trailed off, lost momentarily in memory.

A sharp knock at the front door interrupted their conversation.

"That will be the Inspector," Mrs. Penfield declared, smoothing her skirts as she rose. "I'll tell him you'll be down shortly, once you're properly dressed."

Clara closed The Gilded Leaf, but her finger remained between the pages, marking The Magician's wisdom. As Mrs. Penfield bustled away, Clara gazed once more at the card's illustration. What appears to defeat you may become the instrument of victory. With newfound resolve, she prepared to face not just the Inspector.

eighteen

Clara descended to the sitting room to find Inspector Redgrave standing by the window, still in his uniform from the previous night. He turned at her entrance, and she noticed the subtle changes in his demeanor —the formal mask had slipped, revealing genuine concern beneath his professional exterior.

"Miss Wetherly," he greeted her, automatically reaching for his hat before remembering he wasn't wearing it. "I trust you managed some rest despite the circumstances."

"A little," Clara replied, noting the shadows beneath his eyes that suggested he had fared worse. "You've come with news of the investigation?"

Redgrave nodded, waiting until Mrs. Penfield had discreetly withdrawn before continuing. "The pattern of burning confirms my initial assessment. Turpentine was used as an accelerant, applied systematically around entry points." His jaw tightened. "This was deliberate, Miss Wetherly. Executed with malicious intent."

"Hardly surprising," Clara replied, settling into a chair near the fire. "Too many coincidences have accumulated to be accidents. Barrett's murder, Pinkett's death, the attempt to run me down with a carriage, and now this fire—all connected to my refusal to sell."

"You've constructed a pattern," Redgrave observed, taking the seat opposite her. "One I confess has occurred to me as well, though with some divergent interpretations."

Clara leaned forward slightly. "May I ask your current theory, Inspector?"

Redgrave studied her for a moment, as if weighing how much to share. His professional reserve warred visibly with some newer impulse.

"The property assessments Barrett conducted for both Blackstone and Halston create our first connection," he began, his tone shifting from official to analytical. "His death occurred precisely when his double-dealing between developers was discovered."

"A betrayal that benefited Halston," Clara pointed out.

"Or eliminated a liability for Blackstone," Redgrave countered. "Both had motive to silence Barrett."

"And Pinkett?" Clara asked.

"As Blackstone's financial agent, his death initially appeared to implicate Halston further. But he was also the one person who possessed complete knowledge of Blackstone's railway investments."

Clara nodded, following this logic. "Making him dangerous to Blackstone if he decided to change allegiances."

"Precisely."

"Yet neither developer would benefit from burning my shop," Clara reasoned. "The destruction would only strengthen my resolve not to sell, while simultaneously creating unwanted attention from authorities."

"Unless they believed you had evidence that might implicate them," Redgrave suggested. "Something worth destroying despite the complications it creates for acquisition."

"Or someone else entirely orchestrated these events," Clara added. "Someone who benefits regardless of which developer ultimately acquires my property."

A gleam of approval appeared in Redgrave's eyes. "A third party with interests in the railway development."

"The Medical Research Fund," they said simultaneously.

Clara allowed herself a small smile despite the gravity of their discussion. "Their investment in both development companies creates an intriguing connection."

"As treasurer of that Fund, Dr. Morris would have intimate knowledge of these investments," Redgrave noted, his tone carefully neutral.

"And as Scotland Yard's examiner, he would have access to evidence," Clara added, watching Redgrave's reaction closely.

A muscle twitched in Redgrave's jaw. "I'm examining all evidence thoroughly, Miss Wetherly, even when it leads in directions my superiors find... uncomfortable."

"You suspect someone within Scotland Yard," Clara observed, not a question but a statement.

Redgrave's expression remained carefully controlled. "I've learned through bitter experience that position and authority do not preclude criminal behavior. Indeed, they often facilitate it."

"The amber bottle found with Barrett's body," Clara said. "Has it been thoroughly examined?"

"It contained traces of a botanical mixture. Primarily aconite, with several other compounds." Redgrave leaned forward slightly. "The combination is unusual – not one typically found in medical preparations."

"Nor in my botanical remedies," Clara stated firmly. "I would never combine those particular elements – they create an unnecessarily toxic compound with no medicinal benefit."

"Someone with knowledge of both conventional medicine and botanical compounds, then," Redgrave suggested.

"A rarer combination than one might think," Clara replied. "Most physicians disdain botanical remedies as primitive superstition. Few would study them seriously enough to create such specialized combinations."

Redgrave nodded, his expression thoughtful. "I've been investigating Barrett's medical history. He had been seeing a Harley Street physician regularly in the weeks before his death."

"For his tremors," Clara supplied. "Which worsened over time rather than improving with treatment."

"Yes," Redgrave confirmed, a flicker of surprise crossing his features. "How did you know?"

"Mrs. Winters mentioned Barrett's deteriorating condition. His hands shook so badly during his last visit to her shop that he could barely hold her measuring tape." Clara paused, another connection forming. "Progressive symptoms that worsened after treatments would be consistent with slow poisoning."

Redgrave's eyes narrowed. "A bold theory."

"But consistent with the evidence," Clara countered. "Barrett's handwriting showed increasing deterioration over time. If one wished to eliminate him while avoiding suspicion, a gradual decline in health followed by a final, fatal dose would be far less conspicuous than a sudden death."

The intensity of Redgrave's gaze increased. "You have a remarkably analytical mind, Miss Wetherly."

"Botanical medicine requires precision, Inspector. One must observe patterns, identify causality, and apply knowledge methodically." Clara met his gaze directly. "Not unlike detection, I imagine."

Something shifted in Redgrave's expression—a subtle reassessment. "Indeed."

Their conversation was interrupted by the arrival of Mrs.

Penfield, Mrs. Winters, and Harriet Collins, all carrying parcels of various sizes.

"I hope we're not intruding," Mrs. Winters said, though her interested glance between Clara and the Inspector suggested she rather hoped they were. "We've brought a few necessities."

"Your timing is excellent, actually," Clara replied. "The Inspector and I were just discussing certain patterns in recent events. Your observations might prove valuable."

"How diplomatic," Mrs. Winters remarked dryly, arranging herself on the settee. "Most would simply call it gossip."

"Information," Redgrave corrected, surprising them all with a hint of dry humor. "Which, when properly collated, often reveals truths formal investigations might miss."

"Well!" Mrs. Penfield exclaimed, clearly delighted by this official endorsement of neighborhood intelligence. "In that case, you should know that Lord Blackstone's solicitor was seen entering Pinkett's office the very morning of his death."

"And Barrett was observed arguing with someone outside the Medical Research Fund offices two days before he was killed," Harriet added. "My colleague at the registry witnessed it—said Barrett appeared quite agitated."

"The Medical Research Fund," Redgrave repeated thoughtfully. "Their name seems to appear with surprising frequency in this matter."

"They've been acquiring properties throughout Bloomsbury," Mrs. Winters contributed. "Always through intermediaries, never directly. My late husband handled some of their legal documents before his passing."

"And their trustees include several prominent physicians," Harriet added. "I processed their annual registry filing just last month."

Clara exchanged a meaningful glance with Redgrave. Each piece of information added to their emerging pattern.

"Mrs. Winters," Clara asked, "did your husband ever mention who controlled the Fund's financial decisions?"

"The treasurer, naturally," Mrs. Winters replied. "Though I don't recall the name. A Harley Street physician, I believe."

"Dr. Malcolm Morris," Harriet supplied promptly. "His signature appears on all their financial documents."

"The same Dr. Morris who examined Barrett's body for Scotland Yard?" Clara asked, careful to keep her tone merely curious rather than accusatory.

"I believe so," Harriet confirmed. "The signature is quite distinctive—just an elaborate 'M' with a flourish beneath."

Clara felt a chill that had nothing to do with the rain outside. The prescription she'd recovered bore exactly such a signature—an elaborate "M" with a distinctive flourish.

Before she could pursue this revelation, they were interrupted by a commotion from the street below—the clatter of horses' hooves, the rattle of fine carriage wheels on cobblestones. Through the sitting room window, Clara glimpsed an impressive vehicle drawing to a halt outside Mrs. Penfield's modest home. The carriage was lacquered black with gilt trim, the matching horses groomed to perfection, their harnesses gleaming with polished brass.

A liveried footman descended to open the carriage door and lower the step with practiced precision.

Mrs. Penfield hurried to the window, her composure momentarily abandoning her. "Good heavens! That's the Thornfield crest! What on earth would bring the Duchess to Bloomsbury?"

Clara noticed Redgrave stiffen almost imperceptibly at the mention of the Duchess. His reaction was quickly masked, but not before she glimpsed something like wary recognition in his expression.

Before anyone could speculate further, a sharp, authoritative knock echoed through the house. Mrs. Penfield's maid could be heard scurrying to answer, followed by the murmur of voices—one deferential, one unmistakably commanding.

The sitting room door opened to reveal a tall woman of imposing presence. Though well into her sixties, the Duchess of Thornfield carried herself with the confident posture of a much younger woman. Her silver hair was arranged in an elegant coiffure beneath a modest hat, and her traveling costume, though not the height of fashion, was clearly tailored by expert hands from the finest materials.

"Mrs. Penfield," she announced without waiting for introduction, "I understand Miss Wetherly is staying with you following last night's unfortunate events."

Mrs. Penfield executed a flustered curtsy. "Yes, Your Grace. We've been providing what comfort we can after such a terrible—"

"Quite right," the Duchess interrupted, her keen gaze already moving past her hostess to settle on Clara. "Miss Wetherly. I came as soon as I heard."

Clara rose automatically, years of her grandmother's instruction in proper manners taking over despite her confusion. "Your Grace. I'm afraid we haven't been formally introduced—"

"No need for such formalities under the circumstances," the Duchess declared, removing her gloves with precise movements. "I've known of you—and your remarkable grandmother—for thirty years. Your valerian and feverfew preparation has been the only effective treatment for my migraines since 1826."

Clara stared in surprise. "You've been using our remedies?"

"Every month like clockwork. Delivered discreetly to my housekeeper's entrance." The Duchess seated herself with the easy confidence of someone accustomed to command. "I was distressed to hear about the fire. My lady's maid informed me this morning when I inquired about obtaining a replacement for my migraine remedy."

The Duchess's direct reference to the fire silenced the room. She, however, appeared untroubled by the effect of her words.

"Thirty years I've relied on Hawthorne remedies," she continued, "and I'll not see that legacy end in ashes. Particularly not when it seems your troubles coincide with these railway development schemes."

Clara's curiosity was piqued. "You know about the railway plans, Your Grace?"

"My dear, little occurs in London property circles without my knowledge. The Thornfield estates hold considerable investments throughout the city." Her gaze moved to Redgrave, who had remained standing, his posture reflecting instinctive deference despite his official position. "Graham. You look precisely as your father did at your age. Though with more purpose in your expression, I'm pleased to note."

"Your Grace," Redgrave acknowledged with a slight bow. "It's been some years."

"Too many," she replied, her tone softening momentarily. "Your mother asks after you, you know. Even now."

A shadow passed across Redgrave's features. "You're kind to say so."

The Duchess turned her attention back to Clara. "I lost a remedy recently, you know. Most peculiar circumstance. One of my amber bottles—distinctive with my personal label— disappeared from my dressing table several weeks ago. My lady's maid was quite distressed, believing she'd misplaced it."

Clara's attention sharpened. "An amber bottle?"

"Yes. Quite similar to those you use in your shop, I believe. I had recently purchased it from Hawthorne & Wetherly." The Duchess's gaze was penetrating. "When I mentioned needing a replacement this morning, my maid told me about the fire, making me wonder if my bottle might be among the losses."

Clara exchanged a quick glance with Redgrave before responding. "It's possible, Your Grace, though I keep careful inventory of my stock. I'd need to check my records, what remains of them."

"A matter for another time, perhaps." The Duchess turned to address the room at large. "Ladies, I require a private conversation with Miss Wetherly regarding certain botanical matters. I'm sure you understand."

Mrs. Penfield, Mrs. Winters, and Harriet exchanged glances, clearly torn between propriety and curiosity. Propriety won, barely.

"Of course, Your Grace," Mrs. Penfield replied, rising quickly. "We'll give you privacy. Perhaps some refreshment?"

"Tea would be acceptable," the Duchess replied, in a tone suggesting she was granting a great favor.

After the others had withdrawn, leaving only Clara, Redgrave, and the Duchess, Her Grace fixed Clara with a direct gaze.

"Now, Miss Wetherly, let us dispense with pleasantries. Your shop has been deliberately destroyed. Your life is clearly in danger. And all this coincides with railway development plans that require your property to proceed."

"You seem remarkably well-informed, Your Grace," Clara observed.

"I make it my business to be informed, particularly when it impacts interests I value." The Duchess leaned forward slightly. "Your grandmother provided remedies that allowed me to function when conventional medicine failed me. When the medical establishment dismissed my symptoms as 'feminine hysteria,' Genevieve Wetherly offered effective treatment without condescension."

Clara nodded, understanding this connection. Many of

their clients sought botanical remedies after being dismissed by physicians who viewed women's complaints through a lens of prejudice rather than science.

"In return," the Duchess continued, "I provided her with access to botanical specimens from the Thornfield greenhouses—plants brought back from three continents during my late husband's diplomatic postings." Her expression softened slightly. "A mutually beneficial arrangement that I had hoped would continue with you."

"I would have welcomed such an arrangement, Your Grace," Clara replied. "But as you can see, circumstances have rather altered my capacity to continue my grandmother's work."

"Temporarily," the Duchess corrected firmly. "My estate includes three greenhouses and extensive gardens with many of the herbs you'll require to reestablish your practice. They are at your disposal."

"Graham," she continued, turning to Redgrave, "I assume your investigation has encountered certain... difficulties."

Redgrave's brow furrowed slightly. "We are pursuing all available evidence, Your Grace."

"Of course you are, my dear. But evidence has a curious way of disappearing when powerful interests are involved." The Duchess's tone was matter-of-fact rather than accusatory. "I remember when your father, the Earl, was so troubled by those mysterious circumstances at the Harwick estate. Such reluctance he encountered from officials when asking questions."

Redgrave's expression tightened, a reaction Clara filed away for future consideration.

"My carriage is at your disposal, Miss Wetherly," the Duchess declared, returning to the immediate matter. "I suggest you accompany me to Thornfield House today to survey what botanical specimens might serve your immediate needs."

Clara hesitated, glancing toward Redgrave. "Inspector, would my absence impede your investigation?"

"Not at all," he replied. "In fact, it might be prudent for you to be away from Bloomsbury briefly while we secure the area around your property. I can continue our discussion when you return."

"Excellent," the Duchess pronounced. "Graham, do join us for dinner at Thornfield this evening. Eight o'clock. I suspect by then you'll have information worth sharing with Miss Wetherly, and I've always found conversation flows more freely over decent claret."

Though phrased as an invitation, the Duchess's words carried the unmistakable weight of command. Redgrave, to Clara's mild surprise, accepted with a polite inclination of his head.

"Until this evening, then," he said, addressing both women but allowing his gaze to linger on Clara a moment longer. "Do take care, Miss Wetherly."

After Redgrave's departure, Clara gathered her few possessions and wrapped herself in a borrowed shawl. Marmalade emerged from wherever he had been observing the proceedings, regarding the Duchess with his usual inscrutable expression, tail twitching slightly.

To Clara's surprise, the Duchess addressed the cat directly. "Yes, I see you've inherited your predecessor's role as guardian. Genevieve's Callisto was similarly discerning."

Marmalade blinked slowly, then, in an unprecedented display of feline approval, rubbed briefly against the Duchess's skirts before returning to Clara's side.

As they prepared to depart, Clara paused to secure The Gilded Leaf and its precious contents safely in a small satchel Mrs. Winters had provided. Her hand lingered on the book's worn cover, the morning's discovery of The Magician card still resonating in her thoughts.

As the carriage pulled away, Clara caught sight of her shop's blackened skeleton in the distance. Rather than despair, she felt resolve hardening within her like steel tempered in that very fire.

"The destruction of my shop was meant to break me," she said quietly, more to herself than her companion. "I think it's time to show them how mistaken they are."

The Duchess smiled, a sharp expression that held satisfaction rather than simple pleasure. "I believe, Miss Wetherly, that this marks the beginning of a most productive association."

Behind them, Marmalade settled on the plush seat, golden eyes fixed on the passing street as the carriage carried them away from destruction and toward the means of Clara's counterattack.

nineteen

"This Chinese ginseng survived a two-month journey in my husband's diplomatic trunk," the Duchess explained, her fingers brushing the delicate leaves with surprising tenderness. "The Imperial gardener who provided it was later executed for his generosity—a rather extreme response to botanical sharing, even by Manchu standards."

Clara followed the Duchess through the vast glasshouse, each step revealing new wonders. Thornfield's botanical collection rivaled anything she had glimpsed during rare visits to Kew Gardens, though these specimens were arranged not for public education but for practical study and cultivation. Medicinal plants from five continents thrived in careful micro-climates, their Latin names inscribed on small copper plates in elegant script.

"And this," the Duchess continued, pausing before a sheltered alcove where delicate purple blossoms hung from woody stems, "is where your grandmother performed what I consider her greatest triumph of botanical identification."

Clara leaned closer, recognizing the plant immediately.

"*Rauwolfia serpentina*," she murmured. "Grandmother mentioned studying it, but I've never seen a living specimen."

"The Director of Kew Gardens had classified it incorrectly," the Duchess said with evident satisfaction. "Genevieve corrected him to his face during a botanical society meeting. The poor man turned the most fascinating shade of purple— rather like the flower itself. Genevieve never did suffer fools gladly, particularly men who assumed their education trumped her experience."

The memory brought an unexpected smile to Clara's face, the first since the fire had consumed her shop the previous night. The botanical wealth surrounding her both soothed and sharpened the loss—here among the rhythmic drip of condensation and the humid, loamy scent of exotic soils, she could almost feel her grandmother's approving presence.

Marmalade padded between the elaborate wooden planters, his orange coat vibrant against the greenery. The Duchess had raised no objection to the cat's presence in her prized greenhouses—indeed, she had specifically requested he accompany them "to assess the quality of the specimens in his own feline way."

"Your grandmother saved my life, you know," the Duchess remarked, pausing beside a collection of rare Indian orchids. "Not with any of these showy blooms, but with common foxglove when my heart was failing. Three Harley Street physicians had given me up for lost, recommended I settle my affairs." She chuckled, the sound incongruously warm in her otherwise austere demeanor. "Fifteen years later, I've outlived all three of them. Genevieve understood dosage in ways those medical men never grasped."

Clara was opening her mouth to respond when Marmalade suddenly stiffened, his attention fixing on something behind a large potted palm. A slight rustle confirmed they weren't alone among the plants. The cat's tail swished once, deliberately, before he settled into watchful stillness.

A moment later, a young woman in a chambermaid's uniform appeared at the far end of the greenhouse aisle, carrying a copper watering can. Upon seeing them, she startled visibly, nearly dropping her burden.

"Forgive me, Your Grace," she stammered, executing a hasty curtsey. "I didn't realize you were touring the east greenhouse this morning."

"Quite all right, Eliza," the Duchess replied with a dismissive wave. "The ferns do require their moisture regardless of my visits."

Clara observed the girl carefully, noting her evident distress went beyond being surprised by her employer. Eliza's fingers twisted anxiously in her apron, and her gaze darted repeatedly toward Clara before skittering away like a frightened sparrow.

"This is Miss Wetherly," the Duchess continued, apparently oblivious to the maid's discomfort. "The botanical specialist I mentioned at breakfast."

"Miss Wetherly," Eliza acknowledged with another bob, her face paling further at the name. "I... I'm pleased to make your acquaintance."

The girl's eyes fixed briefly on Clara's face before she abruptly turned, the watering can forgotten as she fled toward the greenhouse exit.

"How curious," the Duchess observed, watching the maid's retreat. "Eliza is normally quite composed. One of my better staff, actually—responsible for the more delicate specimens."

Marmalade's tail twitched decisively as he stared after the fleeing girl. Clara had learned to trust the cat's judgment of character—a skill that frequently surpassed her own.

"She seemed distressed specifically by my presence," Clara noted.

"Indeed," the Duchess agreed. "Most concerning, given that she couldn't possibly have known you were here. Unless..." She paused, her shrewd eyes narrowing slightly. "Well, that's a matter to address shortly. Let us continue—I've something particular to show you."

They proceeded deeper into the glasshouse complex, passing through chambers of increasing warmth until they reached a circular room at the center where plants from equatorial regions thrived in carefully maintained tropical heat. The air was so thick with moisture that breathing felt like sipping warm tea.

"These specimens require the greatest care," the Duchess explained, moving toward a locked cabinet built into the wall. "Some are medical treasures, others are quite deadly."

She withdrew a small key from within her sleeve and unlocked the cabinet, revealing rows of amber bottles similar to those Clara used in her own shop. Each bore a custom silver label with elegantly engraved Latin names.

"Your grandmother helped me establish this collection," the Duchess continued, selecting a bottle and passing it to Clara. "Essential oils and tinctures from specimens too delicate or dangerous to trust to conventional preparation."

Clara examined the bottle, noting the distinctive craftsmanship—the same pattern as her own specialized containers, with one crucial difference. Where her bottles bore paper labels in her own handwriting, these featured engraved silver plates permanently affixed to the glass.

"These are beautiful," Clara observed. "The same maker as my amber bottles, but with considerably more elaborate labeling."

"Genevieve arranged the commission," the Duchess confirmed. "I believe your bottles were crafted as part of the same order, though with more practical labeling for daily commercial use."

As Clara placed the bottle back in its position, movement caught her eye. Through the glass wall of the tropical chamber, she saw Eliza the chambermaid hovering nearby, watching them with undisguised anxiety. When the girl realized she'd been spotted, she dropped the garden shears she'd been holding, the metal tools clattering loudly on the stone path before she once again disappeared from view.

"Your Grace," Clara said carefully, "I believe your chambermaid may have something she wishes to tell us. She appears most distressed."

The Duchess followed Clara's gaze, glimpsing Eliza's retreating form. "It would appear so," she agreed. "Let us return to the house. I believe a conversation in my study is required."

As they exited the greenhouse, Clara noticed the chambermaid lurking near the garden entrance, her posture suggesting she might bolt at any moment. The Duchess seemed to sense this as well.

"Eliza," she called with quiet authority, "you will join us in my study in fifteen minutes. There seems to be something troubling you that requires discussion."

It wasn't a question. The girl's shoulders slumped in apparent relief at having the decision made for her. "Yes, Your Grace," she murmured, ducking her head.

The Duchess's study proved to be a remarkable blend of traditional opulence and practical function. Alongside leather-bound volumes and ancestral portraits stood scientific instruments and botanical diagrams. A large desk dominated one end, its surface arranged with military precision—inkwells, correspondence, and ledgers all in perfect alignment.

Marmalade immediately claimed an embroidered footstool near the hearth, arranging himself with the air of a cat resuming his rightful throne. The Duchess observed this with visible amusement.

"Your companion has excellent taste," she noted. "That was my husband's favorite seat—though he required somewhat more of it."

Precisely fifteen minutes later, a soft knock announced Eliza's arrival. The girl entered at the Duchess's command, her eyes downcast, hands trembling slightly as she curtsied.

"Sit down, Eliza," the Duchess directed, gesturing to a chair positioned directly before her desk. "You've been behaving strangely all morning. Has something occurred that I should know about?"

The girl perched on the edge of the chair, her fingers twisting in her apron. "Your Grace, I didn't know—truly I didn't," she began, her voice barely above a whisper. "Not until I heard about the fire, and the murders, and then I realized—"

"Calm yourself," the Duchess interrupted, her tone gentler than her words. "What exactly has happened that concerns Miss Wetherly?"

Eliza took a shuddering breath, her gaze darting briefly to Clara before fixing on the carpet. "Three weeks ago, a young gentleman came to the servants' entrance asking for me specifically. Said his name was Philip—that he was a medical student working for a prominent Harley Street physician."

"And this man wanted something from you?" Clara prompted when the girl hesitated.

"One of Her Grace's amber bottles," Eliza admitted, her voice cracking. "He said it was for a medical study—comparing different vessels for storing botanical compounds. Offered five pounds for it." She swallowed hard. "It seemed harmless—just an empty bottle—and five pounds is more than I earn in two months."

"Which bottle did you give him?" the Duchess asked, her expression sharpening with concern.

"An empty one from your dressing table, Your Grace. I'd just finished cleaning it after your lavender water was used up." Tears welled in the girl's eyes. "He promised it was for scientific purposes. I never imagined..."

"And when did you begin to suspect otherwise?" Clara asked gently, recognizing genuine distress rather than calculated deception.

"Yesterday, when I overheard the housekeeper talking about the apothecary shop that burned in London—how the owner was suspected of poisoning a man, and how evidence was found in an amber bottle." Eliza's fingers twisted more frantically in her apron. "When I heard the name Wetherly, I remembered the gentleman had asked specifically about the bottles used by Hawthorne & Wetherly. Said the comparison was central to his study."

Clara felt a cold certainty settling in her chest. "Did this young man mention who he worked for? The name of the physician?"

"He didn't say directly, miss," Eliza replied, "but I did hear him mention a 'Dr. M' when another servant asked who had sent him. Said Dr. M was conducting important research that might change medical practice entirely."

The Duchess and Clara exchanged a questioning glance. "Did he give his full name?" the Duchess asked.

"Philip Evans, Your Grace." Eliza hesitated. "Actually, I remember thinking it strange—he spoke as if I should recognize the name. Said something about his aunt being in service here."

The Duchess straightened, understanding dawning. "Evans... that name sounds familiar. I believe it's connected to my household somehow."

After a moment's consideration, she turned to Eliza. "Do you know which member of my staff might be related to this Philip Evans?"

"I couldn't say for certain, Your Grace," Eliza replied. "He seemed to assume I would know his connection, but didn't specify which servant was his relation."

The Duchess dismissed Eliza with instructions to speak with no one else about the matter, then rang for tea. As a footman arranged the service between them, Clara's mind worked through the implications of what they'd learned.

"An empty bottle from your collection," she mused once they were alone. "Found beside Barrett's body, bearing what appeared to be my label."

"It suggests a deliberate attempt to implicate you," the Duchess observed, stirring her tea with precise movements. "Perhaps you should tell me exactly what has occurred, Miss Wetherly. I've heard rumors, of course, but would prefer facts."

Clara hesitated only briefly before recounting the events of the past week—Barrett's death, the evidence pointing to her, Pinkett's murder, and finally the fire that had destroyed her shop the previous night. She explained the railway development plans and the financial interests involved, watching the Duchess's expression grow increasingly grave.

"And Inspector Redgrave?" the Duchess inquired. "What is his role in this matter?"

"Initially, he suspected me," Clara admitted. "But as evidence accumulated, he became... less certain. He's been pursuing the investigation despite opposition from his superiors."

"I see." The Duchess set down her cup with a decisive click. "And you believe this 'Dr. M' Eliza mentioned might be connected to your troubles? Perhaps this Dr. Morris you mentioned—the medical examiner who analyzed the evidence?"

"It seems a remarkable coincidence," Clara replied.

"Though I cannot imagine why a Scotland Yard examiner would involve himself in Barrett's death or my framing."

"Let us see if we can establish a connection between this Philip Evans and someone in my household." The Duchess considered for a moment, then rang a small silver bell beside the tea tray.

A middle-aged woman in the black dress and keys of a senior lady's maid appeared. "Your Grace?"

"Mrs. Crawford," the Duchess began, "I'm trying to identify a young man who visited the estate recently. A medical student named Philip Evans who claimed some relation to my staff. Does that name hold any significance to you?"

The woman's expression registered immediate recognition, followed by evident concern. "Evans is my family name before marriage, Your Grace. Philip would be my sister's boy."

"I see," the Duchess replied, watching her maid carefully. "And is your nephew by chance employed in a medical capacity?"

"Yes, Your Grace," Mrs. Crawford confirmed, growing increasingly uncomfortable under scrutiny. "Philip secured a position with a physician some months ago—has been quite pleased with the opportunity."

"Would you happen to know the name of this physician?" the Duchess asked with deliberate casualness.

Mrs. Crawford nodded. "Dr. Morris, Your Grace. Philip speaks highly of him—says the doctor has connections that could advance his medical career significantly. Always was an ambitious lad, perhaps too much so for his own good."

"Dr. Morris?" Clara repeated, her voice rising with genuine shock. The name struck her like a physical blow. The man who had examined Barrett's body—who had declared the poison came from her shop—was connected to the bottle used to frame her. The implications were staggering.

"Thank you, Mrs. Crawford. That will be all," the Duchess dismissed her with a nod.

When the door closed, Clara set down her teacup with a hand that was no longer perfectly steady. "Dr. Morris," she whispered. "The medical examiner himself. I never suspected..."

"It appears we've established a connection between your case and my bottle," the Duchess observed, studying Clara's reaction carefully.

"More than a connection," Clara replied, her voice strengthening as pieces fell into place. "Dr. Morris examined Barrett's body. He declared the poison came from a botanical source—specifically, from my shop. He controlled the evidence that implicated me from the very beginning."

She rose, moving to the window as thoughts raced through her mind. "There was something about him that troubled me during our brief encounters, though I couldn't identify what. His examination of my herb drawers was too knowledgeable—he recognized specimens most physicians wouldn't. And later, when I suggested a different examiner analyze my tea sample..."

"Your tea sample?" the Duchess inquired.

Clara turned back to her, explaining about the attempted poisoning at Mrs. Penfield's house. "I was certain my tea had been tampered with—I could smell the distinctive bitterness of certain mineral compounds. Yet Dr. Morris's analysis found nothing. When Inspector Redgrave arranged a second examination at my insistence, that analysis also came back negative."

"Most troubling," the Duchess observed. "It suggests Dr. Morris may have allies within Scotland Yard."

"But why?" Clara asked, returning to the central question. "What possible motive could Scotland Yard's medical examiner have for killing Barrett and framing me?"

"I think you should reconsider what you already know,

Miss Wetherly," the Duchess suggested thoughtfully. "There must be connections you've already discovered but perhaps not fully recognized."

Clara paused, mentally reviewing everything she had learned. "Barrett was evaluating properties for development companies. My shop stands in the way of a valuable railway station entrance. And according to the documents Inspector Redgrave found, there are financial connections between developers and a medical charity fund."

"The Medical Research Fund," Clara continued, pieces suddenly connecting. "With substantial investments in properties along the proposed railway route."

"Is there perhaps a connection between Dr. Morris and this fund?" the Duchess asked.

Clara's eyes widened. "The documents Inspector Redgrave discovered showed the Fund's trustees—I hadn't reviewed them fully before the fire. But if Morris serves on that board..."

"It would establish a financial motive," the Duchess concluded. "A physician with investments in property development would have significant interest in removing obstacles —such as stubborn shop owners who refuse to sell."

Clara paced the room, mind racing. "I had assumed Mr. Halston was behind Barrett's death—that he'd arranged to eliminate the man when Barrett's double-dealing with Lord Blackstone was discovered."

"You were not entirely wrong to consider the developers," the Duchess replied, rising to join Clara at the window. "Men like Halston operate through proxies. They create circumstances, apply pressure, then express shock when someone takes the necessary steps. Plausible deniability is a currency in itself—one that keeps reputations intact while others bear the consequences."

Clara considered this perspective—one that only someone like the Duchess, with her intimate knowledge of power structures, could provide. "You believe Halston may have been aware something would happen to Barrett, without directly ordering it."

"I believe he created a climate where Barrett's elimination would benefit certain parties significantly," the Duchess clarified. "Whether he specifically knew of any plan is almost irrelevant. Such systems work because everyone understands their role without explicit instructions."

Marmalade appeared at their feet, weaving between them with a soft chirp that signaled his participation in the conversation. His amber eyes seemed unusually bright in the afternoon light filtering through the tall windows.

"Inspector Redgrave should hear of this immediately," the Duchess declared, turning back toward her desk. "The connection between Morris, your case, and my bottle must be investigated properly."

"If he can persuade his superiors to pursue a Scotland Yard examiner," Clara cautioned. "It seems a difficult proposition."

The Duchess nodded thoughtfully. "That could indeed present challenges. However, the evidence must be presented, regardless of institutional resistance."

As the Duchess considered their next steps, Clara turned her attention back to the window, her mind processing the shocking realization that Dr. Morris might be behind everything—from Barrett's death to the destruction of her shop. The man had been present at every turn of the investigation, directing suspicion toward her while concealing his own involvement.

Most troubling was the tea analysis. If both examinations had found nothing despite Clara's certainty that the tea was tampered with, it suggested Morris had either influenced the second examiner or had accomplices within Scotland Yard itself. The thought sent a chill through her—how deep did this conspiracy extend?

Before the Duchess could complete her thoughts, a knock interrupted them. The butler entered with his usual dignified bearing.

"Your Grace, Inspector Redgrave has arrived. He asks to speak with Miss Wetherly urgently."

The Duchess raised an eyebrow. "That was remarkably swift. Show him in immediately."

Redgrave entered with none of his usual measured composure. His coat was unbuttoned, his hat clutched in one hand, and his expression held an intensity Clara hadn't previously witnessed. He bowed briefly to the Duchess before his gaze found Clara.

"Miss Wetherly," he began without preamble, "Finch regained consciousness briefly at the hospital. Before lapsing back, he mentioned something about a doctor, a bottle, and you being in danger."

"Inspector Redgrave," the Duchess greeted him, "your arrival is most timely. We've just uncovered a troubling connection regarding Dr. Morris."

Redgrave nodded in acknowledgment. "Your Grace, I appreciate your assistance to Miss Wetherly in these difficult circumstances."

Clara intervened, quickly explaining their discovery about Philip Evans, the bottle from the Duchess's collection, and its connection to Dr. Morris. Redgrave listened intently, his expression growing steadily grimmer.

"This aligns with what I've discovered," Redgrave confirmed, removing a folded document from his coat pocket. "Financial records showing Morris's substantial investments in the Medical Research Fund, and the Fund's property acquisitions along the proposed railway route."

He handed the document to Clara, who scanned it quickly, her eyes widening at the unmistakable evidence. "Dr. Morris is not only an investor—he serves as the Fund's treasurer. And these dates—" she pointed to several entries, "—show he was treating Barrett regularly in the weeks before his death."

"It appears we've found our connection," the Duchess observed. "Dr. Morris had financial interest in the railway development, access to Barrett as his physician, and arranged for a bottle that would implicate Miss Wetherly to be present at the scene."

"A perfect conspiracy," Clara said, shock giving way to clarity. "He used his position to control the investigation from the beginning."

Instead of sharing their sense of resolution, however, Redgrave's expression remained troubled. He set his hat on a side table and paced a few steps before turning to face them again.

"I discovered the financial connections yesterday," he admitted. "I attempted to raise my concerns with Chief Inspector Holloway this morning, presenting the evidence about Morris's investments and his treatment of Barrett."

"And?" Clara prompted, though something in Redgrave's demeanor suggested the response had not been favorable.

Redgrave's jaw tightened momentarily. "He explicitly forbade me from pursuing allegations against Dr. Morris." His voice held tightly controlled frustration. "Holloway reminded me that Morris is not only a Scotland Yard examiner but also physician to several prominent members of Parliament. He dismissed my evidence as 'circumstantial' and ordered me to focus on Mr. Halston as the primary suspect."

Clara felt a spike of indignation. "Even with these financial records? Even knowing Morris treated Barrett before his death?"

"Without irrefutable proof—evidence that cannot be explained away—any accusation against someone of Morris's standing will be dismissed," Redgrave explained, his tone revealing how deeply this institutional limitation troubled him. "Holloway made it clear that pursuing Morris without such proof would result in my removal from the case. I would be replaced by someone with no interest in looking beyond the obvious suspect."

"You," the Duchess observed.

"Indeed," Redgrave confirmed with a grim nod.

"What of the tea sample?" Clara asked suddenly. "You said the second analysis also found nothing unusual, despite my certainty it was tampered with. Could the second examiner also be compromised?"

Redgrave hesitated, discomfort evident in his posture. "I've considered that possibility," he admitted. "The second analysis was conducted by Dr. Wilkes—a man I believed beyond reproach. But he and Morris trained at the same medical school and belong to the same professional societies."

"Suggesting the corruption may extend beyond Morris himself," the Duchess concluded.

"I can trust very few people at Scotland Yard in this matter," Redgrave acknowledged. "Which is why I must proceed with extreme caution. I need to build a case so substantial it cannot be dismissed, even by those inclined to protect their own."

He outlined his strategy: locate Philip Evans and secure his testimony about the bottle; document every financial transaction between Morris, the Medical Research Fund, and the railway development; establish a timeline of Barrett's treatments and declining health.

Clara listened with growing frustration. "Barrett is dead. Pinkett is dead. My shop is in ashes. How many more losses while you gather documentation?"

"Morris has already demonstrated he's willing to eliminate threats to his plans," she continued, moving toward Redgrave with uncharacteristic intensity. "We need action now, before he realizes how much we've discovered."

Their fundamental disagreement hung in the air between them—Redgrave believing in working within the system, however flawed; Clara convinced some situations demanded more immediate response. Both perspectives contained validity, creating genuine tension rather than simple stubbornness.

The Duchess observed their disagreement with evident interest from behind her desk. When Redgrave asked Clara to return to London with him, she declined with a gesture toward the greenhouse visible through the window.

"The Duchess has offered me access to her botanical specimens to begin restoring my preparations," she explained. "I believe my time is better spent here for the moment."

Redgrave accepted this with visible reluctance. "Promise me you won't confront Morris directly, Miss Wetherly. The man is clearly dangerous."

Clara chose her words with deliberate care. "I assure you, Inspector, I shall be exactly where the Duchess needs me."

Something in her careful phrasing caused Redgrave's eyes to narrow slightly, but he merely nodded, retrieving his hat from the side table. After expressing his gratitude to the Duchess for her assistance, he departed with a final, searching look at Clara.

When the door closed behind him, the Duchess rose from her desk with unexpected energy for a woman of her years. "Well, my dear," she said, a spark of mischief animating her aristocratic features, "I rather think Inspector Redgrave suspects you of planning something independent of his methodical investigation."

"I wouldn't dream of undermining the inspector's careful approach," Clara replied, her tone innocent while her expression suggested otherwise.

"Of course not," the Duchess agreed with equal insincerity.

"Though perhaps a certain amount of... parallel inquiry might prove beneficial while he navigates his institutional constraints."

Clara turned to her fully, decision crystallizing. "Your Grace, I find myself in need of your assistance."

"I suspected as much from your careful phrasing," the Duchess replied with evident satisfaction. "What do you propose?"

"Inspector Redgrave is constrained by his position, but I am not," Clara began, the outline of a plan forming in her mind. "If we could arrange for Dr. Morris to reveal his involvement more... directly..."

The Duchess's smile contained centuries of aristocratic calculation. "I believe I understand your thinking precisely. And I happen to possess several botanical specimens that might prove useful for such an endeavor."

"First," Clara said, her determination hardening into resolve, "I'll need to return to Mrs. Penfield's house this evening."

As Marmalade stretched on his footstool, whiskers twitching with what appeared to be approval, Clara began outlining her strategy to trap the man who had destroyed her shop and framed her for murder. Whatever institutional protection Morris enjoyed would prove insufficient against the combined resources of a woman with botanical expertise, an aristocratic patron, and a remarkably observant orange cat.

twenty

Clara arrived at Mrs. Penfield's Bloomsbury home in the late afternoon, her mind still processing the revelations from Thornfield Estate. The amber bottle, Philip Evans, Dr. Morris's connection to both—each piece fitting together with disturbing precision. As she climbed the familiar steps, bone-weary from the previous night's fire and the emotional weight of her discoveries, she expected to find Mrs. Penfield alone with her tea service and ready sympathy.

Instead, when the housekeeper admitted her to the morning room, Clara found herself facing not one concerned face, but five.

"There she is," Mrs. Penfield declared from her armchair positioned for optimal street observation. "I told you she would arrive precisely on the hour."

The room hummed with feminine energy, a gathering that at first glance might be mistaken for an ordinary social call. Mrs. Penfield's morning room reflected its owner's personality —comfortable rather than fashionable, with faded William Morris wallpaper in a pattern of twining roses, substantial furniture arranged for conversation rather than display, and glass cabinets housing porcelain figurines collected over decades. Family daguerreotypes in silver frames crowded every available surface, watching the proceedings with frozen Victorian solemnity.

The scent of lavender sachets mingled with freshly baked seed cake on the substantial tea service—a collection of mismatched but cherished pieces already arranged on the central table. Through the large windows with their strategic lace curtains, the late afternoon light illuminated the gathering with a gentle glow that belied the gravity of their purpose.

Clara paused at the threshold, momentarily taken aback by the assembly. Mrs. Winters, the neighborhood dressmaker, sat with her ever-present tape measure draped around her neck, her thin fingers unconsciously smoothing the tablecloth's wrinkles. Harriet Collins from the Registry Office occupied the corner chair, her wire-rimmed spectacles catching the light as she adjusted them with practiced precision. Two other women Clara recognized but knew less intimately completed the gathering—Mrs. Turner, a physician's widow whose imposing height and self-possession commanded attention even in repose, and a plain-faced woman with striking blue eyes whom Clara couldn't immediately place.

"I didn't realize I would be addressing a committee," Clara said, removing her gloves as Mrs. Penfield's housekeeper closed the door behind her.

"Not a committee, dear—a council of war," Mrs. Penfield corrected, patting her steel-gray curls arranged in an outdated but immaculate style. "I took the liberty of summoning reinforcements."

"Word of your shop has traveled through the neighborhood," Mrs. Winters explained, her quiet voice carrying the precision that came from decades measuring clients to the quarter-inch. She tilted her head slightly as she regarded Clara, the habitual gesture of a woman accustomed to assessing people at a glance. "Such a dreadful business."

"These ladies have all expressed concern," Mrs. Penfield continued, gesturing with her lorgnette like a general indicating positions on a map. "And more importantly, each brings particular skills that may prove useful in our current predicament."

Clara sank into the offered chair, Marmalade immediately claiming the footstool beside her. The cat's gaze swept the assembled women with imperial assessment before settling into watchful attention.

"I'm grateful for your concern," Clara began, "but the situation has grown more complicated—and considerably more dangerous—than a mere fire."

A constable passed by the window, his shadow momentarily darkening the room. The ladies fell silent until he had moved beyond hearing range, then resumed their positions with subtle adjustments that suggested collective awareness of surveillance.

"We suspected as much, Miss Wetherly," Mrs. Turner spoke for the first time, her educated accent occasionally revealing traces of her merchant-class origins. She tapped her silver-topped walking stick against the carpet for emphasis. "Which is precisely why we have assembled."

"Perhaps introductions would be appropriate," Harriet suggested, organizing the teacups with unconscious precision. "Not all of us have been formally presented to Miss Wetherly."

Mrs. Penfield nodded approvingly. "Indeed. Clara knows most of you, of course, but Mrs. Emmeline Turner—" she gestured to the imposing widow, "—was married to Dr. Turner of St. Bartholomew's Hospital. She maintains extensive connections in medical circles that may prove invaluable."

Mrs. Turner inclined her head. "My late husband often

spoke highly of your grandmother's botanical knowledge, Miss Wetherly. He considered her a colleague rather than a competitor, unlike certain physicians in Harley Street."

"And this," Mrs. Penfield continued, indicating the plain-faced woman with ink-stained fingers, "is Miss Beatrice Finch."

Clara's attention sharpened. "Finch? Are you relation to Thomas Finch, Mr. Barrett's assistant?"

"His sister," Miss Finch confirmed, her nervous voice contrasting with the precise clarity of her diction. "Thomas spoke of you after Barrett's visits to your shop. Said you were the only person who treated him with any consideration." Her fingers twisted in her lap. "I've been worried sick since his disappearance. When Mrs. Penfield mentioned your connection to the case, I thought perhaps..."

"Your brother is alive," Clara assured her quickly. "Though seriously injured. He's under guard at St. Mary's Hospital."

Miss Finch's hand flew to her mouth, her eyes immediately filling with tears. "Oh thank God!" she exclaimed, her composure crumbling. "I thought—I feared—" She struggled to collect herself, dabbing at her eyes with a handkerchief. "They told me nothing at Blackstone Development. Just that he had 'departed his position without notice.' I've been searching for days, imagining the worst."

"Each lady present has some connection to our situation," Mrs. Penfield explained, pouring tea with military precision. "Mrs. Winters observes our neighborhood with unmatched attention to detail. Miss Collins has access to registry documents that conventional channels might find inaccessible. Mrs. Turner's medical connections may prove essential in understanding the medical aspects of the case. And Miss Finch brings insider knowledge of Blackstone Development that even Inspector Redgrave might envy."

Clara accepted the offered teacup, momentarily over-whelmed by this unexpected alliance. "I'm grateful, truly. But I

must be clear—this situation has become genuinely dangerous. I've discovered evidence suggesting the murders are
connected to something much larger than a simple property
dispute."

"Do tell us what you've learned, dear," Mrs. Penfield
urged, leaning forward with keen interest. "We can hardly
assist without understanding the true nature of the threat."

Clara took a deep breath, considering where to begin. "I
believe I know who murdered Mr. Barrett and Mr. Pinkett,
and who arranged the fire at my shop."

The ladies exchanged glances of surprise and anticipation.

"Not Lord Blackstone or Mr. Halston?" Mrs. Winters
asked.

"No," Clara replied firmly. "Dr. Malcolm Morris, the Scotland Yard medical examiner."

A moment of stunned silence followed this declaration.

"The police doctor?" Mrs. Turner exclaimed, her medical
connections clearly making this revelation particularly shocking. "Are you certain?"

"Let me explain the evidence I've gathered," Clara said,
setting down her cup.

She proceeded to relate everything she had learned—
Morris's position on the Medical Research Fund board, his
treatment of Barrett before the man's death, and his financial
interest in the railway development. Most crucially, she
explained her morning's discovery at Thornfield Estate about
the amber bottle found with Barrett's body.

"The bottle bearing my partial label that implicated me in
Barrett's death was taken from the Duchess of Thornfield's
collection," Clara explained. "By Philip Evans, who is Dr.
Morris's assistant and the nephew of the Duchess's lady's
maid."

The ladies exchanged glances, clearly impressed by both

the aristocratic connection and the significance of this evidence.

"Her Grace is involved?" Mrs. Turner asked, a new respect entering her voice.

"She has been most supportive," Clara confirmed. "But more importantly, we now have direct evidence connecting Dr. Morris to the fabricated evidence against me."

Clara continued explaining Morris's elaborate scheme—how he had treated Barrett while slowly poisoning him, how he had killed Pinkett when the banker discovered his financial connections, and how he had used his position at Scotland Yard to direct suspicion toward Clara.

"Inspector Redgrave has uncovered financial documents connecting Morris to both development companies," she added. "But when he attempted to bring this evidence to his superiors, he was explicitly forbidden from pursuing allegations against Dr. Morris."

"The police protecting their own," Mrs. Penfield observed with a disapproving sniff.

"It's more complicated than that," Clara explained. "Morris is physician to several members of Parliament. The Chief Inspector warned Redgrave that without irrefutable proof, any accusation would be dismissed, and Redgrave would be removed from the case entirely."

"Leaving you as the primary suspect," Harriet deduced shrewdly.

"Precisely," Clara confirmed.

She had just reached the explanation of these institutional constraints when a sharp pang of loss struck her unexpectedly. The simple act of laying out evidence on Mrs. Penfield's table —an action she had performed countless times on her own shop counter—brought the reality of her loss crashing down.

"My dear, what is it?" Mrs. Penfield asked, noticing her sudden silence.

"I apologize," Clara said, attempting to master her emotion. "It's just... speaking of evidence reminded me..."

To her mortification, she found herself unable to continue as grief tightened her throat. The shop had been more than mere walls and inventory—it had been her connection to Genevieve, to three generations of Wetherly women. The place where she had learned her craft, where her earliest memories had formed.

"The shop wasn't merely my livelihood," she managed finally, her voice soft but steady. "It was... Grandmother seemed to linger there, in the creak of that third drawer that always stuck, in the scent of dried lavender hanging from the ceiling beams. Even after three years, I'd sometimes turn quickly and expect to see her standing at the counter, mixing something I'd forgotten. Now that's gone too."

Mrs. Winters reached across the table, her thin fingers gently covering Clara's hand. The unexpected gesture of comfort from the usually reserved dressmaker nearly undid Clara's composure entirely.

"Not gone," Mrs. Winters corrected softly. "Merely waiting to be rebuilt."

Marmalade, as if sensing her distress, abandoned his customary aloofness to press against Clara's skirts—a rare public display of feline affection that drew subtle smiles from the assembled women.

"When this business is concluded," Mrs. Penfield declared with absolute certainty, "we shall rebuild Hawthorne & Wetherly better than before. There isn't a shop in Bloomsbury that doesn't owe something to your grandmother's remedies, myself included."

Clara felt a surge of gratitude for these women who under-stood precisely what she had lost—not inventory or income, but connection and heritage. Their understanding trans-formed her grief into renewed determination.

"You're right," she said, straightening her shoulders. "And before we can rebuild, we must ensure Dr. Morris faces justice for what he's done."

"Inspector Redgrave seems unwilling to pursue the most obvious suspect," Mrs. Turner observed, clearing her throat disapprovingly. "Despite the evidence you've presented."

"It isn't unwillingness but constraint," Clara corrected, surprising herself with her defense of Redgrave. "Inspector Redgrave operates within limitations we can scarcely imagine. He risks not merely his position but the very authority that allows him to seek justice at all. We have the luxury of working outside those boundaries precisely because we have never been granted the power to work within them."

Mrs. Penfield's eyebrows rose slightly, her gaze sharpening with assessment. "Indeed. But if the Inspector cannot act through official channels..."

"Then we must create circumstances where the truth becomes unavoidable," Clara finished, returning to the task at hand. "I've developed a plan, but it will require your assistance."

Clara leaned forward, using Mrs. Penfield's teacups to demonstrate positions and movements as she outlined her strategy for trapping Morris. With precise botanical terminology and methodical logic, she explained how the correct preparations could create symptoms without causing harm, how timing and placement would be crucial, and how evidence must be preserved for Redgrave to utilize within legal boundaries.

The ladies listened with remarkable focus, each contributing refinements from her unique perspective. Mrs. Winters suggested optimal observation points from neighboring buildings. Harriet outlined which documents would most effectively divert Scotland Yard's attention temporarily. Mrs. Turner provided insights into medical protocols that would make Morris's actions appear legitimate until the crucial moment.

"Men like Dr. Morris have always succeeded because they believe our conversations revolve around ribbon and lace," Mrs. Penfield observed with satisfaction. "They never suspect that while discussing the quality of this season's muslin, we've mapped every weakness in their carefully constructed positions of authority."

"I've dressed enough gentlemen to know their vanities," Mrs. Winters agreed, smoothing an invisible wrinkle from her sleeve. "Dr. Morris's waistcoats always match his pocket squares—I've noticed it during his visits to my shop. A man that concerned with appearance will never believe himself capable of being seen through, particularly by women."

"The registry holds thirty-seven property transfers connected to the Medical Research Fund," Harriet added, adjusting her spectacles. "I checked the records after Clara explained the connection. Each document bears the same signature pattern—a decisive downstroke followed by a hesitation. The hand that signed those documents was not confident in the transactions they represented."

"My late husband always said the most dangerous physician was one who believed himself infallible," Mrs. Turner contributed, her walking stick tapping the floor for emphasis. "He once attended a lecture where Dr. Morris disputed a senior physician's diagnosis. His arrogance was notorious even then."

"Thomas believed Barrett discovered something in the railway plans that went beyond mere property values," Miss Finch revealed, her voice gaining strength as she spoke. "He mentioned it in a letter to me just days before he disappeared. Something that made Barrett dangerous enough to eliminate rather than simply bribe or threaten."

As each woman shared her knowledge, Clara began

assigning specific responsibilities to create their trap. Mrs. Penfield would craft a letter to Dr. Morris expressing concern about Clara's respiratory health following the fire. Mrs. Winters would establish an observation post from her shop directly across from Mrs. Penfield's house. Harriet would create a false lead that would occupy Scotland Yard temporarily without compromising Redgrave's investigation. Mrs. Turner would spread word through medical circles about Clara's declining health, ensuring Morris heard it from multiple sources. Miss Finch would position herself near the hospital to monitor any changes in her brother's condition and ensure no further harm came to him.

"The letter is the crucial element," Clara explained. "It must contain precisely the right balance of concern, deference to medical authority, and implied vulnerability."

Mrs. Penfield nodded, already reaching for her writing desk. "He must believe you are alone and unprotected, yet his medical expertise is deeply required. Men like Morris cannot resist demonstrating their superiority, particularly over women they believe have challenged them."

Clara unpacked the botanical specimens she had brought from the Duchess's greenhouse, carefully arranging them on the table as she explained each preparation's properties.

"This mixture of cayenne and bergamot creates significant discomfort when applied to mucous membranes, but causes no lasting damage," she explained, displaying a small vial of russet powder. "A medical examiner would recognize the symptoms as consistent with certain mineral poisonings."

"And this?" Mrs. Turner inquired, indicating a pale green mixture.

"Valerian tincture, but prepared with a specific ratio that induces disorientation rather than relaxation," Clara replied. "Combined with this hawthorn extract, it creates temporary but significant confusion—ideal for encouraging unguarded speech."

Marmalade batted at the valerian bottle with evident disapproval, then deliberately pushed forward a different preparation—a clear liquid Clara had set aside.

"You prefer the white willow extraction?" Clara asked the cat with amused solemnity. "An interesting choice."

The ladies exchanged glances, clearly uncertain whether Clara was simply humoring the animal or genuinely consulting him. Marmalade's decisive meow and subsequent rearrangement of several vials only deepened their uncertainty.

"The cat appears to have opinions on pharmaceutical preparations," Mrs. Turner observed dryly.

"Marmalade has unexpected insights," Clara replied, adjusting her arrangements to match the cat's apparent preferences. "I've learned not to dismiss them."

As afternoon faded toward evening, the final plan took shape. Mrs. Penfield completed her letter, reading the masterpiece of subtle manipulation aloud for approval:

"Dear Dr. Morris, I write with some concern regarding Miss Clara Wetherly, who has been staying with me since the unfortunate fire at her establishment. While she insists she is recovering well, her breathing seems increasingly labored, particularly in the evenings when the temperature drops. As I will be attending my Thursday literary society meeting this evening (I am presenting a paper on Mrs. Gaskell's works that simply cannot be postponed), I find myself distressed at the thought of leaving her alone during what appears to be the worst period of her symptoms. I would be eternally grateful if you could find time in your busy schedule to examine her professionally around eight o'clock. Your reputation for diagnostic excellence gives me confidence that under your care, any lingering effects from smoke inhalation would be properly identified and treated. Your servant, Mrs. Agatha Penfield."

"Perfect," Clara approved. "That appeal to his professional vanity while emphasizing my isolation is precisely right."

"He'll find it impossible to resist," Mrs. Turner agreed. "Particularly the implied vulnerability of being alone in the evening."

"Now for the timing," Clara continued. "Mrs. Penfield will depart visibly at half past seven, ensuring neighbors notice her leaving with a substantial portfolio for her literary presentation."

"I shall be most theatrical about it," Mrs. Penfield promised, patting her curls with anticipation.

"Mrs. Winters will observe from her shop window, which provides the clearest view of the front entrance. When Morris arrives, she'll dispatch this message to Inspector Redgrave, timed to bring him here just as our confrontation reaches its conclusion."

Mrs. Winters took the sealed note with a precise nod. "My apprentice can deliver it while remaining inconspicuous. The boy has a talent for vanishing into street crowds."

"Miss Collins will ensure certain documents occupy Scotland Yard's attention without directly implicating Morris, creating the necessary distraction without compromising the eventual case against him."

"I've prepared registry excerpts highlighting Blackstone's connection to the properties," Harriet confirmed. "Enough to keep them busy without revealing our true focus."

"Mrs. Turner will position herself at the neighboring house, ready to provide medical testimony if required, while Miss Finch maintains watch at the hospital to ensure her brother remains protected."

Both women nodded their agreement as Clara concluded her instructions.

"Remember, ladies—we are not seeking revenge. We are creating circumstances where truth becomes unavoidable. The distinction matters. Each of us must play her role with precision while appearing to play no role at all. It is, in essence, what society has trained us to do our entire lives."

"My grandmother used to say that rules exist for the benefit of those who make them," Clara added, looking around at these remarkable women who had rallied to her cause. "When they no longer serve justice, they become merely suggestions. I believe we have reached that point, ladies."

"Indeed we have," Mrs. Penfield declared, rising to her feet with surprising energy for a woman of her years. "Well then, to your positions, everyone. We have a murderer to catch."

The ladies dispersed with purposeful determination, each departing with specific instructions and a sense of shared purpose that transformed what might have been mere neighborhood gossips into a formidable investigative network. Clara remained at the window with Marmalade beside her, watching as they disappeared into the gathering dusk like an invisible web spreading throughout Bloomsbury.

"Tonight we end this, Marmalade," she murmured, her hand resting lightly on the cat's warm fur. "One way or another."

Marmalade's tail swished once in decisive agreement, his amber eyes fixed on the street where, in just a few hours, justice would finally find Dr. Morris.

twenty-one

The soft knock at Mrs. Penfield's front door came precisely at eight o'clock. Clara, positioned in the back parlor with strategically arranged botanical specimens surrounding her, took a final deep breath and arranged her features into an expression of wan fragility. Marmalade assumed his position on the windowsill, amber eyes fixed on the entrance hall with unblinking attention.

"Dr. Morris to see Miss Wetherly," announced Mrs. Penfield's housekeeper from the doorway, her practiced neutrality betraying no hint that she was part of an elaborate trap.

Dr. Malcolm Morris entered with the confident bearing of a man accustomed to commanding respect. His immaculate frock coat and precisely knotted cravat spoke of meticulous attention to appearance, while the silver-topped walking stick he carried suggested both status and authority. The leather medical bag in his left hand completed the image of professional concern.

"Miss Wetherly," he greeted, his voice pitched to the perfect note of medical solicitude. "Mrs. Penfield's message suggested you're experiencing respiratory distress following the unfortunate fire."

Clara allowed a slight tremor to enter her hand as she gestured to the chair positioned across from her. "How kind of you to come, Dr. Morris. The smoke... it seems to have affected my breathing more than I initially believed."

"Quite common with smoke inhalation," Morris replied, setting his bag on the small table beside him. "The damage can manifest days later, particularly in delicate constitutions."

He removed his gloves with practiced precision, each finger extracted deliberately before folding them into his pocket. Clara noted how his gaze swept the room in a single assessing glance—taking in the tea service, Marmalade's watchful presence, and the scattered botanical specimens with the careful attention of a man who missed nothing.

"I've brought several preparations that might ease your discomfort," Morris continued, opening his bag and withdrawing a stethoscope. "But first, a proper examination. If you would breathe deeply while I listen."

Clara complied, allowing him to place the cold metal against her back as she manufactured a convincing wheeze. She had positioned herself so that reaching for her "medicine" would bring her hand within inches of the cayenne mixture hidden behind a decorative vase.

"Your pulse seems elevated," Morris observed, fingers pressed to her wrist. "And there's a concerning rasp in your lower lungs. Have you coughed up any dark phlegm?"

"Not dark, precisely," Clara replied, her voice deliberately weak. "But there is an unusual bitterness to it—rather like certain alkaloid compounds."

Morris's fingers paused almost imperceptibly on her wrist. "An unusual comparison for a patient to make, Miss Wetherly."

"Perhaps," Clara agreed. "But when one works with botanicals, one develops sensitivity to such distinctions. Rather like certain poisons, I imagine? Progressive symptoms that worsen over time?"

She watched Morris's expression, noting the subtle shift in his eyes—professional concern giving way to careful assessment. He released her wrist and returned to his bag, removing a small bottle of dark liquid.

"This will ease your breathing," he stated, measuring drops into a glass of water from the nearby table. "An extract of wild cherry bark with certain additions known only to medical practitioners."

"How fascinating," Clara remarked, accepting the glass without drinking. "I've found the chemical properties of wild cherry quite remarkable myself. That distinctive bitter almond scent—reminiscent of prussic acid in its pure form, though considerably less lethal in botanical preparations."

"You have an unusual medical vocabulary for a shop proprietor," Morris observed, his tone pleasant though his eyes had cooled significantly.

"My grandmother believed knowledge should never be restricted by convention," Clara replied, carefully setting the untouched glass on the side table. "She was particularly interested in the progressive effects of certain compounds when administered in small doses over time. Rather like Mr. Barrett's symptoms before his death—the trembling hands, the increasing weakness."

Morris's posture shifted subtly—the change imperceptible to anyone without Clara's trained observation. "Mr. Barrett's case was most unfortunate," he remarked, closing his medical bag with a decisive click. "Though I fail to see its relevance to your current condition."

"Don't you?" Clara asked, abandoning her pretense of weakness as she met his gaze directly. "I found it rather enlightening when examining the amber bottle found with his body

—the one taken from the Duchess of Thornfield's collection by your assistant Philip Evans."

The transformation in Morris's demeanor was immediate and chilling. His professional mask fell away, revealing something harder and colder beneath—like ice forming over deep water.

"You've been quite industrious in my absence, I see," he remarked, his voice no longer carrying any pretense of medical concern.

"The bottle from the Duchess of Thornfield. Your assistant Philip Evans. The Medical Research Fund's investments. Your treatment of Barrett before his death." Clara enumerated the points calmly. "Quite a pattern, wouldn't you agree?"

Morris reached for his pocket watch, checking the time with deliberate slowness. The light from the lamp caught the distinctive medical emblem on its case—a caduceus with entwined serpents around a staff. Clara's breath caught as recognition flashed through her mind—this was the same watch she had glimpsed in the lamplight the night Pinkett was murdered.

"It was you outside the bank that night," she stated, certainty replacing suspicion. "You killed Pinkett when he discovered your financial connections to the development companies."

"Mrs. Penfield chose an unfortunately timed literary society meeting," Morris observed, ignoring her accusation as he returned the watch to his waistcoat pocket. "Though I suppose I should thank her for the opportunity. This resolves several complications simultaneously."

He rose from his chair with fluid grace, moving toward his bag with unhurried confidence. "A shame. You might have rebuilt your little shop and continued your quaint botanical dabbling. Now you'll join Barrett and Pinkett instead."

Clara maintained her position, keeping the table between them. "How many others have you gradually poisoned while pretending to treat them, Dr. Morris?"

The question seemed to catch him off guard, a brief flicker of uncertainty crossing his features before the cold mask returned. "More than you might imagine," he replied with clinical detachment. "The human body is remarkably vulnerable to subtle chemical influences."

"So you lured him behind my shop with the promise of henbane for his symptoms," Clara deduced. "After your initial plan failed when I refused to provide the henbane you had recommended to him."

"Yes, that was unfortunate," Morris admitted, sounding almost academic despite his discomfort. "Had you provided the henbane as I suggested to Barrett, the combination with the compounds already in his system would have killed him instantly—and implicated you directly. When you refused him, I was forced to implement a less elegant solution."

"The final dose administered in a location that would implicate me, with my bottle planted beside him," Clara continued, piecing it together. "The perfect solution to both problems."

"The railway station entrance requires your property," Morris confirmed, his scientific pride evident even through his discomfort. "The development cannot proceed without it. Barrett's elimination and your discrediting were simply efficient problem-solving."

"You speak of murder as if it's a medical procedure," Clara observed, genuine revulsion coloring her voice.

"All progress requires sacrifice," Morris stated with clinical certainty. "The railway will transform this neighborhood, bringing modern advancement where backward tradition once prevailed. Your quaint little shop is merely a casualty of inevitable progress."

Heavy footsteps in the hallway interrupted his mono-
logue. The parlor door burst open to reveal Inspector
Redgrave, revolver drawn, with two constables close behind.
He surveyed the scene with a single comprehensive glance—
Morris hunched forward with eyes streaming; Clara standing
calmly behind the writing desk; Marmalade sitting with
impossible dignity beside the cabinet that concealed the
poison vial.

"Inspector Redgrave," Morris greeted, attempting to
straighten despite his compromised vision. "Excellent timing.
Miss Wetherly has assaulted me with some manner of chemical
irritant. I was attempting to treat her respiratory condition
when she became hysterical."

"Indeed?" Redgrave replied, his tone revealing nothing as
his gaze moved to Clara. "Miss Wetherly. I see you've been
precisely where I left you."

"Indeed, Inspector," Clara responded, her expression
betraying the barest hint of satisfaction. "Merely receiving a
medical consultation that took an unexpected turn."

"She attacked me without provocation," Morris insisted,
his composed façade crumbling further as he continued
dabbing at his streaming eyes. "Clearly unstable after the
trauma of the fire—likely affected by smoke inhalation to her
brain."

Marmalade chose this moment to abandon his post by the
cabinet. With deliberate purpose, the cat approached
Redgrave directly—an unprecedented behavior that caught
the inspector's attention immediately. The cat circled
Redgrave once, then returned to the cabinet, pawing meaningfully at its base.

"I believe your cat is attempting to direct my attention,
Miss Wetherly," Redgrave observed, a note of surprise evident
in his voice.

"Marmalade has an excellent eye for evidence, Inspector,"

Clara confirmed. "You might find Dr. Morris's vial of poison beneath that cabinet—the one he intended to administer to me before our consultation took its unexpected turn."

Redgrave signaled to one of the constables, who knelt to retrieve the small glass container. "And how did this consultation progress, exactly?" he inquired, maintaining his professional tone despite the extraordinary scene before him.

"Dr. Morris was kind enough to share his involvement in Barrett's poisoning," Clara explained. "How he administered progressive doses during medical treatments, then arranged the final dose behind my shop to implicate me. He also explained his unfortunate necessity in eliminating Mr. Pinkett when the banker discovered suspicious financial transactions."

"Preposterous," Morris sputtered, though his denial lacked conviction. "The word of a hysterical woman against a medical professional. No court would entertain such unfounded allegations."

"Perhaps not," Redgrave agreed, his tone measured. "Though they might find the testimony of several witnesses compelling."

On cue, Mrs. Penfield emerged from behind the connecting door where she had been listening, followed by Mrs. Winters and Mrs. Turner. "I believe I heard every word, Inspector," Mrs. Penfield announced with evident satisfaction. "As did my companions."

Morris's face drained of color as he realized the trap's full extent. "This... this is entrapment. Conspiracy."

"This is justice, Dr. Morris," Clara corrected quietly. "Something your position and influence nearly allowed you to escape."

Redgrave signaled to his constables, who moved to take Morris into custody. "Dr. Malcolm Morris, you are under arrest for the murders of Silas Barrett and George Pinkett, the attempted murder of Miss Clara Wetherly, and the assault on

Thomas Finch, who has now identified you as his attacker and is recuperating at St. Mary's Hospital."

As the constables escorted Morris from the room, Redgrave turned to Clara with an expression that mingled exasperation and reluctant admiration. "You promised to remain exactly where the Duchess needed you."

"And so I did," Clara replied innocently. "The Duchess needed me precisely here, setting this trap."

Redgrave shook his head, unable to entirely suppress the twitch at the corner of his mouth that might, in a less disciplined man, have become a smile. "You deliberately misled me."

"I chose my words with care," Clara corrected. "As did you when you forbade me from confronting Morris 'directly.' I believe I confronted him through careful botanical intervention instead."

"A distinction that might have resulted in your death," Redgrave observed, his professionally detached tone betrayed by the intensity in his eyes.

"A risk I deemed necessary when institutional constraints prevented official action," Clara countered. "Though I took reasonable precautions." She gestured to the assembled ladies who stood watching this exchange with undisguised interest.

Redgrave surveyed the unlikely alliance with a raised eyebrow. "I see you assembled quite the formidable team, Miss Wetherly."

"The Ladies of Bloomsbury," Mrs. Penfield supplied proudly. "We may not carry badges, Inspector, but we observe more than most realize."

"Indeed," Redgrave acknowledged with a respectful nod. "Though in future, I would appreciate being informed of such... collaborative investigations."

"Would you have approved?" Clara asked directly.

"No," Redgrave admitted after a moment's consideration. "Which is precisely why you didn't inform me."

"I believe we understand each other perfectly, Inspector," Clara replied, the ghost of a smile touching her lips.

Marmalade, as if sensing the shift in atmosphere, abandoned his guard position to wind between Clara's skirts, his mission evidently completed to his satisfaction.

"Your...assistant seems remarkably attuned to investigations," Redgrave observed, watching the cat's movements with newfound respect.

"Marmalade has many talents beyond mere mousing," Clara confirmed, bending to stroke the cat's orange fur. "Though he prefers to maintain an air of mystery about his methods."

As Mrs. Penfield organized tea for the victorious conspirators, Clara found herself standing beside Redgrave near the window, temporarily separated from the others.

"I believe this is the beginning of a new chapter for Hawthorne & Wetherly," she said quietly. "Though I suspect the railway plans will proceed regardless of Morris's fate."

"Indeed," Redgrave agreed. "Lord Blackstone has already issued a statement distancing himself from Morris's 'regrettable actions,' though I suspect he's not entirely innocent in this affair."

"The aristocracy rarely dirties its own hands," Clara observed. "The Duchess explained as much to me."

"Her Grace is remarkably perceptive," Redgrave commented, a note of personal knowledge in his voice that Clara found intriguing.

"Perhaps our paths will cross again professionally, Inspector," Clara suggested, studying his expression carefully. "London seems full of mysteries that might benefit from both detective methods and botanical knowledge."

"A rather uncommon combination," Redgrave observed.

"Indeed," Clara agreed. "Almost as uncommon as a police inspector with aristocratic connections and a botanical specialist with a talent for uncovering truth."

Something shifted in Redgrave's expression—a subtle acknowledgment of the partnership Clara was proposing. Before he could respond, however, Mrs. Penfield summoned them to the tea table with imperious authority.

As they joined the celebration, Clara caught the scent of lavender water—her grandmother's signature perfume—though no such preparation was present in the room. The temperature near the mantelpiece dropped perceptibly, and the candle flame wavered without a draft.

Marmalade, seated once again on his preferred footstool, tracked something invisible across the room with his unblinking amber gaze. Clara smiled, certain that her grandmother was present for this moment of triumph—the justice that her legacy had helped secure.

Justice that had come not through official channels, but through the determined collaboration of women whose observations society routinely dismissed—guided by the subtle influence of one who had transcended death itself to protect what she had built.

twenty-two

M*armalade's Observations*

HUMANS ARE REMARKABLY RESILIENT CREATURES. Particularly the female variety.

Three months ago, my domain was reduced to ashes and smoke. My carefully selected sleeping spots, my strategically positioned observation posts, my extensively curated collection of tiny objects hidden beneath furniture—all gone in a single night of flame and destruction. A catastrophe by any reasonable feline standard.

Yet here we stand, or in my case, recline upon the newly installed window ledge (wider than its predecessor by precisely two paw-widths—a rare improvement I concede with grudging approval).

The reopening of Hawthorne & Wetherly has drawn half of Bloomsbury to our doorstep this morning. The narrow street teems with humans in their best attire, all exclaiming with tedious enthusiasm over the rebuilt shop. From my elevated position, I observe their movements with the detached interest of a natural philosopher studying particularly animated insects.

The shop itself has maintained its essential character despite being entirely rebuilt. The same oak counters, though unmarked by decades of use. The same wall of herb drawers, their brass handles polished to a gleam that borders on offensive to sensitive feline eyes. The same glass jars arrayed on shelves, though these lack the comforting layer of dust that properly distinguishes a well-established establishment.

Clara moves among the visitors with newfound confidence, her voice carrying notes I hadn't heard before the fire. The Ladies of Bloomsbury orbit around her like satellites around a planet, each playing her assigned role with the obsessive attention humans devote to their arbitrary social rituals.

Mrs. Penfield presides over the tea service, her steel-gray curls bobbing as she dispenses wisdom and Darjeeling with equal authority. Mrs. Winters adjusts the new curtains she has sewn, fussing over their drape with the obsessive attention to detail that makes humans simultaneously exhausting and occasionally useful. Mrs. Turner intimidates a delivery man who dared to question whether the botanical specimens were properly addressed. Miss Collins quietly updates the shop's new ledgers with her precise handwriting, while Miss Finch arranges freshly printed labels with the enthusiastic energy of youth.

The Duchess of Thornfield arrived an hour ago in a carriage that momentarily blocked all traffic on our humble street—a dramatic entrance entirely consistent with her character. She now holds court in the corner, explaining to a circle of rapt listeners how she personally selected certain rare specimens from her greenhouses for Clara's new stock. The Duchess catches my eye across the room and inclines her head slightly in acknowledgment. I return the gesture with a slow blink. We understand each other, the Duchess and I—both accustomed to managing those around us while maintaining an air of aristocratic detachment.

The transformation of my human over these months has been particularly notable. Clara moves with purpose now, her earlier hesitation replaced by quiet certainty. She no longer glances over her shoulder expecting to see her grandmother; instead, she seems to carry Genevieve's presence within her. Her conversation flows more easily, her laughter comes more readily, and she handles the various botanical preparations with the confident grace of someone who has tested herself against fire and emerged tempered rather than consumed.

Most intriguingly, Clara has taken to consulting The Gilded Leaf with new regularity. The book now occupies a place of honor on a small reading stand behind the counter—precisely where Genevieve always kept it. I have observed Clara opening it at seemingly random moments, her fingers tracing the handwritten notes while her expression shifts through complicated human emotions I cannot fully decipher but recognize as significant.

I stretch luxuriously on my new perch, extending each paw to its full length before settling into a more dignified position. The window ledge offers an excellent vantage point for both the street and the shop interior, allowing comprehensive surveillance of all relevant activity. I have graciously permitted Clara to place a small cushion here—royal blue velvet that complements my orange coat to advantage—though I've made it clear through strategic rearrangement that its position is subject to my approval.

The bell above the door chimes as another visitor enters. My whiskers twitch with recognition before my eyes confirm the identity—Inspector Redgrave, his tall figure momentarily blocking the morning light. He has visited the reconstruction site seven times during the rebuilding process, each time with some transparent excuse about "following up on the investigation." Today he has abandoned his usual severe black coat for a slightly less severe navy one, and carries a package wrapped in brown paper and string.

Clara's reaction to his arrival is telling. Her hands pause in arranging dried lavender, her posture straightens almost imperceptibly, and her voice takes on a quality that humans might not notice but that no self-respecting cat could possibly miss—a slight brightening, like sunlight breaking through clouds.

"Inspector Redgrave," she greets him, her tone carefully calibrated to convey pleased surprise rather than expectation. "How kind of you to join our small celebration."

Redgrave removes his hat, revealing the silver at his temples that has increased noticeably since our first encounter. "Miss Wetherly. I hope I'm not intruding."

The Duchess observes this exchange with thinly veiled amusement, while Mrs. Penfield and Mrs. Winters exchange glances of such transparent meaning that I'm embarrassed on behalf of my entire species. Humans believe themselves subtle in matters of courtship. They are mistaken.

"Not at all," Clara assures him, gesturing toward the tea service. "Mrs. Penfield has prepared enough refreshment for half of London."

"I've brought something for the occasion," Redgrave says, offering the package with uncharacteristic uncertainty. "A small token for the reopening."

Clara accepts it, her fingers brushing his momentarily—a contact that causes Mrs. Penfield to suddenly develop an intense interest in the ceiling beams. My own interest, I confess, is genuinely piqued. The inspector has demonstrated better taste than I initially credited to him.

Clara unwraps the package carefully, revealing a book

bound in aged leather, its cover embossed with botanical illustrations in faded gold. Her breath catches audibly as she reads the title.

"'Botanical Toxicology and Medicinal Applications'—by Dr. Elizabeth Montgomery," she reads, her voice soft with genuine wonder. "Inspector, this is extraordinarily rare. How did you possibly—"

"Found it at an estate auction," Redgrave explains with a small shrug that fools no one but himself. "Seemed the sort of thing that might be useful here."

The moment between them stretches, weighted with unspoken significance. I yawn pointedly, which breaks the spell as Clara laughs softly.

"Even Marmalade approves, it seems," she says, stroking the book's spine with careful fingers. "Thank you, Inspector. I shall treasure it."

The gathering continues, conversations flowing around the shop like currents in a stream. I take the opportunity to perform my regular inspection of the premises, leaping gracefully from my window perch to the counter, then to the floor. My patrol takes me past the small table where The Gilded Leaf rests open, its pages stirring slightly though no draft disturbs the air.

I pause, whiskers forward with interest. The book has settled on a page I've seen Clara studying with particular attention recently—an illustration of a tarot card labeled "The Magician." The figure on the card stands between heaven and earth, one hand raised toward the sky, the other pointing downward. Above his head, the symbol of infinity. Before him, the tools of his craft: cup, sword, coin, and wand.

Around the illustration, Genevieve's flowing script explains: "The Magician represents the power to transform one reality into another. He stands at the threshold between worlds, channeling divine wisdom into earthly form. When he appears, look for one who transforms ordinary elements into something greater—a healer, a creator, or perhaps... a truth-seeker."

Below this familiar text, a line I've seen Clara reading repeatedly: "The seeker becomes the sought. Those who cannot find justice elsewhere will find their way to your door."

I contemplate this with appropriate feline gravity. The air around the book seems charged with subtle energy, as it often does when Clara reads from its pages. A faint scent—not lavender this time, but the dried roses Genevieve favored for headache remedies—drifts through this corner of the shop. The silver bell on the counter chimes once, though no one stands near enough to touch it.

These phenomena no longer surprise me. I have long been aware that my human is not the only female presence inhabiting this shop. Genevieve's spirit lingers, particularly around this book, asserting influence with varying degrees of subtlety. Humans may debate the existence of ghosts, but cats have never required such debates. We see what is there, whether others perceive it or not.

Clara approaches, drawn to the book as if by invisible thread. She notices the page, fingers hovering above the text with quiet recognition.

"Grandmother," she whispers, so softly that only I could possibly hear.

I press against her skirts once, acknowledging the moment, before continuing my inspection. Human sentimentality, while occasionally touching, should not interfere with necessary patrol duties.

The rebuilt shop has subtle improvements that meet with my approval. The counter now includes a small shelf precisely at my preferred sitting height. The herb drawers have been redesigned to close more securely, presenting an enjoyable challenge for paws determined to access forbidden treasures.

The floor near the hearth retains a warm spot ideal for afternoon contemplation.

Most importantly, my tarot drawer has been recreated exactly as before—third from the left, lined with faded blue velvet salvaged from the fire, sized perfectly for a cat of distinguished proportions to nap among the wisdom of the cards.

Redgrave has moved to examine the book with Clara, their heads bent together over the page in a tableau of scholarly intimacy.

"Your grandmother's handwriting was quite distinctive," Redgrave observes, his finger tracing the line about justice. "Did she write much about divination?"

"She believed botanical knowledge and spiritual insight were two paths to the same understanding," Clara explains. "This book contains both her scientific observations and her more... intuitive wisdom."

Redgrave studies the page with careful attention. "Intuitive indeed. Though I must admit her predictions often seem remarkably applicable to current circumstances."

"Grandmother had an uncanny sense of what might be needed in the future," Clara agrees with a small smile.

Their conversation continues, moving to safer topics of the shop's renovation and future plans. I maintain a position of strategic observation, noting how they navigate around each other with careful attention to proper distance while simultaneously finding reasons to occupy the same space.

The afternoon advances with predictable human patterns —chatter, consumption of refreshments, repeated explanations of the rebuilding process, and tedious expressions of goodwill. I retire to my tarot drawer for a necessary restoration of energy, though I maintain awareness of significant developments through half-closed eyes.

The gathering begins to disperse as evening approaches. The Ladies of Bloomsbury depart one by one, each with a promise to return soon. The Duchess is the last to leave, drawing Clara aside for a private conversation that concludes with a significant glance toward Redgrave, who pretends great interest in a botanical illustration while obviously straining to overhear.

Finally, only Clara, Redgrave, and I remain in the shop. Clara moves about lighting lamps against the gathering dusk, while Redgrave assists by closing shutters with unnecessary precision. I stretch and emerge from my drawer, leaping to the counter to observe this final interaction of the day.

"Your shop has been beautifully restored, Miss Wetherly," Redgrave says, straightening a row of amber bottles that required no adjustment. "Even improved, I would venture."

"Thanks to many generous hands," Clara acknowledges, completing her lamp-lighting circuit to stand opposite him at the counter. "The Ladies of Bloomsbury have been remarkably determined in their support."

"A formidable alliance," Redgrave agrees, a smile briefly lightening his serious countenance. "One that proved more effective than official channels in certain respects."

"Different approaches serve different purposes, Inspector," Clara replies diplomatically. "I've come to believe that justice sometimes requires both."

"An insightful observation," Redgrave comments, his expression thoughtful. "Too often those who need justice most are denied access to official channels."

"Perhaps that's why my grandmother wrote what she did," Clara says, gesturing toward The Gilded Leaf still open to The Magician. "About those seeking justice elsewhere finding their way here."

"I imagine she would be proud of what you've accomplished," Redgrave offers, the compliment clearly genuine despite his formal delivery.

"I hope so," Clara replies softly. "Though I suspect she would say my work is only beginning."

Their exchange of glances communicates more than their words—a foundation of respect layered with something deeper neither appears ready to acknowledge. Humans are remarkably complex in their mating rituals, proceeding with a caution that would exhaust the patience of any sensible cat.

As Redgrave prepares to depart, Clara accompanies him to the door. The evening air carries the scent of approaching rain, and gaslight creates pools of amber illumination along the darkening street.

"Until our next meeting, Miss Wetherly," Redgrave says, replacing his hat with practiced precision.

"I look forward to it, Inspector," Clara replies, her smile visible even in the gathering shadows.

After Redgrave's departure, Clara returns to the counter where I have maintained my dignified observation post. She strokes my fur absently, her thoughts clearly elsewhere.

"What do you think, Marmalade? Has Grandmother set us on a new path entirely?"

I blink slowly in response, which Clara correctly interprets as feline wisdom too profound for human language. She laughs softly, scratching behind my ears in exactly the manner I prefer though I have never explicitly instructed her in the technique.

"You're right, of course. We shall simply have to wait and see what tomorrow brings."

I permit her this presumption of understanding. Humans require such comforts.

The shop settles into evening quiet, lamps casting gentle light across new surfaces that will, in time, acquire the patina of use that transforms mere objects into extensions of their keepers. Clara moves to close The Gilded Leaf, her fingers lingering on the mysterious text before carefully shutting the cover.

As she turns away, I observe the shop with my superior feline senses. The evening shadows seem to move with subtle purpose in the corners. A dried rosebud falls from the ceiling bundle though none was loose moments before. The silver measuring scale on the counter balances perfectly without weights on either side, defying natural laws with casual disregard.

I stretch, acknowledging these signs with the casual acceptance unique to my kind. We cats have always understood that reality has more layers than humans perceive, that some presences remain after their physical form has gone.

The Magician indeed.

epilogue

The first drops of rain had just begun to tap against the windows when the bell above the shop door chimed. Clara glanced up from her inventory ledger, expecting Mrs. Penfield returning for her forgotten shawl. Instead, Inspector Redgrave stood in the doorway, his greatcoat darkened with moisture, hat in hand.

"Inspector," Clara greeted him, setting aside her pen. "Twice in one week—the neighborhood will talk."

"Miss Wetherly." Redgrave's customary formality was present, but something in his bearing suggested this was not a social call. "I apologize for the late hour."

"Hardly late," Clara replied, noting the tension in his shoulders. "The shop is open until six. Though I suspect this isn't about purchasing valerian root for sleeplessness."

A ghost of a smile touched Redgrave's features before vanishing beneath professional gravity. "No. I find myself in a... difficult position regarding a case. I wondered if I might consult with you. Unofficially."

The word hung between them, weighted with significance. Clara gestured toward the small parlor behind the shop where she sometimes conducted consultations. Marmalade, who had been dozing atop a stack of freshly laundered tea towels, raised his head with interest before stretching languorously and following them.

The parlor was modest but comfortable, with two armchairs positioned before a small fireplace where a coal fire provided gentle warmth against the autumn chill. A small table between them held a brass lamp and several botanical reference texts. The walls were lined with shelves of books salvaged from the fire or donated by well-wishers during the reconstruction.

Redgrave remained standing until Clara seated herself, then took the opposite chair, removing a small envelope from inside his coat.

"There has been a death," he began without preamble. "One that presents certain... botanical peculiarities. The official examination concluded natural causes, but circumstances suggest otherwise."

As he spoke, Clara's gaze was drawn to The Gilded Leaf, which rested on the side table. The book lay open, though she was certain she had closed it earlier. From her angle, she could see it had fallen open to the illustration of The Magician card.

The figure on the card stood between heaven and earth, one hand raised toward the sky, the other pointing downward. At his table lay the tools of his craft—cup, wand, pentacle, and sword. As above, so below.

Her grandmother's flowing script surrounded the illustration: *"The Magician commands the elements not through force but through understanding. When he appears, look to those who manipulate the natural world for unnatural gain. The herbs that heal in proper measure will destroy when ambition outweighs wisdom."*

Clara's attention returned to Redgrave, who was watching her with that keen observation that seemed to miss nothing.

"You believe someone has been poisoned," she stated, "and the evidence has been dismissed or overlooked."

"I believe justice is being impeded by influence," Redgrave replied carefully. "The deceased was from a prominent family. Certain avenues of investigation have been... discouraged."

"And so you've come to me," Clara concluded. "Someone without official standing or institutional constraints."

Redgrave met her gaze directly. "I've come to you because you possess knowledge that even our medical examiners lack. Because you see connections others miss. And because I believe you care about truth as much as I do."

The rain intensified outside, drumming against the windows and casting rippling shadows across the room. Marmalade had settled on a footstool near the hearth, his amber eyes reflecting the firelight as he observed their conversation with feline intensity.

"What specifically would you like me to examine?" Clara asked, her decision already made.

From the envelope, Redgrave produced a small glass vial containing what appeared to be dried plant material and a folded handkerchief with a rust-colored stain.

"These were preserved by the lady's maid before evidence could be... misplaced," he explained. "I would value your assessment of what they might tell us."

Clara accepted the items, her trained eye already analyzing the botanical specimen. "This will take some time to properly examine."

"Of course," Redgrave nodded. "I wouldn't expect immediate conclusions on something of this importance."

A moment of understanding passed between them—the recognition of a partnership forming, one based on shared purpose rather than official sanction. Clara found herself thinking of her grandmother's words beneath The Magician card: *The herbs that heal in proper measure will destroy when ambition outweighs wisdom.*

"The authorities have already closed the case, I presume?" she asked, though she already knew the answer.

"There will be no official investigation," Redgrave confirmed. "Which leaves only unofficial means to pursue truth."

"Those who cannot find justice elsewhere will find their way to your door," Clara murmured, echoing the words from The Gilded Leaf.

Redgrave's brow furrowed slightly. "Pardon?"

"Something my grandmother wrote," Clara explained, gesturing toward the open book. "It seems she anticipated this path for me long before I recognized it myself."

Redgrave studied the tarot illustration with quiet interest. "She was a remarkably insightful woman, your grandmother."

"She understood that some truths cannot be found through conventional channels," Clara agreed. "That sometimes the most important evidence is that which others overlook or dismiss."

Outside, the rain continued its steady percussion against the windows. A faint draft stirred the room, causing the lamp flame to flicker momentarily. Marmalade's ears pivoted toward a corner where no one stood, then back to the conversation with deliberate attention.

"I'll need my examination equipment," Clara said, rising with newfound purpose. "And access to my grandmother's references on toxic plant compounds."

"I can return tomorrow for your findings, if that would be convenient," Redgrave suggested, standing as well.

"There's no need to leave," Clara countered, moving toward her workbench visible through the connecting door. "You're welcome to observe the process, Inspector. Two perspectives often reveal what one might miss."

Something shifted in Redgrave's expression—relief, perhaps, or appreciation. "I would be most interested in your methods," he admitted, following her into the shop's preparation area.

As Clara arranged her equipment with practiced efficiency —glass retorts, spirit lamp, testing papers, and several reference books—Marmalade positioned himself atop a nearby shelf, his tail curled around his paws as he observed their activities with feline interest.

The evening deepened outside the windows of Hawthorne & Wetherly, the gas lamps along Bellrose Lane creating hazy orbs in the rain-swept darkness. Within the shop, the familiar scents of dried herbs and beeswax candles merged with the distinctive botanical samples Redgrave had brought.

Clara worked methodically, her hands moving with the confident precision that came from years of practice. Occasionally she would explain a particular test or reaction to Redgrave, who listened with genuine interest, asking questions that revealed an unexpectedly scientific mind.

In that rain-soaked evening, something new began—a partnership forged in the quiet understanding that justice sometimes required unconventional methods. That there were truths official channels could not or would not pursue. That some mysteries could only be solved by those willing to look beyond accepted wisdom.

Marmalade watched them with inscrutable feline understanding, amber eyes gleaming in the lamplight. The Gilded Leaf remained open to The Magician card, its illustrated figure standing at the threshold between worlds, just as Clara now stood at the threshold between her familiar life and something new unfolding before her.

The Magician's path had opened. Where it would lead remained to be seen.

from the remedy book of genevieve wetherly

CALMING SLEEP TINCTURE

As prepared at Hawthorne & Wetherly since 1832

This gentle sedative tincture has been dispensed to our London customers for three generations. Unlike the dangerous sleep preparations containing chloral hydrate or opium sold by less scrupulous establishments, this blend works with the body's natural rhythms rather than forcing unnatural stupor.

INGREDIENTS:

- 2 parts dried valerian root, coarsely chopped
- 2 parts dried passionflower
- 1 part dried hops flowers
- 1 part dried lemon balm
- 1 part dried skullcap
- High-proof spirits (brandy preferred, vodka acceptable)
- Clear glass bottle with tight stopper

PREPARATION:

1. Fill a clean glass jar one-third with the dried herbs.
2. Pour spirits over herbs until completely covered plus one inch above.
3. Seal tightly and place in a cool, dark cupboard.
4. Shake vigorously once daily for 4-6 weeks.
5. Strain through muslin cloth into amber dropper bottles.

TRADITIONAL USAGE:

Take 15-20 drops in a small cup of warm water half an hour before retiring.

For particularly troubled minds, a cup of lime blossom tea may accompany the tincture.

HISTORICAL NOTE:

This preparation was first created by Genevieve Wetherly for the famous actress Sarah Nightingale, who suffered terrible insomnia after witnessing a tragedy at the Lyceum Theatre in 1831. After taking this remedy, she reportedly slept soundly for the first time in months and went on to deliver her most acclaimed performance.

CAUTION:

This information is provided as historical interest only. Readers should consult with qualified herbalists or physicians before attempting any herbal preparation. Valerian may interact with certain medications and should not be taken by pregnant women.

A note from Clara:

The tincture I prepared for our mysterious visitor was similar to this recipe, though I chose to emphasize lemon balm for its uplifting properties. Sometimes what presents as sleeplessness is truly a troubled heart seeking peace rather than mere unconsciousness. The difference is subtle but essential—much like the difference between truth and lies.

author's note

Dear Reader,

Thank you for joining Clara Wetherly on her first adventure. While crafting this story, I was fascinated by several historical elements that I'd like to share with you.

The railway expansion that drives our mystery was inspired by the actual transformation of London in the 1850s. During this period, railway companies aggressively purchased properties throughout Bloomsbury and other districts, often using agents to acquire land without revealing the true purpose. Many small business owners and residents found themselves displaced as London's first underground railway (the Metropolitan Line) began construction in 1860. The tension between progress and preservation that Clara experiences reflected real conflicts that reshaped Victorian London's landscape.

Scotland Yard's Detective Branch, where Inspector Redgrave serves, was still in its infancy during our story. Formed in 1842 with just eight plainclothes detectives, by the 1850s it remained a small, elite unit that handled London's most serious crimes. Unlike today's forensic procedures, Victorian detectives relied heavily on observation, interviews, and logical deduction—making medical examiners like Dr. Morris particularly influential in murder investigations.

The botanical preparations described in Clara's shop reflect authentic herbalism practices that bridge both Victorian and contemporary approaches. What fascinates me is how many of these traditional methods remain effective today. The folk preparation method for the Calming Sleep Tincture featured at the end of this book is not merely historical fiction —it's a remedy I personally prepare and use, following the same essential techniques Clara would have employed in her shop.

The amber bottles, maceration periods, and plant combinations mentioned throughout the story are grounded in both nineteenth-century apothecary records and modern herbal practice. As a dedicated herbalist myself, I take great care in researching and testing the remedies that appear in Clara's world. However, I should note that readers should consult healthcare professionals before experimenting with medicinal herbs, particularly if taking prescription medications.

In each book of the Tarot & Tea Leaves Mystery series, you'll find a different authentic herbal preparation from my personal collection—remedies I've refined through years of practice and study. These aren't simply historical curiosities but living traditions that continue to offer gentle, natural support in our modern world.

I hold an MFA in writing popular fiction and have spent years studying both historical and contemporary herbalism while creating Clara's world. My writing desk is often scattered with botanical texts, nineteenth-century maps of London, and fresh herbs from my garden as I work to ensure authenticity in each detail.

The next book in the series will find Clara facing new

botanical challenges as her partnership with Inspector Redgrave evolves and Genevieve's ghostly influence grows stronger—along with another of my favorite herbal preparations for you to discover.

Until our next adventure,

Zia Bellamy

Printed in Dunstable, United Kingdom